THE TWO TARTARS:

Or, Tom and Ned among the Moors.

TOM TARTAR SEIZED THE EMIR BEHIND AND UNDOUBTEDLY SAVED NED'S LIFE.

No. 25.

Price One Penny.

THE TWO TARTARS;

OR, TOM AND NED AMONG THE MOORS.

CHAPTER I.

THE EMIR AND HIS FACTOTUM—AN INTERRUPTED SIESTA.

 T was a hot day in Algiers, burning, blazing hot, overpowering to the strangers within its gates and trying even to the natives.

Take the year all round it is pretty warm there; but this was an especial day, when it seemed as if the furnaces in the sun had received an extra stir and additional fuel. Its rays were shafts of hot air that baked the already arid earth as if bent on making it into bricks to last for ever.

The streets of the old town—we refer to the Moorish quarter—are narrow, and wisely so, for it is shade the native wants; but the stillness of the air on this day made them suffocating.

All who could abandon business had stolen away into cellars and dark corners, to lie there panting and praying for the cooler evening to come.

The only place where it was possible to escape the full power of the sun was on the shady side of the great and grand old fortress, the Cabash, which is built upon a rock five hundred feet above the sea, to dominate the town, and is about a mile long, English measure.

If you want to know what simplicity and sublimity combined means in the way of architecture you could not find a better illustration than this great work of the Moors of olden time.

The chief characteristics of the noble structure are solidity and harmonious composition. Look at it from what point you may, it is impressing to the eye and touches the chord of sublimity within us.

In the shadow of one of its huge towers were two men—natives—the Emir Abdul-ab-Bourad and Si Hamick, his confidant, spy, factotum—anything you please.

The Emir, as became his position, squatted on the hard rock, taking things easy; Si Hamick, as a servitor, stood beside him, making strenuous efforts to bear up against the relaxing power of the heat, outwardly calm, but inwardly cursing his master for depriving him of his accustomed noonday siesta.

The fact was the Emir was in an unsettled state of mind.

A pious fit was upon him, which, as usual with his race, took the form of additional rancour against the Christians.

As a guide to the cause of his religious perturbation let him speak for himself.

"Si Hamick," he said, addressing his wily servitor, "my soul is weary."

"My lord is good and great," softly responded Si Hamick. "His right hand is powerful; he smites with a two-edged sword."

"To-day," continued Abdul-ab-Bourad, without acknowledging the compliment by so much as a depression of the eye, "I humbled my spirit to seek audience with the accursed Frank who rules us!"

"General Boureau is a French dog!" said Si Hamick. "He has the ears of a pig; his skin is afflicted with sores!"

"But he rules us, you ass!" said the Emir, without any change in his even-toned speaking; "he puts taxes on us; he treats us as unclean swine! Even to-day he would not give me audience."

"For which my lord shall put the Frenchman's neck under his heel," said Si Hamick.

"You speak as one with a head that is a potsherd without water in it," replied the Emir. "What matters it whether he does it or another? The Franks have come upon the land like the locusts that swarm up from the blazing sands of the desert. May they be withered by a blast of poisonous wind!

"See yonder," he resumed, after a pause, during which Si Hamick kept a discreet silence, "another form of the Frank—an Englishman with his yacht. Ah! he is of the race that is the most accursed; but our women will not see it. They say the men are bold and beautiful."

"They are mad!" said Si Hamick, with a sly look at his master. "I have seen the two men from the yacht—one is but a boy. They tell me they are brothers—Tartar by name."

"Si Hamick," queried Abdul-ab-Bourad, raising his voice a little, "am I well favoured?"

"My lord is shaped for Paradise," replied Si Hamick; "the houris await his coming with impatience."

"It may be so," said the Emir, rubbing his chin; "but I trust they will have to wait awhile. I am more concerned with the wife I have. But yesterday, in the Bab-el-onad, as she rode in her palanquin, she passed these strangers—these brothers—when she pushed aside her veil and showed them one of her lustrous eyes."

Si Hamick's face showed a strong tendency to expand into a grin; but by dint of much practice he had acquired the art of controlling his features, and with a stone-like expression on his face he replied—

"Some evil spirit must have prompted her to this sin."

"What shall be done?" asked the Emir, spreading out his hands.

"If my lord loves her not so well after her sin as

he did before it," replied Si Hamick, "she must die!"

"Pig—camel!" said the Emir, wrathfully; "is it punishment for her I ask? Can I live without my Alea? It is of the Franks I speak. Devise something, thou offspring of a scapegoat ass! for their confusion. Get them in HERE!"

The Emir waved his hand in the direction of the fortress, slightly turning his head at the same time.

"Here I command," he went on. "General Boureau has granted so much to me, because it is a place which he cares not for himself—curse him!"

"It rules the city," hinted Si Hamick.

"And if I so much as lifted my finger to rule it would they not with their ships and guns—may they be blighted!—pound it to pieces in a few hours—eh! thou son of a mangy jackal?"

"It is so, my lord, I fear," replied Si Hamick; "but of these Englishmen? Will it be good for my lord to lay a finger on them?"

"Of a verity thou art an idiot," said the Emir. "Is there now any love between the French and English? Are they not embittered against each other? True, there is no war, but there is no liking."

Si Hamick was not up in the subject, and, fearing his master might be laying a trap to lure him into a false position, he kept silent.

"It is so," continued the Emir; "they are rival robbers, and the English have gathered in most of the plunder. But enough. It wastes my breath in talking to such an eyeless pig as you. Quick! tell me what is to be done to this man who has lured my Alea to unveil an eye?"

"Speak to him," said Si Hamick.

"I speak to the dog!" cried the Emir.

"Speak to him," proceeded Si Hamick, with a leery eye, "even as thou dost to me. Let him learn that he is an English pig, and then—he will STRIKE YOU. Eh! my lord?"

"Ha!" exclaimed the Emir, "do you dare to suggest that an infidel hand should be laid on ME, Abdul-ab-Bourad, whose forefathers swept the desert like the wind, and—"

"My lord—my lord!" cried Si Hamick, "if he strikes one so mighty he shall be taken away to prison—to this prison where thou alone rulest. Which, my lord, did my queen cast one eye upon?"

"I know not," said the Emir, "but methinks it was the younger one. The elder, they say, hath a wife with him, not that that would matter much. He would be ready to give her up for my Alea."

"She is a peri," said Si Hamick, "a pearl of the sun, a—a—"

"Silence! thou scurf of a man," returned the Emir, savagely; "devise a plan and let it be carried out ere the sun sets. Think while I sleep awhile."

Abdul-ab-Bourad shifted his position a little, so as to get his back against the wall, and closing his eyes seemed to sleep immediately.

Si Hammick would dearly have liked to follow his example, but he dare not.

It was possible—nay, very probable—that his lord and master was shamming for the nonce, with the object of bowling him out in an attempt to neglect his duty.

So he kept erect for a time, with an immovable face, in no way an index to his thoughts, which ran as follows—

"So the old beast is jealous. Who shall marvel, for is he not as the bristly hog that the devils kicked over the city wall? May he lose his Alea! May some leper steal her and the itch afflict him for ever! May locusts eat up his substance and insects pick his bones!"

This we give as a sample of the amiable thoughts that crossed through his brain for a quarter of an hour.

Then, assured by the mellifluous sound which came from the nose of the Emir that he really slept, Si Hamick sank into a sitting position and speedily forgot the woes of servitude in profound slumber.

An hour's peace was vouchsafed him, and then he was aroused by a kick that brought him back to the realities of life in something under the tenth of a second.

"What, you dog! dare you sleep?" cried the Emir.

"My lord, I was thinking," replied Si Hamick, skipping up and gliding out of reach; "I have conceived a plan for the confusion of the two English brothers. Bear with me if I appeared to sleep."

The Emir, with every hair on his head and face bristling with wrath, moved away without another word down some steps cut in the rock towards a small gate in the face of the Cabash.

Si Hamick followed him, softly rubbing that part of his anatomy which had been so roughly assaulted, his eyes half closed to conceal the gleam of bitterness in their depths.

"Go, pig!" he muttered; "imprison the Englishmen, and they will bring you ruin. Ere you are much older you will be prowling about alone like a toothless lion in the desert. Allah send the hour speedily!"

CHAPTER II.

ON BOARD THE WHITE WING—A PLEASANT PARTY OF THREE—THAT LADY OF THE ONE EYE—CHIPPY CHUNKS.

AND what was Tom Tartar doing in sunny Algeria?

Very few words of explanation will suffice to account for his presence there.

Tom had done well in the world, and at five-and-twenty was passing rich. A girl and a boy had been born to him, and his home was a very happy one; but Lottie, one of the sweetest of sweet wives, showed signs of not being in perfect health.

"Give her a short sea trip," said the doctor, "away from the cares of home and children."

It was good advice, and Tom resolved to go with her. His mother offered to take care of the little children, so there were no grounds for uneasiness on their account.

Then Ned, Tom's favourite brother, came to the fore—he wanted to go too.

He was just the age when every day of travel was likely to be of benefit to him, and of course Tom said yes.

So a yacht named the White Wing was purchased; a competent master in the person of Captain Starfish, a regular old salt, was engaged; and he selected a crew of the right sort of men. Then away they went to the place selected, the Mediterranean, in due time arriving, without extraordinary adventure or mishap, at Algiers.

There was one man on board who was not a seaman, nor ever likely to be one, but he was a very useful man for all that.

His name was Chippy Chunks, and he had been a porter and odd man in Tom's place of business.

He adored his master, believed in him without any reservation whatever. Napoleon was very small potatoes compared with Tom Tartar in Chippy Chunks' eyes.

He begged to be taken on the yacht.

"You'll find me handy, master. A man like me, with a hammer, a few screws, and sich like, is sure to be wanted."

Chippy was an old man, a character in his way, with an ineffable disdain for mankind in general and women in particular, bar one.

He thought Mrs. Tom Tartar a koh-i-noor among her sex—high above them all in brilliancy and value.

Chippy Chunks was no longer young, but nobody knew how old he was, and his favourite attire was that of a working-carpenter. Without his paper-cap, apron, and shirt-sleeves rolled up, he was like a fish out of water—nowhere.

But you will hear more of Chippy as we go along, so now to our story.

It was on the afternoon of the day when Abdul-ab-Bourad and Si Hamick conversed under the shadow of the walls of the Cabash that Tom, Ned, and Lottie—we must stick to the dear, familiar names throughout ("Mrs. Tartar" doesn't come trippingly to the pen)—sat on deck under an awning covering the aft of the White Wing.

The noon-day siesta had been indulged in by all. Not a creature on board but had to give way under the heat and sleep in the shade somewhere, and some tea had been made as the best of drink at that hour and in that climate.

"Coffee is the drink of the east, but is not so good as tea by long chalks," said Ned, as he sipped the warm beverage. "It is strange that the hotter you drink it the more it cools you"

"In summer," said Lottie; "but in the winter it warms you."

"Don't for goodness sake go into physiological or gastronomical mysteries!" said Tom, as he took out his cigar-case. "May I smoke, Lottie?"

"Of course you can, you dear old boy," replied Lottie.

"I suppose it is necessary to ask that question even after one is married?" said Ned.

"A man ought to show to his wife the courtesy he exhibits to other women," said Tom; "perhaps a little more."

Ned laughed, and brought out a small inlaid cigarette-case.

"Well, may I smoke?" he asked.

"I don't know," replied Lottie, doubtfully. "You are very young, but, as you are something like Tom used to be when I first knew him, I suppose I must grant permission to you."

"Am I really like what Tom used to be?" asked Ned, delighted.

"Yes; but not so handsome."

"Oh!"

It was Tom's turn to laugh now.

"You mustn't mind what Lottie says on that score," he said; "she's prejudiced."

"Oh! never mind my good or bad looks," returned Ned, good-humouredly; "I don't want to develop into a puppy or an ass."

"Some of the women ashore think a lot of Ned," said Tom, with a smile; "they make eyes at him."

"It is only one woman," replied Ned, "and she makes but one eye at me. It is deuced funny. I can't help laughing at her; but, of course, I don't let her see it."

"Where do you see these women?" asked Lottie, with matronly stiffness.

"Oh! in the Bab-el-onad or the Bab-azome," replied Ned.

"Ah! those are the two main thoroughfares of this savage town."

"Yes, they run nearly through it."

"And how often have you seen this one-eyed person?"

The way Lottie put this question set Tom off into a perfect fit of laughter. His wife gradually tilted her nose in the air and tried to look at him scornfully, but the effort was not completely successful.

"Speak the whole truth, Ned," said Tom.

"Well, four or five times," replied Ned; "on every occasion, in fact, when we have gone ashore. As soon as we get into one of the Babs along comes this woman in a palanquin, carried by four niggers; as she passes she draws aside her veil and shows me one eye."

"A sparkler," said Tom.

Lottie turned quickly upon him.

"A what do you call it?" she asked, with fourteen degrees of frost in her voice.

"I am quoting Ned," said Tom, with becoming humility; "he said it was a sparkler."

"I am ashamed of you both," retorted Lottie, "and the next time you go ashore I will accompany you."

"My dearest girl," said Tom, "Algiers is no place for you. It is filled with the ruffians of every nation under the sun, and a woman without a veil —such a pretty one, too—would bring on a riot. The narrow thoroughfares—and they are so narrow that I can almost stretch across them—would be filled with a staring mob of scoundrels of every shade of colour."

"Then you must not go ashore again," said Lottie.

"Once more, and once only," returned Tom. "There are two or three things I want to buy at one of the bazaars. I began to bargain for them yesterday with a thief of a Mussulman, who asked six times as much as they are worth. I have already got him down to half what he demanded."

"Mind, it is for the last time," Lottie cried, laughing. "I can't have our Ned run away with by a one-eyed woman. Who is the creature?"

"Don't know," said Ned. "How should we? We have never exchanged a word. I did ask—"

"Oh! indeed."

"Be quiet, Lottie, and let Ned fully explain.'

"Tom, I get more ashamed of you every day. Go on, Ned."

"I asked one old fellow—a dealer in crockery—as old as the hills outside Jerusalem, and what do you think he said?"

"How should we guess what answer the old wretch would give?"

"'She is the daughter of the evening star,' said the old man, 'and the moon hides its feeble light when she walks abroad at night.' What do you think of that?"

"The man was an old fool, Ned."

Lottie's reply set them all laughing. She was out of humour with them, but was comforted by the assurance that the "one-eyed lady" was not likely to be abroad at eve, as they had usually met her in the morning.

"In fact," said Tom, "I don't believe that any woman is allowed to be about the town after three o'clock."

Little more was said upon the subject.

The sailors—with the exception of two in the bows keeping watch—were below, and Captain Starfish was in his cabin studying the chart of the coast, for on the morrow the White Wing was to fly away to Tunis.

Chippy Chunks by-and-bye appeared on deck, coming out of the fore-cabin with a hammer lightly poised in his hand.

He was not handsome, nor ever had been. A nose half an inch too long and shaped like the teat of a baby's feeding-bottle is a serious bar to beauty.

Small lips are also considered a disadvantage to those who wish to go a-mashing; but Chippy had never been a dandy, and was not likely to be one in his sere and yellow leaf.

The one absorbing thought in his mind was to make himself useful.

As soon as he was on deck his small eyes were glancing here and there in search of a job. A vacancy of a nail or a screw soon caught his eye.

Down went his hand into his left trousers' pocket, and out came a collection of nails, screws, bits of chip, and sawdust.

Closing one eye he carefully selected the nail he wanted, and with two or three flourishing taps drove it home.

"Yer see what a man can do if he's only got the conweniences about him," he said, addressing the men on watch. In the perfect stillness around every word he uttered could be heard by all on deck. "Now, 'spose for the sake o' argyment, that I hadn't got that nail about me and this yere hammer in my hand—"

"Well, maybe you'd ha' gone down and fetched 'em," replied one of the men.

"I might," said Chippy Chunks, "but YOU wouldn't. You would ha' put off the job till by-and-bye and forgot all about it."

"How do you know that?" asked the man, with asperity.

"Because I DO know it," answered Chippy Chunks. "Do you think I've lived all these years in the world without knowing what I know?"

"What yer fancy yer know," said the man.

"Fancy," echoed Chippy Chunks, "me a dealin' in fancy! Why, you talk like a owl."

"Owls don't talk," said the man.

"Can you swear to that?" asked Chippy Chunks.

"No, I can't," was the reply.

"Then what you can't swear to don't put forward as solemn truth. If I was in your place I should feel ashamed to do so."

"All right, old Tintacks," said the man; "if you are satisfied I am."

"Tintacks!" retorted Chippy Chunks, eyeing him up and down. "I'd like to know—"

"Well, not Tintacks— Mister Screws, Two-inch Brads, Tenpenny-nails—any name you like. We ain't partikler."

"All through my life," said Chippy Chunks, as he moved away, but still keeping his face to the men, "I've thought that words in season and good advice is pearls fit for kings, but it's no use giving things to them as ain't got no use for 'em. Afore I'd go about the useless creatures some of you are I'd—a—I'd—a—I'd— It's a waste o' time to tell you what I'd do.'

And Chippy Chunks, all aglow with scorn and hatred of useless men, made for the companion and vanished swiftly below.

CHAPTER III.

THE MEETING WITH THE EMIR—A HASTY BLOW —THE DARK DISTRICT OF THE CITY—SI HAMICK AGAIN.

O, Starfish," said Tom Tartar, "I shall not take any of the crew. Here is a fellow with a boat. He can land us."

Captain Starfish —a stout, sunburnt, reserved-looking man, one of few words but of considerable action in an emergency —looked aloft as he replied, "It's as you like, of course, sir."

"Yesterday," said Tom, "when I left Mason and Binks in charge of the boat for an hour they got wrangling with some of the scurvy loafers on the shore."

"Men don't like to be cheeked by niggers, sir," said Starfish. "If, instead o' talking, they'd ha' chucked 'em into the water, the argument would soon have been over."

"To avoid all argument," said Tom, "I'll hire this boat."

He had hailed one commanded by a swarthy Moor, whose sole attire consisted of a turban and a cloth round his loins. Three or four fellows at the oars brought the boat alongside.

Ned was in waiting, and the two brothers dropped into the boat.

As they were being rowed away a small white hand fluttered a handkerchief from a porthole of the chief cabin.

Tom and Ned kissed their hands by way of reply.

"Dear Lottie!" said Tom; "she is the best woman in the world."

"Barring One Eye," retorted Ned, laughing.

"Bar nobody," said Tom. "Where is this fellow going to?"

"Perhaps he is making allowance for the tide," answered Ned.

"There is little or no tide in the Mediterranean," said Tom. "You are going too far that way," to the man; "I want to land lower down in the town."

The man grinned, showing his white teeth, and murmured something in Arabic. English seemed an unknown tongue to him.

Tom pointed in the direction he wanted to go, but the man shook his head and motioned with his hand that he was going towards the Cabash fortress.

"But I don't want to go there," said Tom; "I am not sight-seeing. Hang it, Ned, why didn't you study Arabic at school?"

"For the same reason as you avoided it," replied Ned. "It wasn't taught, and if it had been neither of us would have cottoned to it."

Tom was determined the fellow should not have his own way, and he sternly pointed in the direction he wished to be taken.

"Let him do as he likes," said Ned; "if you have a row with the fellow you will upset the boat."

"I'll throw him out of it," Tom returned, "if he doesn't do as he is told."

They were now getting near the shore, the boat pointing in the direction of a landing-stage near the great fortress—the Cabash.

For the last time Tom signalled for the boatman to steer lower down.

The answer was another exhibition of the gleaming teeth and a few more unintelligible words.

"Confound you!" cried Tom; "do as you are told, or I'll pitch you out of the boat."

If the fellow did not understand the words he fully comprehended the imperative action of Tom, and, giving the right hand line an extra pull, he headed the boat for the lower part of the town.

But he had already come far out of the way, and was near the shore, so Tom angrily bade him steer for land.

There was a lot of meaning in the eyes of the swarthy boatman as he complied, and the boat shortly after bumped against the stonework of the landing-pier.

Tom gave the fellow a coin and jumped out. Ned followed him, and the boatmen, a moment later, leaped up and vanished.

"Those fellows are in a hurry to get home," said Ned. "Perhaps they have bloaters waiting for tea."

"They had some reason for bringing us here," replied Tom. "Your pardon, my good man!"

It was the Emir Abdul-ab-Bourad who had brushed rudely by him, and Tom's apology was, in a measure, sarcastic.

But it was not so much Tom as Ned that the Emir was bent on insulting, which he did by deliberately giving the latter a push that nearly drove him into the water.

Ned was made of the stuff that does not take an insult with serenity, and, without waiting to consider the consequences, he sprang forward and struck Abdul-ab-Bourad a smart blow in the ribs.

For a moment the Moor was palpably short of breath, but on recovering he drew a scimitar he wore by his side and slashed at him.

Ned dodged his first stroke, but the second might have been fatal if Tom had not seized the Emir behind and tossed him off the quay into the boat they had just quitted.

The Emir fell with a mighty whack upon the bottom, his head coming into contact with one of the seats, and there he lay, with his eyes staring and his mouth opening and shutting like a dentist's model going by machinery.

His weapon as he fell flew out of his hand and sank under the sea.

There were a few people about, but as far as Tom could see none had observed what had taken place.

It was all, indeed, the work of a few moments, and beyond the noise made by the Emir as he fell there was no sound to speak of.

"What an insolent old brute!" said Ned. "He won't try the bouncing game again in a hurry."

"Let him lie there," returned Tom, airily; "he will have time to reflect on his folly."

They crossed an open space before them and came to a wall, in which was a gateway leading to the city.

Passing through, they found themselves in what was clearly one of the lowest quarters of the town.

The street was so narrow that two ordinarily stout men could scarcely have passed without knocking against each other. The houses were of two stories, square-built, with narrow doorways and slits for windows, where there were any windows at all, which was the case in about one house in three.

In every doorway laid one or more men—a mixed class, in which every degree of swarthiness was represented.

Here and there a lean, hungry, wild-eyed dog prowled in search of food.

Neither Tom nor Ned were particularly sweet upon the quarters in which they found themselves; but pride and their indomitable courage kept them from expressing any opinion or of feeling any actual fear.

With a light, swinging step they went on side by side, Ned occasionally falling behind when they had to pass another wayfarer.

All the people they met or saw were grimly silent. There was neither music nor laughter nor sound of human voice anywhere. It was about as cheerful as a stroll through the catacombs of Rome.

They got through the first street, and found themselves in one which was, if anything, worse.

With the exception of the strip of clear evening sky overhead there was not one redeeming point in the picture.

Tom knew in what direction he ought to bear, and was looking for some opening on the right which would take him towards the two great thorough-fares, Bab-el-onad and Bab-azome, but could find none.

Openings there were here and there between the houses, but they only led to short blind alleys, rank with the refuse of a naturally dirty population.

Here, as elsewhere, they caught glimpses of men and occasionally children, but there was no talking, no playing—nothing but grim silence and faces on which a scowl was stamped as an indelible thing.

"What a hole!" exclaimed Ned, suddenly.

"We shall soon be out of it, that's one comfort," replied Tom.

"I feel," said Ned, with a slight twist of his shoulders, "as if I were collecting specimens of all the objectionable insects under the sun."

Tom laughed softly in spite of the loathing which the place inspired in his heart. A similar feeling had laid hold of himself.

At the top of the second street there was a short turning to the right, and then another narrow way appeared.

Ere they had gone far a startling discovery was made by Tom.

The street was a short one, and at the end of it was a high wall; there was no outlet whatever.

"Well," he said, "we shall have to go back."

"I don't think I can stand those streets again," said Ned.

"But, my dear boy, you must," urged Tom. "We have made a mistake by entering that gate. This is some close quarter of the town, reserved for a particular class—lepers, perhaps; who knows?"

"Come on," said Ned; "let's run. I feel, if I am here much longer, that I shall faint away."

They wheeled round, to find, to their amazement, their way blocked by a number of dark-skinned men, armed with long rifles, which they were aiming at them.

They were grimly silent, but their air was unmistakable.

Somebody behind gave a word of command, and they began to slowly advance.

"Tom," said Ned, "what is to be done—fight?"

"Fight with what?" asked Tom. "I have a revolver and you also have one. We might take the lives of two or three of the poor devils, but then we should be no better off. It is some mistake."

He advanced towards them with his arms upraised in sign of peace.

"What do you want?" he asked. "We are strangers here and have lost our way."

The men did not answer, but with a quick movement broke into single file, passed by, and fairly surrounded them.

A moment later and ropes were thrown over their shoulders. Then the two brothers instinctively struggled for freedom; but it was too late.

It was a big struggle but a short one. Overpowered by numbers they were thrown down and securely bound.

That done they were raised to their feet, and then Tom saw before him the man who was in command.

He was tall and lean, with a dark face, hook nose that almost met his chin, and little, dark eyes set deep in his head quite close to his nose.

A Turkish *fez*, Albanian jacket, short white trousers, and slippers, formed all that could be seen of his costume.

In his hand was a huge scimitar, and four pistols were stuck in his sash.

This notable personage was Si Hamick, whom we have not before attempted to describe, so we have taken a convenient opportunity to give a sketch of him to the reader.

"Sons of camels!" he said, in respectable English, "yield yourselves to the sword of the faithful."

"What is the meaning of this outrage?" demanded Tom. "Do you know who we are? What have we done? Our coming here is purely accidental."

"The voice of Abdul-ab-Bourad has spoken," said Si Hamick. "His wrath is as a simoon of the desert. It carries death with it."

"I tell you," said Tom, "that we have done nothing. We are two Englishmen here on a visit, and were trying to find our way to the bazaar."

"You have laid infidel hands on the chosen Emir," said Si Hamick; "you have smitten the elected one of the Prophet. He awaits you in the Hall of Justice."

"Very well," replied Tom, "conduct us to him, and we will explain matters. But you need not keep us bound like felons. Take off these cords and we will go quietly."

"Shall the man-eater of the desert when snared ask for the net to be removed?" said Si Hamick. "Accursed ones! you shall tremble before the Emir of Cabash this night—Abdul-ab-Bourad He shall make ashes of your flesh and give your bones to the lions."

"I don't think we want any more of the penny plain and twopence coloured stuff," said Ned; "take us where we have to go and let us settle the business."

"The time of going is not for pigs to choose," said Si Hamick. "When the sun goes down you will be taken to the Emir—he of the mighty hand. Until then here you remain awaiting my voice to speak."

Tom was in an agony on Lottie's account.

If he and Ned were kept there until after dark, or possibly until the morning, what apprehensions she would have on his account!

For himself he had no fear.

His idea of the position was that he had strayed into some forbidden quarter of the city, which could be rectified by an apology or that eastern open sesame—a bribe.

"Take us at once, I say," he returned, angrily. "Beware how you put too great an indignity upon us."

But Si Hamick smiled in his special way, which consisted of compressing the lips, stretching the corners of the mouth, and bringing his nose and chin together.

A more exasperating smile it would be difficult to imagine.

"Who are you?" asked Ned, regarding him as he would have viewed some loathsome reptile.

"I am my lord's servant," he said.

"But what are we charged with?" asked Tom.

"Is it for me to say?" answered Si Hamick. "In time and season my lord will speak, and then you infidels will think of lightning and thunder and tremble."

"Oh! you are an infernal ass," said Ned, testily.

"Keep as quiet as you can," whispered Tom. "This fellow is only the creature of someone higher in authority. We shall know in good time what we have done to offend. Poor Lottie! she will have a bad hour or two of it, I fear."

"I say, Tom," said Ned, as an idea flashed upon him, "do you think old lightning and thunder is that antiquated old humbug you toppled into the boat?"

"It may be," returned Tom. "Beggar the fellow! I had forgotten him."

The men on guard had kept silent, and Si Hamick, not being spoken to again, was silent also.

He contented himself with surveying the prisoners with a most irritating smile on his aggravating countenance.

"He's as bad as some of those figures they have

in the shops at home," said Ned—"missionary things, you know. You put a penny on a tray and touch a spring, then away goes the penny into his gullet."

"Better be quiet, Ned," said Tom.

So they were all quiet, and the sun, being in the west, speedily went down.

As soon as the rapidly-darkening sky announced the close of another day, Si Hamick gave the word for a move to be made.

Some of the guard walked on ahead, the rest fell in the rear, and with the prisoners they threaded the narrow streets back towards the small postern gate.

The men who had been lounging at the doors were lounging still, but as the cavalcade passed they made no sign. Some did not so much as raise their heads.

Onward to more open ground, where the soft breeze from the sea was welcome to all, then away to the right to a flight of steps.

From thence upward, by a path cut by the hand of man, winding here and there as some huge stony obstacle barred the way—up full five hundred feet above the town to the far-spreading fortress, the Cabash.

A large door stood open to receive them, and armed men lined the way on either side in the direction of a lamp, dimly lighting a huge hall—cool and quiet.

Then a halt was called, and Si Hamick, leaving the prisoners under the care of the guard, glided away to report to his lord, the mighty Abdul-ab-Bourad, the entire success of his mission.

"Tom," said Ned, in an undertone, "what is to be the outcome of THIS pretty business?"

"I am not good at problems," replied Tom, "but I would give something to be able to send word to Lottie. She is in a terrible state by this time, and her health won't enable her to stand it."

"I hope that one of these days I may have a private interview with that nose-and-chin party," said Ned; "I ask no more than a quiet corner and a pliable cane. By Jingo! I'd make him skip."

Tom did not answer him—his mind was on board the White Wing with Lottie. The picture he drew of the mental agony she was enduring nearly drove him mad.

Back, like some spectre from the gloom, came Si Hamick, with his nose and chin and mocking eyes.

Bending low in sham reverence, he said—

"My lord awaits you, oh! sons of the infidel—swift is his hand, sure his vengeance. All the earth trembles when he is angry."

CHAPTER IV.

THE EMIR AND HIS PRISONERS — ALEA THE HUMBLE AND ALEA THE PASSIONATE—GRACE TILL THE MORNING COMES.

 MIR ABDUL - AB - BOURAD, seated on a pile of cushions in one of the chambers of the huge fortress, awaited the coming of the prisoners.

By his side was a woman, closely veiled, who crouched low, with her head bowed, to express anguish or contrition, or some similar emotion; but if the Emir could have got a peep at the face under the folded muslin he would have seen that she was laughing.

This woman was Alea, the Emir's favourite wife, who had been so wicked as to exhibit one of her lustrous eyes to an infidel.

Overhead a suspended lamp was burning.

It did not give a very powerful light, but it revealed all things in the room with tolerable distinctness, from the jewels in the Emir's robes to the swarthy face, of half-a-dozen Nubians, who, with drawn swords, were ranged as a bodyguard behind him.

"Alea," said the Emir, "I have brought thee here to see the humiliation of these accursed sons of the Evil One, who have dared to raise their eyes to the wife of Abdul-ab-Bourad. Lift thy head but an inch to return their gaze, veiled though thou be, and thou diest! Hear all, see nothing."

"Is not the word of my lord a written law in my heart?" answered Alea, in her lightest tones. "Why should I look upon those I do not know? Though the Wicked Spirit led me to draw aside my veil I saw nothing. I was thinking of my lord."

"It is well," said the Emir, with a repressed smirk of satisfaction upon his dark countenance. "Be still—they are approaching."

The door opened and Si Hamick entered, bowing low at every third step, and finally prostrating himself before his master.

"Lord of the earth," he said, "the infidel prisoners are approaching."

The Emir took no notice of him whatever, but straightened his back and composed his face to the expressionless appearance of an image of stone.

Just for one moment he turned his eyes down into the corners to look at the humble Alea, whose chin was resting on her breast.

A rattle of arms announced the coming of the prisoners.

First of all entered half-a-score armed men, who divided and ranged themselves on either side of the apartment close to the Emir. Then Tom and Ned advanced, with more armed men behind them.

Tom looked very grave, for he was bitterly angry, and had to make an effort to control himself. The outrage inflicted upon him had roused all that was fiery in his nature, and if he could have got his arms free, and been favoured with a private interview with Abdul-ab-Bourad, that mighty potentate would have had a bad five minutes with him.

Ned, on the other hand, could not resist a tendency to treat the whole thing in a somewhat jocular spirit, little dreaming how very serious the end might possibly be.

Not even the discovery that the Emir was the pugnacious Moor whom Tom had pitched headlong into the boat roused in him more than a temporary feeling of uneasiness.

"What can the old fool do?" was the question he asked himself.

The "old fool" stared at them with venomous, basilisk eyes for several minutes, until, becoming conscious of Si Hamick still prostrate before him, he cursed him as "a son of a dog," and bade him get out of the way.

Si Hamick, thus released from prostration, arose and stood erect on the right-hand side of the Emir, glancing across at Alea, whose humble position seemed to tax the risible muscles of his face, for

WITHOUT A MOMENT'S HESITATION TOM KNOCKED ALL THE FIGHT OUT OF THE EMIR.

something like the ghost of a grin passed over his features.

"Infidels," said the Emir, "what hast thou to say?"

"Only this," replied Tom, curtly, "that you will have to pay dearly for this outrage upon two British subjects."

"All men are subject to me," replied Abdul-ab-Bourad. "Thou hast insulted my wife by casting evil glances upon her. Thou hast bewitched her."

Ned, laughing in a quiet way, drew all eyes upon him. Those in the Emir's head sparkled with fury.

"Darest thou mock me, boy?" he demanded.

"It seems to me," returned Ned, "such utter bosh to talk as you do. Who wanted to look at your wife, or you, or any of the precious lot about here?"

"You had better be quiet, Ned," said Tom, "and leave this affair to me. Emir," he added, addressing the wrathful potentate, "first of all I demand one thing — that our arms be freed of these bonds."

"You must be a cowardly lot," put in Ned, "to be afraid of two Britishers."

"You MUST be quiet," said Tom. "Well, Emir I am waiting for your answer."

"Your bonds," replied Abdul-ab-Bourad, "shall be removed when I desire it."

"But why bind us? What have we done?" demanded Tom.

"You have insulted an Emir's wife," said Abdul-ab-Bourad.

"That's a lie," answered Tom. "What have I to do with your wife? Have I not one of my own?"

"But the young Frank," said the Emir, with a cunning look. "He—"

"Upon my word," interposed Tom, "I think you are the most foolish old man I ever met with. If you are seeking an excuse to heap indignities upon us because I pitched you off the landing-stage, please to remember that you behaved most grossly. We are not accustomed to take insults from any-one."

"Especially foreigners," said Ned.

"Knowest thou that it is in my power to order you to instant execution?" said the Emir, bristling with jealous fury.

"It would be risky work to carry out," said Tom. "Come, have done with this foolery. What is it you want? What are you going to do?"

The Emir was about to reply when he happened to look down at his wife. He saw that she had raised her head sufficiently to look at the handsome infidels who stood so proudly and defiantly before the mighty Emir.

An exclamation in Arabic, which we do not intend to translate, on account of its volcanic nature, burst from his lips.

"Thou art sorcerers—both!" he hissed, "and shall die! Away with them to the Eastern Tower, and thou, brother to a lame camel?" to Si Hamick, "on thy life guard them well."

Tom, worked up to a pitch of fury by the bearing of the Emir, drew in a deep breath, and then with an effort expanded his chest, with the intention of bursting the ropes that held him.

But they were too strong and the fastening much too scientific to yield to the efforts of an ordinary man.

Violent hands were laid upon him, and Ned and Tom, bound as they were, both struggled with their guards, who had their work cut out to drag them from the room.

Ned got near Si Hamick in the temporary riot, and bestowed upon him a kick on the right shin which brought him gasping to his knees.

The two brothers were finally hustled from the room, Tom vowing vengeance and Ned bestowing all sorts of left-handed compliments upon his assailants.

Si Hamick, oblivious of all things for the time outside the agony he felt, knelt upon the floor holding his injured shin with both hands, and expressing his feelings with face-contortions that would have made him invaluable to a circus proprietor in want of a novel clown.

Abdul-ab-Bourad was very much in want of something to assault, and seeing his factotum in a convenient position for punishment he arose and descended upon him.

Thrice he kicked him ere he realised that his master was behind him.

Then, rising, he limped out, cursing the hand that made boots with soles so hard and the legs that were strong enough to put them to such effective use.

Turning upon his original bodyguard, the Emir, with sundry verbal explosions bearing on their birth or one or more of their relations, dismissed them.

He and Alea were alone.

The woman was so lowly now that she was almost double.

Abdul-ab-Bourad slowly drew his sword.

Alea did not look up or flinch.

Not a word escaped her lips, but a slight shudder passed through her frame.

"She trembles before me," thought the half-maddened Emir.

Ah! fool of old fools. If you could have seen her face you would have beheld the smile of a woman who was enjoying some huge joke.

"Alea," he said at last.

"My lord," was the humble answer.

"Art thou prepared to die?"

"If my lord wills it. Why should I live if he is angry with me?"

"Have I not cause for bitterness?" asked the Emir.

"Nay, my lord should laugh," said Alea.

"Laugh?"

"Aye, oh! mighty ruler. Laugh at the infidel—who is as dust beneath his feet—who has dared to love one of the chosen race."

"For which he shall die!"

"Nay, my lord," cried Alea; "let him live—let both live, and knowing how well I love my lord shall not they suffer the tortures of those who give their hearts to persons who despise them?"

"It IS torture," said the Emir, slowly.

"What is death?" asked Alea. "It is sleep, rest, forgetfulness. Is that the punishment my lord in his wrath would heap upon those who wrong him? Nay! my lord will let them live—to suffer, to burn, to thirst, and drink not."

Abdul-ab-Bourad, with a clouded brow of mingled doubt and belief, stood for a few moments looking down upon her in silence.

Slowly she raised her head and threw aside her veil, revealing a face that was beautiful in a semi-savage way.

The cheeks were swarthy and the mouth somewhat coarse, but the nose was well-shaped and the eyes large and lustrous.

"If you love me, my lord," she said, "kill them not."

"Oh! you plead—"

"Because I would have them live and suffer."

"I'll think of it," said the Emir, in a stern, uncertain way. "I will spare them till the morning. With light comes coolness and judgment. For the present, Alea—"

"For the present, my lord, leave me," she said, humbly. "I am sick—weary. I cannot live without your love. On the morrow, if thou sparest these two infidels, and send them back to their people to suffer, I shall know that thy heart is mine still; but if not," here she rose suddenly to her feet with flashing eyes, "if thy will demands their lives, then I shall learn my lord loves me not. What else have I to live for? KILL ME!"

The two last words were spoken with the intensity of a passionate woman, and she threw out her arms as if inviting him to plunge his sword into her heart.

What could the infatuated, jealous, self-torturing old man do?

He could not slay so beautiful a treasure, and slowly returned his sword to its scabbard.

"I must have time to think, Alea," he cried, huskily, "for verily I know not how to disentangle the whirling thoughts within me."

"Leave me," she said, softly.

He backed slowly down the room with his eyes upon her, and she never stirred until he had gone out, closing the door behind him.

Then she threw herself down upon the cushions, laughing silently for a while, and finally bursting into tears.

"Oh! accursed fate," she moaned; "bound to this old ghoul, whom one day, when he comes leering up to me, I will stab to the heart. A bitter lot—hard life! Let me see the beautiful brothers free, and then—welcome DEATH!"

CHAPTER V.

LOTTIE'S ANXIETY—A TRIP ASHORE—CHIPPY CHUNKS ASTONISHES AN INHABITANT—IN THE STREET AT NIGHT.

LOTTIE, left on board the White Wing, was, from the time Ned and Tom went away, filled with vague apprehensions; but she endeavoured to drive them away by busying herself about the cabin.

Wherever there are books, furniture, pictures, or flowers, a woman can find something to do. She can rearrange, if she can do nothing else. It is their mission to beautify and put into order.

Lottie altered some of the pictures, put a bookcase tidy, and finally found a dress that wanted a few stitches in it.

And so the hours passed away.

The sun was dipping into the sea when she went on deck and cast her eyes shoreward, with the hope of seeing the boat with her loved ones returning. But she, of course, was disappointed.

Captain Starfish was leaning on the vessel's side with his stolid face turned in the same direction.

Probably he, too, was anxious, but his face gave no indication of it

Close by, Chippy Chunks was engaged in repairing a small wooden coal-scuttle belonging to the cook.

It was giving out at the back, and Chippy was taking a scientific survey of the whole structure, to find out where a screw or a nail could be most effectually placed.

For it was one of his mottoes, "Always be willing for the job and ready to do it, but don't waste material that may be wanted another time."

"They are a long time gone, Captain Starfish," said Lottie, suddenly.

"Yes, ma'am," he replied; "it's a goodish bit o' time since they went ashore."

"You think they ought to be back?"

"It much depends, ma'am, on what they went ashore to do."

Chippy Chunks looked up, turning his eyes quickly from one to the other.

Instead of going on with his job he softly laid his hammer down and listened.

"Do you know Algiers, Captain Starfish?" asked Lottie, after a pause.

"Very well, ma'am," was the reply.

"It's a very rough place, isn't it?"

"Roughish in some ways, ma'am."

"Do—do you think anything has happened to them?" asked Lottie.

"I think that the governor can take care of himself a'most anywhere," replied Captain Starfish; "but there wouldn't be any harm in a boat going ashore for the gentlemen. Maybe they can't get a boat on hire."

"That's a good thought—a wise thought," said Lottie, cheerfully. "I think it most likely they are unable to get a boat."

The White Wing lay about half-a-mile from the shore—no great distance; but the view of the landing stages was intercepted by intervening crafts, two of which were French cruisers.

A boat with three men was got ready, and they were about to start when Chippy Chunks approached Captain Starfish.

"I'd like to go with 'em, sir," he said.

"What on earth for?" demanded Starfish.

"Oh! in case I should be wanted," replied Chippy Chunks. "You never can tell. Say a rowlock gives, or a seat gets loose, or the leather of the oars starts. In any of 'em a nail or screw's wanted; and if you've got the man and the material handy, why there you are."

Captain Starfish was about to say something about Chippy's taking a journey to his Satanic majesty when Lottie intervened.

"Oh! let him go, Captain Starfish. The boat will hold him."

"Very well, ma'am," said the captain.

Chippy Chunks raised his paper cap and smiled gratefully on Lottie.

"Look 'ee, ma'am," he said, "I'M NOT COMIN' BACK UNTIL I FIND 'EM."

Before she could realise the full portent of these

words Chippy Chunks, who was not entirely unacquainted with rheumatism, and was as stiff in the joints as a Dutch doll, had dropped into the boat in imitation of the agile seamen.

This rash proceeding screwed up his face, and extracted from him a hissing sound as he rubbed his knees.

" You oughtn't to do it, Mr. Chunks," said one of the men. " At your time of life jumping's off."

" Never you mind my time o' life," returned Chunks. " I'm young enough to do anything you are up to, Mason."

" I'd like to run you a mile for a sovereign,' said Mason.

Chippy Chunks made no reply, but expressed his sentiments by curling up one nostril and closing his right eye.

When he did these things it was time for all opponents to make tracks. They indicated a start upon the war-trail.

Darkness soon fell upon the land and sea. Lottie, with growing fears, slowly paced the deck. Captain Starfish silently shifted from place to place with his eyes ever shoreward.

The crew of the yacht had the spirit of fear upon them. Every man was on deck, and all were silent save for an occasional exchange of whispers.

Their eyes travelled from the restless Lottie to the town, where lights were now springing up in every direction.

The sound of oars suddenly aroused all from a semi-dreamy state, and there was a general movement to the side.

Out of the shadow of one of the French cruisers came a boat with two men in her—no more.

It pulled up by the side of the yacht, and Mason, standing up, laid hold with a boathook.

" We thought we would come for orders," he said.

" Have you seen nothing of Mr. Tartar ?" asked Lottie.

" Nothing, ma'am."

" Where's Chunks ?" asked Captain Starfish.

" Oh ! he's gone into the town. He says he's got to find master or bring down the town."

" He will get into trouble, the old fool," muttered Captain Starfish.

" I must go ashore," said Lottie, with sudden determination. " Excuse me, Captain Starfish, but I shall do as I please in this matter. I am an Englishwoman, and can take care of myself."

" But, my dear lady, what can you do ?" asked Captain Starfish, dismayed. " There's an awful rough lot abroad at night in that hole of a town."

" I am going as far as the shore, at all events," said Lottie. " You remain here and take care of the yacht. If my husband should return you can tell him I shall not be long."

" I'll send up a rocket, ma'am," replied Captain Starfish ; " a blue one with a red star, the sort Mr. Tartar arranged to be used as a signal to return abroad."

" Very well," said Lottie, calmly. " I will wait for it."

There was no fuss or nonsense about her—none of the hysteric anxiety some women would have exhibited.

The men had the chair ready for her in a trice, and she was lowered into the boat.

" Plucky," was the mental comment of Captain Starfish, as the boat was rowed away, and with unwonted asperity he turned upon the sailors and asked them " What the deuce they were all lumbering up the deck for ?"

They did not answer, but if they had spoken they would have said something like this—

" We are anxious about the master, just as you are."

The hour and the scene were charming.

A soft breeze blew shoreward from the sea, giving a refreshing coolness to the air. The waves were merely ripples, that scarcely rocked the boat and ships, which rested like sleeping monsters on the bosom of the water.

In the east a moon was setting, throwing its white beams upon the antique city. To the left the large Cabash prison home of Tom and Ned was picturesquely limned against the deep-coloured sky. Ahead a thousand lights were twinkling.

Some were low down upon the shore, others on the summits of high towers. There were no regular lines of lights such as we see in our great European cities. The charm of irregularity was on everything. But Lottie, who at any other time would have been charmed, had no eye for the scene. All her thoughts were with the absent ones.

She imagined a hundred things that might have befallen them, and none were right—not even near the truth—in that short journey to the land.

The boat, as it had done before, pulled up to the western end of the town.

Tom and Ned, it will be remembered, were landed by the obstinate boatman, who was probably in the pay of Emir Abdul-ab-Bourad, in the east or upper end.

The first person they saw was Chippy Chunks, who was engaged in putting his paper-cap into shape.

" I heard you coming," he said to Mason—" and—why—who's that you got ? Beg parding, ma'am, but I didn't expect to see you here."

" You have not seen anything of them ?" said Lottie.

" No, ma'am," replied Chippy Chunks. " But I ain't been able to get up to the city—a nigger chap stopped me. ' Yah—yah !' he says—a holding out a bit o' pointed hoop-iron—sword, I suppose, he calls it. ' Yah, yourself,' says I. ' You let me pass.' Then he shaves my cap orf—meaning, maybe, to take my head—and I give him a crack with my hammer somewhere between the eyes. I then picks up my cap and comes back again. Dern him ! He's spoiled the folds of it."

" I hope you did not seriously hurt him ?" said Lottie, as she stepped out of the boat.

" I can't say, ma'am. He just sat down, and I left him a trying to make out what had happened. He wasn't dead, for his mouth and eyes was a-working, like the beggar I once see in a waxwork show of King John 'spostulating with the Barings afore he signed Magnum's Charta."

" I am going into the town," said Lottie, " to see the French governor, General Boureau. If anything has happened to—to my husband and brother, he will have heard of it."

" May I be so bold as to offer myself as your humble escort, ma'am ?" said Chippy Chunks.

" I am not afraid," replied Lottie.

" But I'll make so bold as to follow you, ma'am. I may be wanted. A man with a hammer and a few nails, let alone screws, is always handy, and—"

But Lottie was gone.

She knew the direction to take, and felt pretty sure of meeting with a French officer or soldier who would be able to direct her.

There was no gate to this part of the town, and having crossed the quay, whereon Chippy Chunks' late antagonist, a dark-skinned man, was still sitting in doubt about matters generally, Lottie entered a street of more than average width, and well lighted up.

A great number of men were abroad, but only a few women, with veiled faces, who showed by their halting gait that they were past the age when their beauty would be dangerous to the peace of man.

But a woman of great beauty without a veil could not fail to create a sensation.

Albanians, Turks, Moors, Frenchmen were there, and every eye was on Lottie, but, indifferent to their gaze, she walked proudly up the street.

There was a "stand-off" expression on her face that kept all gallants at bay.

A few paces behind her walked Chippy Chunks, with his hammer tucked inside his waistcoat and his hands upon his hips.

As everybody there swaggered he swaggered also, but with a mighty poor effect. The stiffness of his knee-joints, an old thing with him, was a bar to easy, graceful motion.

Several young French officers were abroad in twos and threes, and the question was asked among themselves—

"Who is she?"

And the answer was—

"English. There is no other woman in the world who DARE show herself here at such a time."

Presently Lottie saw the sort of man she wanted. It was a grey-headed, amiable-looking officer, standing at the door of a café.

"Sir," she said, "I beseech you to help me! I have lost my husband in this city, and I wish to see the governor about him."

The officer raised his hat and bowed.

"I am General Boureau's brother," he said, "and perhaps I shall serve as well. Tell me the story of his disappearance."

Lottie told him all there was to tell of that ridiculous affair, as she called it, of the meeting with the woman "who was proud of her one eye."

This part of the narrative made the officer look very grave.

"Do you know who this woman is?" he asked.

"No," replied Lottie.

"If that could be ascertained we might possibly get a clue to the disappearance of your husband."

"You think he has been wicked enough to go into the company of this woman?"

"That would not be necessary," said the officer. "I think I have seen him. Your husband is a handsome man, and this creature, whoever she may be, might lure him into some brawl."

"Why?"

"Oh! you cannot go into women's notions. Or her lord and master, as they name husbands here, may have developed a jealousy. In that case—"

He stopped short, and, stroking his moustache, looked thoughtfully at Lottie.

"Do not be alarmed," he said, after a pause. "There may be no cause for fear."

He would have said more, but at that moment a disturbance, as sudden as an unexpected earthquake, arose close by, and two men—a Zouave and a Turk—were seen desperately fighting with swords.

"Step in here, madam," said the officer. "This is no scene for you."

CHAPTER VI.

THE DESPERATE FRAY IN THE STREET—SI HAMICK SHOWS ANOTHER SIDE OF HIS CHARACTER—AT MORN BY THE EASTERN TOWER.

IT was not a time for a woman to hesitate for a moment. Like a match applied to powder, the fight roused all the antagonistic element in the street.

Shouts in half-a-dozen languages were heard on every side, swords were drawn, pistols cocked, and with cries of encouragement there was a general press upon the fighting men.

Lottie stepped into the café, dexterously avoiding half-a-dozen men who, hearing the sounds of a fray, came rushing out, eager to play the part of spectators or assistants in the scene.

Chippy Chunks had no time to get out of the way.

The crush drove him against the wall of the adjoining house, and he was pressed there, with a fat Turk as a buffer. He could hear a great deal, but see very little.

Self-preservation is the first law of nature, and Chippy Chunks, having no desire to be smothered even by a Turk of high degree, dragged his hammer out of its resting-place and gave the man who incommoded him a tap on the head of the tenpenny-nail order.

The turban notwithstanding, it was a tap that would have taxed any ordinary cranium, and the Turk was treated to a pyrotechnic display—vivid, varied, and bewildering.

He staggered to the right, and was immediately fallen upon by three or four savage-looking men, mountaineers of the Kabyle race—the most untameable and rebellious of the Algerian tribes.

Chippy Chunks, having no great interest in the struggling and cursing that ensued at his feet, got out of the scrimmage and tried to make his way to the café door.

But the crowd in the narrow street was now too great, and he was borne away until he succeeded in taking refuge in a doorway.

From thence he had a fine view of what was going on.

At least a dozen men were fighting, and the report of firearms soon began to vary the clashing of swords.

It did not last long.

Down the street came a double line of Zouaves wearing the French uniform, sweeping everything before them like a tornado.

In an incredibly short space of time they had swept the narrow way, and all that was left of the brief but desperate fray were three men, two dead, and one leaning against the wall, with the life blood gushing from his heart.

"It's more like a penny-rammer than real life," gasped Chippy Chunks, who had been unharmed by the passing Zouaves.

He slipped out of his hiding-place and made for the café, where, instead of the officer and Lottie, he found a man wearing a fez and a mixed costume—Si Hamick in the flesh.

He had just arrived upon the scene, coming up behind the Zouaves, whose up-street progress he was following with his eyes.

As he stood in the middle of the rather narrow doorway, Chippy Chunks could not pass him without inconvenience, so he politely asked him to make way. Si Hamick brought his little, leery eyes to bear upon the figure before him.

That he was astounded goes without saying—he was too much astonished to stir

"My lady is inside," said Chippy Chunks. "I want to get at her."

"Your lady, eh ?" said Si Hamick, slowly. "Who is she ?"

"Mrs. Tartar," said Chippy Chunks. "She's lost her husband and his brother, and she wants to find out where they are "

A light leaped into the eyes of Si Hamick, and, spreading out his arms, so as to effectually stop Chippy Chunks, he said—

"Your lady lost her husband ? English gentleman from yacht ?"

"That's him," exclaimed Chippy Chunks, breathlessly. "Do you know where he is ?"

"You come here," said Si Hamick, drawing away. "I tell you, perhaps, IF I KNOW."

Chippy Chunks did not exactly know what to make of him; but he went into the shadow of the next house with Si Hamick.

Already the people were returning, and some men were busy helping the wounded man away; the dead were left lying there awaiting the coming of an ambulance.

Nobody seemed to be particularly interested in them, and the few stragglers passing by scarcely looked at their still, upturned faces

"Your lady wish to know where her husband is ?" said Si Hamick, with a curious leer on his face.

"Yes—yes," said Chunks. "If you know, speak up; if you don't, I'll thank you not to keep me waiting here "

Si Hamick looked round cautiously, and then, thrusting his face close to that of Chippy Chunks, whispered—

"How much ?"

"Here — what do you mean ?" said Chippy Chunks. "Don't try to take a rise out of me, or I'll make a two-inch brad of you. Come, what do you mean ?"

"How much your lady pay ?" asked Si Hamick. "Two English pounds ?"

"I can't say what she'll give," said Chunks, "but I don't doubt she'll come down handsome. Stop a minute; I'll see if I can find her."

He went to the café, leaving Si Hamick standing in the shadow, watchful of all around, and ready to clear off at the least alarm.

Lottie was seated by one of the café tables talking to the officer, who was eagerly expostulating with her. On seeing Chunks she beckoned him to approach, which he did, quite oblivious of the amazed stare of the officer.

"This gentleman says I must return to the yacht," she said, wearily, "and he will see that every effort is made to find my husband and his brother."

Chippy Chunks thereupon told of his meeting with Si Hamick outside and the offer he had made.

Lottie was incredulous, but the officer was of opinion that there might be something in it.

"Go out." he said. "Give him the two pounds and hear what he has to say. Take this," he added, giving her a revolver, "and if he shows his teeth shoot him down. I will see that no harm befalls you."

"If I might make so bold, sir." said Chunks, "may I suggest that you go with Missus—"

"My good fellow," replied the officer, "the bare sight of my uniform would scare him away."

There was so much sound meaning in this remark that Lottie, who had hesitated a moment, did so no longer.

Rising, she took the weapon and went boldly out.

She was absent for awhile, and, getting anxious about her, the officer was about to sally forth when she reappeared.

Her face was very pale, but otherwise she exhibited no sign of agitation.

"My husband," she said, "is a prisoner in the Casbah. The Emir Abdul-ab-Bourad is insanely jealous of him or his brother, and intends to have him shot to-morrow."

"This is serious," said the officer.

"Can you not help him ?" asked Lottie.

"Perhaps," was the reply, " but it is very doubtful. Who is your informant."

"He refuses to give his name "

"But do you think his story is true ?"

"I have every reason to believe in it. If you were to send to the Emir—"

"He would probably have them killed at once, sink their bodies in the sea, and vow he knows nothing whatever about them. Pardon my being so plain, but I see you have an alternative plan to help them."

"My informant has given me one," said Lottie, "but first he bound me to secrecy. If he has told me the truth I think I can save them."

"Dear lady," said the officer, rising, "this is a sad affair. But let us hope all will be well. Whatever we can do shall be done—but we have to deal with cunning villains, who tax us in every way to the utmost. What do you propose to do ?"

"For the present," said Lottie, "I must return to the yacht."

"Permit me to escort you thither."

"I think it will be better," said Lottie, "if we returned as we came "

"As you will," said the officer.

As a parting exhortation to Chippy Chunks he bade him take good care of his mistress.

Chippy, by way of reply, exhibited his hammer.

"You see that ?" he said. "Well, I'll back it against any weapon going that don't shoot powder. The man as harms her will have to 'sperience what BOTH ends can do."

After a meaning tap upon the marble-topped table he declared himself ready to renew the position of escort.

Lottie took leave of the French officer, and with her faithful attendant vanished.

"Sacre !" said the officer, twirling his moustache; "if I were a little younger and she a widow, I would —bah ! Do not give way to sentiment. You have seen her but once, and may never see her again "

In the night, when the lights of the town were lessened to a few lamps scattered about, the White Wing's anchor was raised, and with all her canvas set she slowly tacked to and fro until she was off the upper end of the Cabash.

There she was out of sight of the ships in the harbour, and her anchor was dropped again.

At early dawn the gig was lowered, and two trusty seamen took the oars. Lottie and Chippy Chunks were the two passengers to be conveyed ashore.

Landing at a convenient place at the base of the huge rock on which the fortress stood, they began the ascent, Lottie leading.

Chippy Chunks did his best to keep up with her; but he was no match for the agile woman eager to rescue the man she loved.

Daylight was necessary for the work they had to do, for in the dark Lottie could not have found a certain barred window in the Eastern Tower which Si Hamick had told her of.

In her hand she bore a packet containing files and a small bottle of oil, wherewith to help cut through the bars without making any noise.

There were sentries on the watch for any sound, but probably at dawn they would be weary of the night's vigil and their senses would be dulled. They would also be looking for the welcome relief that took place an hour after the rising of the sun.

Up—up she went over the broken face of the rock, Chippy Chunks making the most strenuous efforts to keep near her.

What it cost him in aching bones is only known to himself. He never spoke of it then or thereafter, but he long remembered that morning climb.

Up, at last, to the summit of the rock, close upon a window strongly barred.

Lottie stood up and whispered one word—

"Tom !"

There was a movement within the cell, a springing up, and two dear faces peered through the bars.

"Don't speak," whispered Lottie; "take this"—she held up the packet she had brought with her—"and be as quiet and as quick as you can."

"My darling !" was all Tom said, as he grasped the packet and the small white hand that held it.

Above, a little way to the right, a swarthy sentry was pacing to and fro.

A slight sound—a stifled gasp which escaped the almost breathless Chippy Chunks—fell upon his ear.

Curiosity more than anything else prompted him to walk to the stone parapet and lean over to see from whence that sound came.

Round the corner of the Eastern Tower he saw a woman's dress gently fluttering in the soft morning breeze.

CHAPTER VII.

ABDUL-AB-BOURAD'S PLANS—THE STRUGGLE IN THE CELL—THINGS LOOK VERY DARK INDEED.

RESTLESS and troubled was the night spent by the Emir Abdul-ab-Bourad.

His private room in the Cabash was a small apartment in the Eastern Tower, high up, so as to get the full benefit of the evening breeze.

It was furnished with Moorish richness and sim-

plicity. The walls were covered, except over the narrow windows, with rich hangings, and the floor hidden with a thick carpet. Two or three hookahs, their long tubes tipped with amber and jewelled mouthpieces, a quaint vase or two, and a pile of sumptuous cushions are all that need be described.

Here the wily, irritable old Moor passed a wretched time, striving in vain to get sleep or rest during the dark hours.

He had no faith in his wife Alea. Neither Turk nor Moor ever trust their woman-folk an inch, and he was furious against her for having cast an eye—literally, one eye—at the Frank. It mattered nothing to him whether the favoured Frank returned her signal of affection or not. As one who had lured away the affection of his wife he must die.

He hated Ned because he was so good-looking, also Tom because he was his brother, and he longed to kill them.

But Alea had said that they must live, and the infatuated old Moor, suspecting all the time that she was mocking him, did not like to go against her.

But there are more ways of killing a pig than by the usual rough-and-ready butchery, and the Emir was busy working out some plan to satisfy his revengeful feelings and yet keep faith with Alea.

He would send them into the interior, to the Atlas mountains, and dispose of them as slaves.

It was a common thing well on into the present century for such an atrocity to be committed by Moors who had plundered and sunk an English or French vessel in the quiet waters of the Mediterranean.

It is not an entirely unheard of thing to this day.

"By the beard of the Prophet," said the Emir, "I will do it."

With the very first peep of dawn he threw open the door of his room and sallied forth to carry out his plan, but first he must arouse Alea and tell her he had decided to set them free.

Her room was in the adjoining tower, which could only be reached by means of a long passage, guarded by grim, silent eunuchs, ten in number, whom the Moor had imported from Turkey as guards over his domestic sanctity.

He knew he would find them, like watch dogs, at their post, sleeping perhaps, but ready to wake on the slightest sound.

To reach the entrance of the passage he had to descend two flights of stairs, and at the bottom of the first he met one of the captains of the ordinary Moorish castle guard, who prostrated himself before him.

"Ah ! Yurra Khan," cried the Emir; "you bring me news ?"

"Oh ! mighty ruler," replied Yurra Khan, "there are infidels without—a white-faced Peri and a strange, unholy man, wearing a paper turban—who are holding converse with the prisoners."

"Pig ! why not seize them ?" cried Abdul-ab-Bourad; "and not waste time in coming to me."

"My lord," was the answer, "it is done. I have sent forth thirty men to waylay them as they retreat to their boat, which lies below upon the shore."

"Bring them before me," said Abdul-ab-Bourad. "But first send hither some men. I will change the prison of the Franks."

Yurra Khan rose up, and, bowing thrice, retreated by the way he came.

In a minute or two the rattle of arms was heard, and a body of men came to the foot of the staircase, where the Emir joined them.

Among them was a big, dark-eyed Nubian, who held a key in his hand.

He was the jailer set over the cell where Tom and Ned were confined.

Another flight of steps were descended, and they were level with the cell. A short passage brought them to the door.

Abdul-ab-Bourad signalled for the Nubian to open it stealthily, and for the men to be ready to use their arms if necessary.

The well-oiled lock was swiftly turned, and the door thrown open.

Then a strange sight saluted the eyes of the astounded Moor.

Tom and Ned had just succeeded in each filing a bar through top and bottom, and were breaking them away.

" Seize but do not harm the Franks !" he cried in the Moorish tongue, at the same time rushing into the cell, sword in hand.

" Yield yourselves, accursed ones !" he shouted in English.

Tom and Ned, each with a detached bar in his hand, startled by his voice and the rattle of arms, turned from the window and faced him.

A drawn sword flashed before Tom's eyes, and without a moment's hesitation he aimed a blow at the Emir, who, unprepared for so daring an assault, received it on his head and fell senseless on the floor.

" Hit out, Ned," cried Tom, "for life and liberty !"

At the same moment a wild scream from Lottie was heard outside.

It was followed by a shouting of men in the Moorish tongue.

Half maddened by the hope of escape being dashed for the time, also the certainty of Lottie being in peril, the brothers laid about them furiously, and terrible blows were received by the foremost of their assailants.

Two were laid out disabled on the floor, one with a cracked skull and the second with a broken arm, but the others pressed forward in a body and hampered the gallant pair.

They fought while they had room to strike a blow, but in the narrow confines of the cell they could do little more.

Pressed close to the wall, they were seized by the arms and legs and dragged down to the stone floor, where they still struggled until they were securely bound.

All this was not done without some trampling upon the fallen.

In the excitement even the sacred person of the Emir was forgotten.

Heavy feet trod upon his body, bruising it in a score places, and trampling his linen garments into ragged disorder, which the men regarded with palpable dismay.

He was insensible, and when they raised him up groaned heavily, but gave no other sign of life.

One of their number directed him to be taken back to his chamber, and a personage named Effendi to be sent for.

His next care was to have Tom and Ned, who in their despair were silent but still defiant, placed in some other place of safety.

They were lifted up, bound hand and foot as they were, and carried down below the basement of the tower to a cell, into which they were cast and left alone.

There all was black as the eternal night—not one single ray of light penetrated the dismal hole from window or elsewhere.

There was not even a keyhole to the closely-fitting door, for the lock was entirely on the outside.

Neither could speak for awhile, and it was Ned who at length broke silence.

"Tom, old fellow," he said.

"Oh ! Ned—Lottie !" Tom groaned.

"It's her I am thinking of."

"It won't bear thinking of. Why did she risk so much for us ?"

"Because she is true blood, Tom, and although they've got her—"

"Killed her, you mean."

"Well, Tom, wouldn't you rather have her dead ?"

There was a short silence after this query. Then Tom spoke.

"Better dead," he said ; "but it is very hard and bitter to bear. All our old troubles are as nothing to this, Ned."

"Nothing."

Another silence.

"Say, Tom," said Ned, "there'll be a row at home when our people hear of this."

"Yes," replied Tom, bitterly ; "but will that help us ? Will it bring Lottie back to life, if she IS dead ? Oh ! Ned, I can't bear to think of it. She may be ALIVE, and, if so, do you know what they will do with her ?"

"I dare not think, Tom."

"They will send her into the interior of this accursed country and SELL her to some brutal chief."

"And don't I pity him !" said Ned, with grim humour. "If he so much as WINKED at Lottie she would kill him. Come, Tom, don't quite give way even now. Starfish was below in the yacht ; he saw what took place—he must have done so !—and, of course, he'll go to the French governor, who will put a stop to the high jinks of these black brutes."

"I'll try to look at matters hopefully, as you do," said Tom, stifling a groan. "But I know that it will all be a matter of diplomatic letter-writing. Our Government will complain, and the French here will assure them that justice shall be done. Half-a-dozen ignorant black devils, innocent of crime as far as we are concerned, will be strung up or shot. The affair will be referred to in the papers at home as an instance of the far-reaching power of the British and the impossibility of those who wrong an Englishman escaping justice, and there will be an end of it."

"I won't see all black just yet," said Ned. "And by the way, Tom, we've forgotten poor Chippy Chunks, who was with Lottie."

"Ah ! yes," ejaculated Tom. "Poor old fellow !"

"He won't find much use for his hammer and tacks here, eh, Tom ?" said Ned.

"I don't know," replied Tom, wearily ; "I can't think of him, or myself, or even you, Ned. It's all Lottie—a prisoner among those brutes ! Curse them ! if once I get free and find they have so much as harmed a hair of her head, I'll—"

THE TWO TARTARS:

Or, Tom and Ned among the Moors.

"BE AS QUIET AND AS QUICK AS YOU CAN," LOTTIE WHISPERED AS SHE HANDED TOM THE PACKET.

"Steady, Tom ; don't waste your energies in threatening now.   Wait until we are free, and then we may do something together "

" I'll try to be quiet, Ned."

And then the two brothers once more lapsed into silence.

CHAPTER VIII.

CHIPPY CHUNKS FINDS HIMSELF IN A FIX—HE VENTURES INTO THE CABASH, AND HAS SOME REMARKABLE ADVENTURES THERE.

HIPPY CHUNKS never had a very clear idea how it had all happened. As he recalled the events of that particular time, when he and Lottie stood upon the rock anxiously watching Tom and Ned work on the iron bars, all he could remember was a sudden yell and a rush of men from somewhere, a scream from his mistress, and scuffling.

He dimly called to mind being knocked down and using his one and only weapon upon a collection of naked feet with considerable effect, the recipients of the blows leaping into the air with the most unearthly yells.

Finally, he recollected that he scrambled to his feet and received another blow somewhere about the head from the butt of a long musket, which knocked him out of time.

On recovering from this blow he found himself alone, some distance down on the eastern side of the cliff, and fairly wedged in between two pieces of rock that rose up like walls on either side of him.

Overhead there was a strip of brilliant sky, and through a fissure he could see the towers of the Cabash a hundred feet above him, but all else was shut out from his sight.

"Well !" he said, as soon as he could collect his thoughts, "I wonder who shovelled me down here, and what's come of that pearty angel-missus ? Blessed if I ain't—no it CAN'T be— Come out of it, Chippy.   Be a man and rise to the occasion."

He had to struggle some little time before he could get himself free from his truly perilous position, and when he succeeded in getting upon his feet he looked about for his hammer.

It had fallen with him, and lay close by, half embedded in the narrow, sandy bottom between the rocks.

Having picked it up and ascertained that it had received no injury he proceeded to examine himself.

Slowly he tapped himself all over, and finally repeated aloud—

" Bruised a bit, but no cracks or breakages."

The next thing to do was to get out of his narrow place of confinement, which was quite twenty feet deep.

It was as upright as a wall on either side of him, and he could not have escaped unaided but for the closeness of the two rocks.

" I must do it sweep-fashion," he thought.

With his back against one rock and his knees against the other he worked himself up, and what it cost him in the way of smart for chafed skin and aches for stiffened joints he alone of mortal man could tell.

But he reached the summit at last, he saw to his amazement that the sun was fairly high up, and that it must be quite ten o'clock.

He had lain insensible for some hours, and there was still a very uncanny buzzing in his head, which in the first excitement of returning consciousness he had taken little notice of.

But the thing that troubled him most was the sense of utter loneliness that came over him.

There were several vessels sailing slowly about far out at sea, and one steamer on the horizon was going west, leaving a long trail of smoke behind her ; but there was not a living creature near, and the White Wing was gone.

He turned his face up to the window of the cell lately occupied by Tom and Ned.   It had the appearance of a black, sightless eye, the bars being gone, and the glare of the white walls by contrast giving the interior an appearance of gloom it hardly possessed.

" Am I a-dreaming ?" asked Chippy Chunks.

He passed his hand over the back of his head and winced.

There was a gash and some clotted blood there —real enough to assure him that he was awake.

" The whole lot's vanished," he muttered, "and I'm left alone, like Robinson Cruiser—blowed if I ain't !"

Without any definite purpose, he slowly climbed up the rocks and returned to the window of the cell.

Two pieces of broken bars stood up like stumps of teeth in a giant's mouth, unsightly in his eye.

Chippy Chunks laid hold of them, and drew himself up to get a clear view of the cell.   It was empty, and the door stood open, showing the passage beyond.

" I may as well go in and have a look round me," muttered Chippy Chunks, wearily.

The buzzing in his head was getting stronger, and a strange indifference to all things mundane was coming over him.

" Why not ?" he murmured.   "As well there as anywhere.   Life's a game o' pitch and toss—one moment it's head uppards and then comes the tail "

He scrambled through the opening and rolled down inside, falling headlong fashion upon the floor.

There he lay awhile, smiling inanely upon the ceiling.

" A little while ago," he said, " it was bees in my head, and now it's muffin bells, two on 'em ringing one agin another.   There ought to be a law agin it.   Them as works all night wants to sleep by day.   Muf-fins !"

He got up slowly, stared about him a little, and staggered off down the passage.   Presently he came to several stone steps, some going up and others going down.

" A man can allus go down," he said, musingly ; " but chances o' goin' up don't come every day.   Up it is."

He found a strange difficulty in getting upstairs, just as if his feet had been shod with lead ; but he managed to reach a small landing.

There he found a passage. It was that which led to the private apartment of Alea; but the eunuchs were not there on guard.

Chippy Chunks staggered and rolled down the passage, occasionally putting his hand to his head, and muttering to himself—

"No muffin bells now—church bells—unkimmon like St. Bride's, Fleet-street. Hawfully strong! What's this? Big Ben a-tolling. Stop it! He's too big to toll, specially in a man's head. There ain't no room allowed in it for vibration. Stop! I say, or my head 'll burst. Hallo! where's this?"

He had passed through an open door, and stood in a private chamber—the boudoir of Alea.

In front of a semi-circle of cushions were three chibooks, one of them faintly smoking, as if only recently abandoned. On the thick carpet lay several musical instruments, among them a crude sort of harp and a zither.

A rich inlaid writing-table stood on the right, and half-a-dozen handsome Moorish vases filled with flowers were dotted about the chamber.

"Apartments to let," said Chippy Chunks, dreamily, "and the price a tidy figger, I'll be bound. Being unkimmon sleepy I'll take 'em. Money no hobject just now. Chippy, old man, YOU'RE DRUNK!"

He reeled across the room, fell upon the cushions, and rolled over to the back, where he curled himself up and lapsed into a state of unconsciousness.

Poor old Chippy was worn out with suffering and fatigue.

He lay on the dark side of the room, and one of the cushions he had disarranged rolled over so as to conceal his face and half his body. If he only kept quiet he would scarcely be noticed, and at the outset he lay as still and as noiseless as the dead.

Now Alea had gone to see her lord and master, who, having the proverbial thick cranium of the Moor, had suffered somewhat, but not so extensively as might have been expected, from the blow Tom dealt him.

Effendi was a doctor, and having administered a restorative, announced that my lord would do well, he being by favour of the Prophet a man whom no pig of an infidel could slay.

Abdul-ab-Bourad also thought it necessary to feign imperviousness to infidel blows, and when Alea paid him a visit of condolence he laughed.

"Be not anxious, sweet one," he said. "I am of the faithful, and the arm of a Frank raised to strike withers away."

"Truly, my lord," she answered, "thou art good and great. And the infidels—what of them? Are they free?"

"I despatched them from here a little while since," he answered; "for lo! the white woman came for her husband, and I sent them away together to the mountains."

"Is that how you keep your word, oh! master mine?" asked Alea, pale under her brown skin.

"I spared their lives, oh! rosebud of women."

"For what? To be slaves For the woman I care not, but the men—"

"Alea," said Abdul-ab-Bourad, "I did as you wish—I spared them—those haughty Franks. They will live in a rage of jealousy—to go mad as they think of my love and me"

"What! when the white wife is with them?" said Alea, innocently.

She looked straight into his eyes and saw something there which raised up a sudden fury in her heart.

They were alone, and no eye saw how the woman dominated the man in private.

She fell upon him like an avenging spirit.

She boxed his ears, pulled his beard, knocked off his turban, and struck him with her clenched fist upon his shaven head.

The fury of a score of fiends for the time possessed her.

"Alea—Alea! love of my heart," he gasped, as he fairly grovelled on the cushions. "Why this anger? How have I offended thee, my dove?"

"Send the white wife AFTER her husband," she hissed. "You hear! AFTER him, or I will tear every stone of this place down to find where thou hast hidden her, you faithless old CAMEL!"

She shot the last word at him like a projectile, and, turning on her heel, gathered her robes about her and left the room.

Outside the eunuchs were in waiting, and, dull, soulless creatures as they were, they could yet see that something entertaining had been going on.

A feeble smile parted their lips as they fell in behind her.

With swift footsteps she hastened back to her chamber, and threw herself down upon the cushions in a transport of jealousy.

"I'll have no rival here," she cried, tearing at the velvet coverings of the cushions like a cat. "I'll only give him a little while ere I begin to pull the castle about his dog-like head."

And so she raged on, unconscious of the vicinity of Chippy Chunks, who slept like an infant through it all.

Abdul-ab-Bourad felt it was time to hurry up matters.

Tom and Ned, bound and gagged, were already being borne away towards the Atlas Mountains, to be disposed of to some chief in the vast unknown tract beyond in need of slaves.

And Lottie was held a prisoner in the Cabash, because she was, for an infidel, very fair.

But now the old scoundrel felt that he must dispose of her. No doubt she would bring in many shekels of silver and gold, more than Alea herself.

So he gave orders in all haste, and Lottie, swathed in robes that hid her face and form, with her mouth gagged and hands bound together under the muslin about her, was got ready to send away.

Then Abdul-ab-Bourad ordered Si Hamick to command the escort, and see that he got a good price for the unbeliever, on pain of having his ears cut off and his eyes made as holes in the earth.

Si Hamick was not sorry.

He had in his pocket the remnant of the bribe he had received from Lottie, and he shrank in his shoes when he found that she had been made prisoner.

If once she was sold as a slave she never would be able to betray him.

And there was another thought in his mind, of which more anon. It was only half hatched as yet.

The old Moor having made these preparations hurried off to fetch his Alea.

She should see the "white wife" taken away, and learn from it how faithful and loving he was.

Straight to her chamber he went, and found her lying quietly with her eyes closed.

The cushion tearing was all over for the present, and she was resting from her labours.

"Pearl of Paradise, awake!" he said.

The Pearl opened her eyes and looked at him sulkily.

"Well!" she replied.

"Come and see the white-faced one carried into slavery," he said.

She rose up slowly and put her arms about his neck.

"And thou DOST love me?" she asked.

"Ay! even more than my life," he replied.

At this moment Chippy Chunks woke up, and, finding something soft upon his face, tossed it aside.

The slight noise he made caused the old Moor to look in his direction. He saw Chippy in a sitting position, in the act of carefully adjusting his paper cap.

He was not as yet fully awake, and in a general way was taking things easily.

"Curses," cried Abdul-ab-Bourad. "Alea—woman, speak. Is this another of your infidel lovers?"

"My lord," she cried, "I have never—before—seen—this—this—thing!"

"A lie—a lie! Ho! there, you guards. In here. Bear the faithless one to a dungeon."

"My lord—my lord," cried Alea, clinging to him. "I am innocent. I know him not. He is as some monster that comes in my sleep. Could I love him?"

Chippy Chunks got up slowly and looked bewildered.

He could not understand what was said, as they spoke in the Moorish tongue, but he could see there was a family disturbance, and felt sure he had something to do with it.

"Excuse me," he said, advancing, "but if I've skeered you a bit I—"

"Guards, there—guards!" cried the Emir.

"Oh! my lord," cried Alea, clinging to him like a leech, "be merciful. If I am to die let it not be for HIM. I know not the creature."

"Wouldst die for any of these Franks?" demanded Abdul-ab-Bourad, trying to free himself.

"Aye, old mummy, I would!" she cried, passionately, throwing him off; "if I had the right. Were I the white face wife I would die—DIE a hundred times for the MAN you have sent into accursed slavery. But for you, shadow of a true blooded Moor, I'd not bear a finger-ache. The guards are at the door—open it. Admit them so that they may hear what I say."

The old Emir clutched his beard and fairly danced with fury. Jealousy, humiliation, and a score of mixed emotions, drove him nearly frantic.

Alea, in one of the most mocking moods that will at times come over woman-kind, shot dart after dart into his rankling wounds.

"Old fool," she cried; "you BLACK FACE—idiot! did you ever think that I loved you? Pah! Here, white man, you are only a poor creature to look at, but you are better than he. Come and comfort me."

She threw open her arms to the staggered Chippy Chunks, who did not understand a word she said.

But the action was that of one who needed protection, and, rising to the occasion, he hopped to her side and put his arm round her waist.

"Look here, Mister Christy Minstrel or Mohawker, whichever you may be," he said, "it's plain to me that you've been a rounding on this pretty poppet in rather an unmanly way."

"Dog!" screamed Abdul-ab-Bourad in English.

"Dog away," returned Chippy Chunks; "you won't rile me. I'm as good a dog as you are any day. Here, Maria, or whatever your pretty name may be, jist stand by and see fair play. Don't holler or make any row. See me polish him off. Now, Old Christy, up with your fives. If you use that flat-iron I've got a hammer, but let's have it out manly and fair."

He tried to get free of Alea, but she would not let him go until, in her wild defiance of the Moor, she had kissed him.

"Well, I'm blowed if that isn't a stimerlant," said Chippy Chunks. "It's made a Sayers of me. You've revived the old grit o' the ring, which have died out of the lot of soft fists of to-day. Let me go, my dear. If I don't upper-cut him in 'arf-a-minute don't you look at me again."

She let him go, laughing wildly, and Chippy, his eyes blazing with the courage of his youth, went for the Emir, who made for the door and threw it open.

The eunuchs were there, hearing all through the flimsy partitions, but standing impassive, as if they had been made of stone.

"Seize him!" yelled the Emir.

Poor old Chippy, with his rheumatism and age and other things heavily handicapping him, was no match for the muscular ebony men who threw themselves upon him.

He hit out, but he might as well have struck as many blocks of wood, and they soon got him down spread-eagled upon the floor.

"Oh! brave Emir; noble Abdul-ab-Bourad!" laughed Alea. "With ten wild BEASTS he conquers a white man, whose bones are bent by age. Ha! ha! ha!"

"Be he white man or white devil, he shall die!" yelled the Emir, "and you, too, hag of the evil eye! I'll bind you both together and burn you."

CHAPTER IX.

GOING INTO CAPTIVITY—THE MIRTHLESS VILLAGE
—NIGHT-TIME AND THE LIONS.

TOM and Ned, bound and strung pannier-fashion across the hump of a camel, were borne away in a south-easterly direction, towards the Atlas Mountains.

To ease them they had boards on which their feet could rest; but this was not done in mercy—for what true Moor would show mercy to a white man—but because the prisoners were valuable merchandise.

A crippled slave will fetch but little—the buyer asks for them strong and sound.

On either side, in advance and in the rear, walked a number of men of mixed breed, commanded by Yurra Khan.

Two Nubians, five Albanians, three Turks, and half-a-dozen Moors formed the body.

They were ruffians every one, raggedly attired but heavily armed, poor to mendicity but swaggering as princes of old.

Crafty of eye, cruel of mind, stealthy of foot, they strode along, the only speaker Yurra Khan, and he breaking silence simply to threaten or to curse.

The sun was blazing above, and the air was like the breath of a blasting furnace.

Sweltering in the heat, the prisoners reclined helplessly in their bonds, silent and thinking.

Death would have been welcome—anything rather than the relaxing torture of the hour, but they had ceased to despair.

Ned had only done so a little at first, and Tom had recovered from the temporary depression that had assailed him.

After all, they were alive, and while there is life there is hope.

Lottie was, as heretofore, their chief anxiety.

Tom could have borne his sufferings lightly if he had but known that she was free of her enemies.

Ned's hopeful words had taken root.

If dead, then her loss would have to be avenged. If living, might she not, in her strong womanhood, be able to withstand the onslaught of a foe?

As on the day before there was no wind.

At noon it entirely ceased, and there was nothing but the rays of the pitiless sun.

Heat, we are told, is motion, but there was no sense of it that day. Even that most impervious of animals, the camel, felt it.

Progress at midday was impossible, so they halted and rested as well as they could, the men making a shady place with a huge blanket spread out upon the points of bayonets. Under this they all gathered, safe in a way from sunstroke, but sweltering with heat.

There was little talking and no laughter. Neither guard nor prisoners had an ounce of merriment in them.

One of the men carried a small keg of water, from which he gave the prisoners a drink. They were in sore need of it and thanked him.

He was a ragged, thin-ribbed, swarthy fellow, a cross between a Turk and an Albanian, with a sash round his waist, in which were stuck a huge knife and two pistols.

"We take care of our captives," he said. "The men must take care of themselves."

The significance of this reply was not to be mistaken. It gave the two brothers, for the first time, a real knowledge of the fate in store for them.

"We are to be sold for slaves," said Tom, "and shall learn for certain whether the stories of hellish misery the Moors and Arabs inflict upon their captives are true.

"It will be interesting so far," returnd Ned, drily. "I remember reading that once in their clutches escape is hopeless."

Tom made him no answer. The heat was overcoming him and he was dozing off. Ned followed his example, and they both slept until it was time to go forward again.

On resuming their route they moved along quickly, and towards evening halted in a village built near a grove of date-trees.

The spare population all came out to look at them—the young, the old, the afflicted.

But the men only came to mock and not to commiserate. Here were two Franks going into a living perdition—two of the accursed race who had invaded their land and left so many traces of their fiery spirit upon it.

With veiled faces the women looked closely at Tom and Ned, who bore the scrutiny with impassive looks.

Some of the women took off their caps, and after a long look at their faces replaced the coverings tenderly, saying—

"The white man hath an Allah who makes them goodly to the eye."

But they spoke in a language the prisoners did not understand, and they could not read the faces they did not see.

One child put a fresh date into Ned's mouth, and clapped his hands as it was eaten with evident relish.

But he did not laugh or even smile. There was no laughter in that lone spot.

Before leaving, Yurra Khan addressed himself to the people, briefly informing them that if ever they spoke of having seen two white men going away captive the wrath of all good sons of the Faithful would fall upon them.

"Your homes will be destroyed," he said, in conclusion, "your eyes put out, and you will be sent to work like beasts in a land where water is not known."

It was late, long after dark, when they halted again, and then only for two hours.

A supper of dates and brown bread was served out, and the prisoners' arms released, so that they might eat it without troubling the guard.

A watchful eye was kept upon them as they ate, simply to preserve their strength, and likewise to assuage their misery if for nothing else.

Tom had got over the first great shock of grief, and was his stronger self again, calm and resolute, inclined to hope for the best, but ready to bear the worst.

They soon resumed their march, the men keeping close together, with guns loaded and cocked, for they were now in the land where the lion prowls in search of prey, and of all his tribe he who wanders near the desert is the fiercest of all.

The native fears nothing so much as the lion.

All the stories and pictures of the Arabs hunting and fighting lions in the open are lies. Neither Arab nor Moor will ever face the king of beasts, unless he be one of a multitude.

They dig holes and trap a lion now and then, and as it lies growling in the depths below they will stone it to death or riddle it with bullets, but that is the boldest thing they will do to rid themselves of a lasting terror.

And the lion knows it, too, for he will sometimes take up his quarters near a village, sleeping by day, and boldly walking into it by night, sure of finding the inhabitants with doors made fast.

In epicurean fashion he will go round and pick out a goat to his fancy, on which he will bestow a nip in the loins, and then calmly carry it away for his wife and cubs waiting outside for their supper.

There were lions abroad that night, roaring here and there, brute answering brute as deep answers unto deep, the still air echoing the fearful sound.

Only two hearts in that cavalcade were without fear. Neither Tom nor Ned quailed or cared for the peril of the hour.

But the mongrel guard quaked and shivered and moved their bloodshot eyes in the direction of each particular roar, cursing the power of the man who had sent them into that country at night.

Suddenly one of the men uttered a cry and pulled the trigger of his gun.

He was by Ned's side, and the flash lit up the ground ahead, so that the gallant boy for a moment saw all things within twenty yards of him.

Of what he saw he only remembered one thing, and that was a huge lion quietly approaching with his red tongue swinging from side to side licking his lips.

As soon as the gun was fired the men broke away, yelling to Allah for mercy, and the camel with its two bound prisoners sank slowly upon its knees.

It was shivering with terror as they could feel, but their attention was distracted from it by a yell the like of which they had seldom, if ever, heard before.

It came from a man, one of the guard, on whom the lion had sprung.

One cry only he uttered, and then followed sounds of the tearing of flesh and crunching of bones.

It was sickening—horrible !

With their arms free and possessed of the simplest weapons the brothers would not have cared.

But bound and helpless as they were, and compelled to listen to the rending of a human body by a beast of prey was more than man could bear with calmness.

The rest of the guard had fled, whither it was impossible to tell.

Soon the taint of blood was in the air. Other lions, lionesses, and cubs, had scented it, and were bearing down upon the spot.

The busy lion knew what they were coming for, and hurried with his feast, grunting and snarling over his awful meal.

" Ned !" whispered Tom.

" Yes, old boy."

" Keep still.   It is our only chance of escape."

" Is there a chance ?"

" I can't say.   If not, good-bye."

" Good-bye, old fellow."

A touch of the hand would have been something. But it was denied them.

Their bonds had been knotted by practised persons, and there was no hope of shaking off or breaking them.

Still the hurried rending of flesh and cracking of bones went on, and nearer and nearer drew other lions, hungering for a feast.

CHAPTER X.

THE TORCHES FROM AMONG THE ROCKS—A GRIM CHIEF AND HIS FOLLOWERS—A SIGH IN THE SILENT NIGHT.

S this the end ?" Tom asked himself.

He had a brave disposition, his heart was sound, and fear, as some of us experience it, was unknown to him ; but the thought of being clawed to death by a wild beast while he was helplessly bound was horrible.

But over and above all thought of himself was the appalling reflection that Lottie was in the hands of the cruel, remorseless Moors. Of her fate he dare not fully think—indeed, he could not.

Like a flash of light the joys of his life during the past year or two flashed before him.   Then again was darkness, and the roaring and snarling of the approaching lions.

Another moment and there was a flash of real fire before his eyes.

At first he doubted the evidence of his senses, but in a little while he made out that it was a number of torches borne by some men whom he could but faintly see.

That they were clad in white garments, and their faces dark, was all that he could discern.

They emerged from behind some huge rocks in the neighbourhood, which, owing to the darkness, he had not hitherto observed.

Behind them he could see the flashing of weapons, spears and swords as far as he could make out, and by their elevation evidently carried by men on horseback.

A few moments after they appeared the men began to shout, and rude instruments of the cymbal class were loudly clashed.

The lion hard by paused in his feast, and after an angry stare in the direction of the torches, seized with his teeth what was left of his prey and dragged it away into the desert.

At the same time the other lions which had gathered round became dumb.

The sight of fire had checked their advance.

On came the men bearing the torches, and as they drew nearer Tom saw they were gigantic Nubians, with faces as dark as ebony. They wore white turbans and short trousers. Their arms and legs were bare.

Behind them rode an Arab or Moorish chief— Tom could hardly say which. He seemed to be something between the two.   In his hand he carried a bright-bladed, light sword.

In close attendance upon him were a score of mounted men of similar appearance but of less majestic mien.   Some carried swords and the others spears.

The foremost Nubian espied the camel and its burden. These swarthy sons of Africa are gifted with the sight of wild beasts, and can with their vision pierce the darkness with the most wonderful distinctness.

A shout burst from their lips, and on a word from their chief the whole cavalcade hurried forward.

A chaos of men and torches surrounded the camel, and the chief, riding up to Tom, cast a curious glance at him.

Then he wheeled his horse—with a touch of his knees, it is to be assumed, for his hands did not move—and rode round to Ned, whom he also favoured with an inspection.

Not a word did he utter, not a sound escaped his grim followers.

In obedience to a sign from the chief one of the Nubians handed his torch to a neighbour, then with a keen knife which he drew from his belt he advanced upon Tom, and after a few flourishes which had an ominous look cut the bonds that bound him.

Ned was also released, and the two brothers got upon their feet, stiff and sore, and hardly able to stand.

Another sign from the chief and the camel was seized and half dragged, half lifted on to its knees.

Reassured by the presence of light and men it scrambled to its feet ; but it still trembled and turned its head slowly to the right and left, its wild eyes looking for the dreaded lions.

The chief regarded the two brothers, who simply bowed their thanks and waited for him to speak.

They were not quite sure whether they had found friends or only fallen into the hands of another antagonistic power.

"You are English?" said the chief, breaking the silence.

He spoke the language very clearly, but with a peculiar lingering on the vowels that strengthened the words and gave them a musical ring.

"We are," answered Tom; "and please accept our thanks for a rescue from almost certain death."

"Keep your thanks for awhile," was the dry response. "Your name."

"Tom Tartar."

"And he—this youth?"

"My brother Ned."

"Who are you, and how is it I find you here in this sorry state?"

In a few words Tom told his story—who he was, his object in being in the country, his unwarranted arrest and subsequent treatment.

Not a muscle of the chief's face moved.

He listened as impassive as a statue, and when Tom had finished his story he made no comment upon it.

Turning to two of his followers, he motioned for them to dismount, and then, with a wave of his hand, requested Tom and Ned to take their places in the saddle.

They could do nothing else but comply with the somewhat curtly-expressed desire, and as well as their stiffened limbs would permit they climbed into the vacated seats.

Once there they sat easily enough, and the chief, with another sign, set the whole body in motion.

They had come from the right of the route Tom and Ned had been taking, and now bore away to the left, going further inland, and not, as Tom hoped, towards Algiers.

He and Ned were apparently unguarded, but the attendants of the chief, who rode on with feigned indifference straight ahead, were practically enclosing the brothers in a roughly-formed circle.

"Prisoners still," said Tom, in a low tone.

"Very likely," replied Ned, cheerily; "but not so closely confined as we should be in the stomach of a lion."

Tom made him no rejoinder.

He feared that they had fallen into the hands of those who would bear them away into slavery.

In a little while the sandy waste was changed to broken, rocky ground, gradually sloping upwards, and winding about through defiles so narrow that a dozen determined men, well-armed, could have held them against an army.

After about three hours' travel a halt took place.

The riders dismounted, and with ropes tethered their horses together.

Small bundles of fodder were untied and placed under their noses, and to each man was given a handful of dates.

Tom and Ned had their share, and ate them gratefully, but of water, which they most needed, there was none.

By chewing the stones of the fruit they succeeded in assuaging thirst, and, glad of respite from this form of suffering, they stretched themselves upon the ground, in imitation of the example of the chief and his followers.

The torches were extinguished and apparently all lay down in search of repose.

Weariness lay heavily upon Tom, and if he had thought there was a chance of escape he could not have availed himself of it.

So he gave himself up to the insidious influence of sleep and found rest in unconsciousness.

Ned also yielded to the allurements of the drowsy god, and the camp was soon at rest.

Absolute stillness reigned around.

The horses had eaten their fodder, and lay prone on the earth.

All the camp slept but one man—a mighty Nubian—who stood still as a figure of bronze just behind the unconscious Ned and Tom, with his naked sword ready to use if either or both made any movement that could be construed into an attempt to escape.

On either side the black cliffs, overhead a strip of sky jewelled with stars, ahead an unknown land, peopled by a race of whom is recorded stories that freeze the blood and stir the heart with longings to avenge.

What is the fate that lies before the brothers?

Hark! what is that. A breath of air coming from where nobody knows, and going no one knows whither. A sigh or a groan heaved out from the bosom of the night.

The still, watchful Nubian hears it, and bends his head in terror or reverence as he distinguishes the sound, while a few muttered words escape his lips.

Then all is still again.

What sound is this? Is it an omen of coming woe, or no more than a wandering eddy of disturbed air, winging its way to the desert, there to raise one of those startling columns of sand that mean death to all who are sucked into its choking embrace?

Who can tell?

It has passed down that narrow defile and gone on its way to the desert unheard and unnoticed by the prisoners, who sleep on in peace.

CHAPTER XI.

THE EMIR'S WRATH—SI HAMICK GIVES GOOD COUNSEL—ON THE ROAD TO SLAVERY.

E left Chippy Chunks in a very perilous position, and for a brief time we will return to the Cabash to ascertain what became of him and Lottie.

The Emir, Abdulab-Bourad, was in a terrible way.

It is doubtful if ever he had been so exasperated in his life as he was by the scene in his wife's chamber.

His first idea was to have Chippy and Alea tied neck and heels together and flung off the summit of one of the towers.

Then he thought he would have them roasted alive, and after that he designed to cut them up piecemeal.

Finally he had them bound hand and foot and flung into one of the rooms adjacent, where he locked them in, and then retired to his own chamber to think over what he should do.

Thinking, however, was well-nigh impossible.

It was maddening for him to dwell on the fact that the woman he knew, and whom he believed once adored him, should jeer his mighty person as she had done, and submit to the arm of a Frank being put round her waist, without his having at once ordered them away for instant execution.

It did not matter that Chippy was an aged Frank, very rocky on his legs, and with no more beauty in him than there was in a gorilla.

He had embraced Alea in the presence of her lord, and if the stars should fall and the whole earth heave up like a bubble of molten lava, it could not be a greater catastrophe in the eyes of the Emir.

As he could not think for himself he sent for Si Hamick, whom he had entrusted with the mission of disposing of Lottie in the most lucrative slave-market he knew of.

Possibly he had not started. If he had shown ordinary activity he would have been off ere then, but as it happened he had not finished his preparations, and having a full knowledge of the explosive state of the Emir he hastened to him.

Having prostrated himself the usual number of times, and thrown in one extra bit of grovelling to soften the soul of his master, he ventured to ask—

"What is it my lord would have me do? Let him command his faithful servant, Si Hamick."

"Thou hast seen the aged Frank," said the Emir—"he who wears a turban of paper and goes about with his arms bared like a woman who washeth clothes?"

"I have seen him, my lord," answered Si Hamick, "and he is poison in my sight."

Abdul-ab-Bourad, in flowery language, garnished with Oriental expressions of a substantial order, told Si Hamick the story of the discovery of Chippy Chunks and also of the sneers and jeers of the handsome Alea.

Si Hamick was so overcome with horror that he was obliged to cover his face and wriggle like a worm upon the floor.

When he was sufficiently recovered to raise his head and speak, he looked like a man who had narrowly escaped an apoplectic fit.

"Speak, thou mangy dog!" cried the Emir. "What shall be done to her who betrays one so mighty as I and he who brings his half-clothed carcase into the secret chamber of my house?"

"Let them be sold—for slaves, oh! Father of the Stars," said Si Hamick.

"Sold—too poor a fate, thou fish-skinned camel!" replied the Emir.

"Oh! my lord," returned Si Hamick, "thou dost want money—thy coffers are empty."

This was a terrible truth. The Emir, like many other little potentates, was terribly hard up.

"Slave! hyena!" he retorted; "I gave thee my purse yesterday."

"Oh! my lord," replied Si Hamick, squirming in agony, "some son of a prowling wolf came upon me in the night, and as I slept didst take the money from the purse and put in its place certain date-stones and two brass buttons from the garment of a French gendarme."

"May he be eaten by locusts," said the Emir, apparently quite overwhelmed by this final financial catastrophe.

He fell into a musing state, calmed by his sufferings, and Si Hamick, in a kneeling attitude, remained quite still before him.

"Would the Frank be bought?" asked the Emir, suddenly.

"My lord," replied Si Hamick, "he would fetch much, for though shrunken of limb and wizen of face he is a skilled man. He is great in the use of the tools which he carries with him."

"And Alea, my wife?" said the Emir. "Would the sons of the prophet desire to buy one who had been degraded by the embrace of a Frank?"

"Oh! my lord," returned Si Hamick. "She is beautiful, and if my lord speaks not of the Frank's embrace who shall know? It hath set no mark upon her that the eye can see."

"Verily, Si Hamick," said the Emir, "though thou hast the hide of a pig and the head of a camel, wise counsel comes at times from thy lips. It shall be so. Go! hasten with all three, bear them away to some market FROM WHENCE THERE IS NO RETURN, and bring back the money speedily. And, hear me, thou gaping ape!"

He bent forward, and Si Hamick took up a position of abject attention.

"LET NONE OF THE COINS STICK TO THY FINGERS," said Abdul-ab-Bourad. "Dost hear?"

"My lord, if I do more than count it," replied Si Hamick, "and seal up the bags that hold the money, may jackals make powder of my bones and a simoon bear the ashes of my father over the desert."

"Enough!" said the Emir. "Away!"

Si Hamick backed out of the room with many reverences.

But outside his manner changed.

He was alone in one of the corridors of the castle, and the floor was covered with a thick green matting. He could dance without being heard, and he cut a variety of capers that would have done credit to any dancing dervish who had unduly indulged himself with strong liquors.

Finally, with much care, he fixed his thumb against his nose and opened his fingers out.

"English laugh," he said, softly. "You old fool —ass—pig—camel—flea—yah!"

After this outburst, necessarily of a subdued nature, he walked softly away.

Whatever preparations he had to make were speedily carried through, and within half an hour the three prisoners were on their way to the mountains.

Lottie and Alea were carried in palanquins, not so much in consideration for their sex as from the necessity of keeping their charms hidden from ordinary eyes, so that they might fetch a good price in the slave-market.

They were, however, carefully secured hand and foot, so as to prevent all attempts at escape.

To each were awarded two negro women as attendants, big, black-skinned women, who, but for the contour of their forms, might have passed for men.

Chippy Chunks had to walk by the side of Si Hamick, with an additional guard of six armed, silent eunuchs, who would have made mincemeat of him if he had attempted to run.

Si Hamick did not seem indisposed to be friendly. His face beamed with smiles, and a succession of

WITH ONE CIRCULAR SWEEP OF HIS SWORD THE CHERIF SMOTE OFF THE FRENCH SPY'S HEAD.

chuckles escaped his lips. Presently he gave Chippy a dig in the ribs.

"Go easy," said Chippy. "I ain't a man o' leather."

It was not the pain he felt, for that was nothing, but the sense of degradation arising from undue familiarity of a "black man," that excited the ire of Chippy.

Si Hamick laughed again.

"You clever," he said. "You give her hug. Old Camel not want her after THAT. But SHE DO FOR ME."

And away Si Hamick went into a long string of chuckles, that threatened to choke him. Chippy Chunks stared at him with amazement.

"Well," he said, after a while, "if you ain't got a few slates loose, I'm a Dutchman. You want a few nails put in your roof. I dare say you are considered a handsome man in these parts, but if I ever see such a image— Well, may I never !"

And, utterly unable to give a clear expression of what he thought of Si Hamick, Chippy Chunks lapsed into silence.

———

CHAPTER XII.

THE SPY—A WILD FLIGHT AND SWIFT DEATH—ARRIVAL AT THE KABYLE HAUNT—A TERRIBLE FIX.

TOUCH from the hand or foot of one of the guards awoke Tom, and, leaping up, he saw the chief and his followers ready to start. By the light of the morning there stood before him a fine man with a handsome dark-skinned face. The eyes were both fierce and intelligent. He was engaged in buckling on his sword as Tom rose to his feet. Ned was also rising, and as a matter of instinctive courtesy they gave him "Good morning."

"It is good for some and bad for others," was the calm reply. "The sun rises and shines on the joyful and tortured alike."

"And on the prisoner and captor too," said Tom.

The chief slightly smiled. It was the merest movement of the lips ; the rest of the face was unchanged.

A native appeared carrying a basket of dates, from which he handed to each person a certain number. The chief helped himself.

Still no water, and Ned asked Tom in a low tone if they had fallen among people who never drank.

Softly as he spoke the words reached the chief's ears.

"We shall reach a well at noon. Is it not sufficient to drink once a day ?"

"Our habits at home," said Tom, "are, I fear, somewhat different to yours."

"Have you not a proverb about your doing in Rome as Rome does ?" asked the chief.

"Yes."

"Then, being with the Kabyles act as a Kabyle."

Tom had heard of the tribe of the Kabyles—a warlike, untameable race, ever at war with whatever power was in authority at Algiers.

Probably they were also at war with inland tribes, but the records of their doings did not in their entirety reach civilisation.

"I," continued the leader of the party, "am the Cherif Bouzian, head and ruler of the tribe. I am merciful to a friend, but merciless to a foe. See here !"

He turned to the Nubian near him, and said something in a tongue Tom did not understand.

About a third of their number vanished by the way they had come the previous night, and after a short delay, during which no man moved or spoke, reappeared, dragging a man wearing the uniform of a French Zouave.

His face was white by nature, and whiter still in the excitement of the moment, but he uttered no sound, and seemingly was not subdued by fear.

"A spy," said Cherif Bouzian, "who crept upon us while we slept, who tracked us when even awake, to fall at last into the trap set for him—a bird snared in the darkness of the night."

The man, with his arms bound, stood upright before the Cherif. There was no shiftiness in his eyes, no quailing.

"Dog !" cried the Cherif, "beg for your life."

The man did not answer, but with a quick movement burst his bonds, and broke through the Nubian guard behind him and ran for his life.

In an instant a dozen men, headed by the Cherif, were in swift pursuit.

Tom and Ned, urged on by the excitement of the moment, would have followed, but a dozen armed men barred the way.

They were, however, permitted to spring up a rock which commanded a view of the chase.

And this is what they saw.

The French spy fled swiftly, and might have escaped but for an untoward mishap.

In his great haste he stumbled, then lost his balance, and finally fell headlong to the ground.

As he sprang to his feet the Cherif, who led the pursuit, was upon him, and with one circular sweep of his sword smote off his head.

The decapitation was so perfectly done that the head lingered upright near its natural position a moment ere it fell.

And when it struck the ground it rolled like a gory ball down the path out of sight, the body simply sinking to the earth.

Tom and Ned, peering over the rock, were transfixed for the moment with horror, and Cherif Bouzian, turning, beheld them.

"See," he cried, "how I prevail with my enemies. Is it not better to be my friend ?"

They did not answer him, but dropped down quietly to their original position on the ground.

"No fear, no trepidation, no emotion whatever, if we would hold our own with these fellows," said Tom. "Be calm, Ned."

They braced their nerves, and both were as quiet and unconcerned when the Cherif came back as if they had witnessed nothing more than an ordinary feat of skill.

Cherif Bouzian scanned their faces closely

He still carried his bloody sword, stained from hilt to tip with the life-blood of the slaughtered Frenchman.

One of the men brought him a cloth wherewith to clean it.

"Thou seest," he said, as he slowly wiped it up and down, "the arm of Bouzian is mighty. He wields a sword better than any man on whom the sun shines."

"You are skilful," said Tom, coolly; "but we have men at home who can do more."

"Can'st thou do more?" demanded Cherif Bouzian, fiercely.

"I am not skilled with the sword," said Tom. "The rifle is our weapon."

The Cherif signalled for the horses to be brought, and sprang into the saddle of his own steed.

He was dissatisfied that his feat had not made a deeper impression upon his prisoners, and yet, on the whole, he was pleased.

"They shall strengthen the arm of Bouzian," he muttered. "The accursed French shall perish."

It seemed a long ride that morning ere the spring or well was reached, but at noon, as the Cherif said, they found it.

It was a natural basin formed by rocks, into which dripped a dribbling spring.

The breadth was about eight feet across, five wide, and ten deep.

The Cherif was in no hurry to drink, and his followers also showed no signs of eagerness to quench their thirst.

A stone vessel was filled and handed to Ned, who drank deep, and then Tom was supplied.

After them the horses were attended to, then the men, and last of all the chief.

It was a point of honour with him to be last, for it showed how strong and enduring he was.

Even when he held the vessel of water to his lips he was in no hurry to drink, but taking it away again gave some general directions to his men.

Then he drank, slowly and sparingly, tossing what was left into the air.

For dinner there was some dried goat's flesh and dates, and as soon as it was partaken of they rode on, halting no more until at eve they came upon Bouzian's home upon the mountain.

They debouched upon it suddenly as they emerged from a defile so narrow that only two men could walk abreast. There was a guard at the entrance of some half-dozen men, who drew aside and knelt as the Cherif rode by.

Nestling between a circle of mountains, with precipitous cliffs and no visible paths or roads, was a level piece of land, the outer fringe of which was rich pasture, where hundreds of sheep, goats, and cattle were feeding.

Near the centre was a collection of plain square houses, built after the pattern adopted in the lower quarters of the city of Algiers, and plump in the middle of this natural arena arose a huge Moorish castle.

The whole area of this strangely enclosed land was about one thousand acres.

As the Cherif Bouzian rode forward, Tom and Ned, who were close behind him, noted that his figure seemed to swell with pride.

Here was his haunt, his fastness, the spot where he ruled as king.

There were few grown people near the houses, but many little children were playing about close by. Their elders were scattered around tending the sheep and cattle.

As the cavalcade drew near the little ones they stopped in their play, and falling on their knees bowed low to the Cherif.

So perfect and regular were their movements that their careful training to do obeisance to the great man was evident.

The whole scene was so strange that Tom and Ned felt for awhile as if it were some vision of sleep. Neither spoke, but they made amends for their silence by staring well about them.

And so they rode on to the gate of the castle, where Cherif Bouzian reined up his steed, and the ride was at an end for all.

"Dismount," he said to the brothers, "and enter the castle—my guests."

The latter word startled them, and a throb of joy warmed their breasts. Could it be possible that in this savage mountain ruler they had found a friend?

Tom had read of the Alhambra in Spain, but had never seen it. By the aid of skilfully executed plates he had formed an idea of its architectural magnificence; and in the castle gate he saw a promise of at last gazing on some of the peerless Moorish work.

The carving and moulding were wonderful. Such sculptured flowers, such cunning interlacing of graceful devices neither of the brothers had ever seen before.

Inside the gate was an archway of about fifty feet in length, where every inch of the sides and roof was filled with some portion of a rich design. The eye failed to take in the full measure of its beauty.

Beyond this archway was an open court, with a cool pool of water in the middle. Around there were arches and pillars like the cloisters of our cathedrals, but infinitely superior in elegance and airy design.

Here, upon the marble floor, a number of armed men were reclining.

As the chief entered they sprang to their feet and saluted him by drawing their swords and holding them for a moment in the air.

He waved his hand and uttered one word. The men departed with a clattering of arms, darting by under the arches and vanishing through passages scarcely visible in the deep shadows beyond.

Tom now noticed for the first time that none of the cavalcade had followed. He and his brother and the Cherif were all that had entered the castle.

"English strangers," said Cherif Bouzian, "welcome!"

What could Tom say? He could only bow his acknowledgment, not knowing whether the words were spoken in mockery or in earnest.

"Cherif," he said, after a pause, "I am grateful for your courtesy, but I have need to return with all speed to Algiers."

"You shall return," replied the Cherif, "with me, when I enter it as conqueror."

A startled look sprang into the listeners' faces. The Cherif observed it with a faint smiling movement of his lips.

"You think, then," he said, "that you will be here for ever? Not so. The cursed invader has ruled us long enough; but the hour of his death advances. We but await the coming of the Mahdi, at whose voice a hundred thousand swords will leap into the air."

"But, pardon me," said Tom, "I do not see how

this concerns us. We are but visitors to your country, and have naught to do with those who rule you."

"Thou talkest idly," said the Cherif, as he drew a scroll of bark-paper from his breast. "Hear the words of the Mahdi, sent to me by the hand of Shusan, the son of Gahliel.

"'Behold two young Englishmen shall enter your land,'" he read, in deep, resonant tones. "'They shall be fair to look upon, and young. They shall be redolent of the sea whereon they rule the world. Take them to your castle and place them in command of your hosts. If they will aid you the invader shall be driven into deep water and perish, but if they refuse to help you let them die.'"

He rolled up the scroll and carefully replaced it in his breast. With eyes that flashed fire he gazed at the brothers, and, in a tone of voice in which there was more pleading than command, said—

"Your answer?"

Ned wisely held his peace.

He knew as well as Tom that by an unfortuitous concourse of events they were placed in a very terrible position, from which he could see no escape.

What knew they of war?

How could they lead these fanatical Kabyles against the tremendous power of France?

And if they rashly attempted to do so what could the end be but defeat and an ignominious death?

Tom stood silent for a few moments, and then answered—

"Cherif, we are by nature or training not men of war, and your words have come upon us as an overwhelming surprise. Give us a little time to dwell upon them."

"You shall have it," said the Cherif. "When the sun rises on the morrow your answer must be given. Follow me."

CHAPTER XIII.

A WEIRD NIGHT-TIME—THE SILENT SERVITORS.

PRECEDED by Cherif Bouzian, the brothers traversed several passages, the walls and ceilings of which were marvellously rich in artistic design and superb colouring.

In the end a tall, airy chamber was reached, and there the Cherif bade them a temporary adieu.

"Do not forget," he said; "to-morrow when the sun rises I will come for your answer. Meanwhile you will be well cared for. Both food and the wine beloved of your race shall be sent you."

He bowed low, and they returned his salute gravely, Ned taking his cue from Tom.

The chamber in which they were left was a magnificent apartment about thirty feet square.

There were no windows, but there was no lack of light, for the ceiling was of open stone work, carved with the neatness and skill exhibited by the Chinese on those wondrous ivory balls held in great esteem by collectors of curios.

Above there seemed to be another chamber, or an open place with a simple roof, supported by unrivalled pillars of Moorish architecture.

But the exact nature of the apartment overhead was not discernible, owing to the delicacy of the tracery of the ceiling. The walls were ablaze with gilt and harmonious colours.

To rest upon there were cushions strewn about the marble floor, and on an ornamental slab or table pipes were ready for those who desired to smoke.

On one side was a doorway covered with heavy tapestry. Tom moved it aside and revealed a bath of rich marble work, with a fountain in the centre which was, however, not playing.

"Tom," said Ned, "it is like a dream."

"I wish it were no more," replied Tom, with a sigh. "It would then be enjoyable. What a magnificent place it is!"

"It looks to me like some of the pictures of the Alhambra in Spain."

"The Alhambra, Ned, cannot compare with this place, I am sure. Although I have never seen it, I have heard about that historical stronghold, and the most glowing description of it would not do justice to the home of Cherif Bouzian."

"It looks quite new," said Ned; "just as if it were fresh built."

"It is probably centuries old," replied Tom; "as old or older than anything we have at home. In a pure climate like this such material as we see around us cannot fall into decay. Heigho! I wonder what has become of Lottie?"

"Let us hope for the best," returned Ned, laying a hand upon his brother's arm. "What do you think of that prophecy read by the Cherif?"

"Humbug!" replied Tom.

"The Cherif's humbug?"

"No, not necessarily. Some fanatic who has worked himself up into a belief that he has a divine mission to foretell the rescue of his country from the invader is more likely to be accountable for it."

"I don't know what to make of the people. They seem to be a rum lot."

"Mahdis come and Mahdis go, but the race goes on for ever," said Tom. "Some rise up from Heaven alone knows where, and in a moment become a power in the land; others perish as soon as they expose themselves to the people. They announce their mission, and take the chance of becoming popular. It is a sort of neck-or-nothing business."

"But the fixing on two Englishmen?" returned Ned, thoughtfully. "There is something odd about that."

"An unfortunate something for us," replied Tom. "Probably the coming Mahdi—whoever he may be—fixed on two Englishmen as the most unlikely people to turn up. He may be trying to trade on an expectation that he feels will never be realised. It's rough upon us, Ned, and, frankly, I tell you we are in a fix."

"Suppose we did lead these fellows against the French, what then?"

"Oh! the usual thing—a licking for these sons of the mountains; you and I shot down, or if captured, killed for aiding and abetting in a rebel outbreak."

"Pleasant, Tom."

"Very!"

They were interrupted by the appearance of half-a-dozen Nubian attendants, who brought them fruit, dried goats' flesh, and some excellent wine in a jar, with a narrow neck, of exquisite workmanship.

Without uttering a word they placed these things upon the floor, and, bending thrice, retired.

"Let us eat and drink if we cannot be merry," said Ned.

The wine was good, but its exact nature neither of them knew. It was the juice of the grape without a doubt, but from whence it came they could not tell.

"It is like a rich claret," said Ned.

"A cross between claret and port," returned Tom; "but whatever it is, it is certainly first-class."

After they had partaken of food the attendants again appeared and removed the remnants.

Then two of the Nubians lifted two pipes or hookahs from the stand, and placed one before each of the brothers. They lighted them with, of all things in the world, an old-fashioned tinder-box.

Not a word escaped these grim, silent attendants, who did not even so much as look into the faces of those they served, but kept on at the work quietly and mechanically.

Neither Tom nor Ned thought proper to say anything. They surmised correctly enough that if they had spoken they would not have been understood.

Once more alone, Tom, who had drawn awhile at his pipe, said to Ned—

"You may smoke, old fellow. It won't hurt you. The tobacco is as mild as milk."

"Thanks!" replied Ned; "it is something to do. I certainly hesitated to tackle a whole jar of tobacco alight.

They smoked awhile in silence, thinking, and then again reviewing their position.

No satisfaction was got out of it, but one thing was clear. Unless something intervened in their favour they would have to do as the Cherif wished, or prepare their necks for the terrible sword.

Of its power of doing its work swiftly and thoroughly they had already had evidence.

By-and-bye night came on, and as the darkness stole swiftly down upon them they heard strange, weird music floating about.

From whence it emanated they could not tell.

Sometimes it seemed as if it came from the chamber above, then from either side of the room they were in, and anon from below. It was anywhere and everywhere.

Presently the voices of men were heard chanting harmoniously, and yet in a manner to cause the blood to run cold.

Higher and higher swelled the music, louder and louder became the voices, until the chorus of sound echoed on every side.

It reached such a pitch of musical clamour that it was becoming unbearable, and then it suddenly ceased. The after stillness, coming without notice, was very startling. There was no sound whatever.

If the hand of death had been laid upon all but those two listeners within the castle walls it could not have been more complete.

Presently Ned gave vent to his feelings by muttering—"How awful!"

"It makes me think of the Assyrian army of old," said Tom, and then in a low, clear voice he recited one verse of Byron's famous poem on "The Destruction of Sennacherib."

"*For the Angel of Death spread his wings on the blast,*
And breathed on the face of the foe as he passed;
The eyes of the sleepers waxed heavy and chill,
Their hearts but once heaved, and for ever were still."

"For mercy's sake, Tom," said Ned, "let us try to get some sleep. I feel as if I were in a haunted place."

So they tried to sleep—and slept.

The strange excitement which had been upon them entirely subsided, and blessed forgetfulness came to their aid.

No dreams—nothing but oblivion for many hours. Was it a hand laid upon him?

Tom did not know, but he woke suddenly, and found a grim Nubian with an armful of towels standing near him.

Another held aside the tapestry of the bath, while a third stood by Ned awaiting his awakening.

Other ebony-skinned sons of Africa were arranging a morning meal.

A word awoke Ned, and the two brothers hastened into the bath, where, having divested themselves of their clothes, they plunged into the marble basin filled with cool water.

An attendant stood waiting with clean linen of European make, and he with the towels expertly rubbed the bathers down as they emerged from their refreshing bath.

There was a luxury about the whole thing which would have been thoroughly enjoyable but for one attendant circumstance—they were prisoners.

On returning to the ordinary chamber they found the Cherif awaiting them.

He gravely saluted them and bade them eat, which they did with fair appetites, notwithstanding the arrival of the portentous hour when they must say Yea or Nay to the Cherif.

The Moorish chief did not eat with them, nor say a word until their fast was broken.

Ned and Tom exchanged a few glances, but nothing more.

Those from Ned meant—"Tom, I must leave all to you;" and Tom's signified that he would, courteously but firmly, refuse to do what was required of them and take the consequences.

Better to die by the hand of a savage, and be buried away in that lone spot, to be never more heard of by civilised man, than be shot as a rebel by the French, and have his name bandied about Europe as an Englishman who had leagued himself with the most ferocious semi-savages on earth.

"I am at your service, chief," Tom said, rising. "You have come for your answer."

"In the night-time," said Cherif Bouzian, "news that turns my heart has been brought to me. The Fanzuals have risen, and are on their way hither to destroy me and mine."

A bitter, savage expression passed over his face, and with his clenched hand he struck an imaginary foe.

"It is not enough," he said, "that we must have our land eaten up by the French locust, but those who should be our friends must rise against us. I must first destroy the Fanzuals. Woe to Ozrim, the son of Melshah, who brings his tribe against my people!"

He paused anon, and Tom maintained silence. By an almost imperceptible movement of his head he bade Ned keep quite still.

"Your swords are ready for you," said Cherif Bouzian, his dark eyes upon Tom. "Their edges are sharp. With you victory is sure. Ozrim and his host will perish."

"I am ready," said Tom.

His face as he looked at Ned for a moment conveyed the comparatively good tidings—

"Here is a respite from the greater danger. Let us be thankful."

Then, addressing the Cherif, he said—

"The news came in the night?"

"Aye!" was the answer. "The Mahdi himself brought it. He is within these walls, and awaits you. He begs to see the white children whom Allah has sent hither to destroy our foes."

The eyes of the chief flashed lightning. His hand, trembling with excitement, was clapped upon the hilt of his sword, and as he drew it from its sheath it flashed out like a band of fire.

"To the Mahdi!" he cried.

Then, in the Moorish tongue, he gave some command, and the tapestry of the door of the room was pulled swiftly aside.

In the passage without were a number of Moorish warriors and musicians, with drums, cymbals, and strange stringed and wind instruments.

How silently they must have stood for no indication of their vicinity to reach the ears of Tom and Ned!

A clash of cymbals was the signal for a general outburst of music—weird, fanciful, thrilling.

The musicians marched on, the warriors fell in next, and last of all came the Cherif and the brothers.

"To the Mahdi!" cried the Moorish chief, and Tom, with an irrepressible feeling in him to cry out something to relieve the surging emotions in his heart, responded, in ringing tones—

"To the Mahdi!"

CHAPTER XIV.

SI HAMICK AND HIS PRISONERS—A RESTABLE PLACE—CHIPPY DOES A DESPERATE THING.

OR two days the party under Si Hamick pursued its way over level ground. Their progress was not remarkably rapid, and a long halt was indulged in every day at noon. At night they put up at one of the scattered villages on their route. Lottie and her sister prisoner, Alea, were lodged in a house on these occasions, not particularly remarkable for cleanliness or comfort, and they had to occupy one room.

The difference between the character of the women was a bar to their close communion.

Alea was frivolous and foolish, empty in her talk, and ridiculously vain.

Lottie was, as we know, an unaffected, high-spirited woman, but too courteous to let her companion know that her company was distasteful.

It was not until the halt on the eve of the second day that Lottie got a clear idea of the fate in store for her.

Alea, who knew a little English, asked her if she "think she fetch much?" and this question led to an explanation. To be sold as a slave!

The awful thought almost killed her.

For a moment reason tottered on its throne, but, recovering, she proceeded to elicit the full facts from Alea.

The Emir's wife did not look forward to her fate with dismay; indeed, she seemed rather to enjoy the prospect.

"I am beautiful," she practically said, "and whoever be my lord he will love me."

Lottie thought of her two children, her husband, Ned, and all at home.

In her anguish she could have cried aloud, but she maintained an impassable demeanour before the frivolous Alea.

Up to the present she had held no communication with Chippy Chunks; but she knew he was of the party, and somehow felt he would be her friend in need.

But how?

Aye! there was the rub.

What could the old man do to release her from her perilous and degrading position?

That worthy was trying to plan out something. From the start he had been endeavouring to scheme a way of escape, but could arrange nothing.

Chippy was not a mental genius—he never pretended to be—but he could be useful at a pinch.

Give him a job to do, and the right tools to handle, and then he was in his element, doing good work like an honest artisan.

He and Si Hamick were outwardly good friends, but there was no real affinity between them. Necessity made them companionable.

Si Hamick could not be chummy with the grim Nubian guards because they were slaves and he was free, so he wanted somebody to talk to, and Chippy was the only available personage.

To him Si Hamick unfolded a notable scheme on the very eve when Lottie learnt the full extent of her misery and peril.

They had partaken of food, and Chippy Chunks was invited to sit in the cool of the evening on the housetop of the residence Si Hamick had requisitioned for his use.

Armed as he was by a firman from Abdul-ab-Bourad, Si Hamick was all powerful. What he wanted for his use he took, and nobody said him nay.

The housetops in this country are flat. They are the evening resting-places of the people, and are literally used as open-air bedrooms—if we may be permitted to use such a term.

On a roll of grass matting sat the pair, Chippy with his legs straight out, Si Hamick with his tucked under him. They were smoking a coarse species of cheroot provided by the wily native.

"Great and good is the Prophet," he said, with a sigh.

"Is he now?" asked Chippy Chunks, in his matter-of-fact way. "A decent sort of chap all round, perhaps?"

"He is good to the faithful," said Si Hamick. "He gives them what they yearn for with a bountiful hand."

"I suppose he's got a reason for it," said Chippy Chunks. "For my part, I allus say, 'Give a man his due.' If a man's done his work well treat him fair—let him have his money; but if he's shirked the job don't pay him."

"The women of your land are fair," sighed Si

Hamick. "They have lustrous eyes. Are you loved?"

"Eh!" exclaimed Chippy Chunks.

"Are you loved? Do you not yearn for beauty?" asked Si Hamick.

Chippy Chunks took a long pull at his cigar and then said—

"I don't know as I ever yearned, as you call it, for anything in that line, not bein' a beauty myself; but perhaps you will explain."

Then it was Si Hamick unfolded his scheme.

Beyond the mountains he said there was a land where they could live in peace.

By selling the Nubian guards, who were valuable and would raise no objection, they could get enough money to buy flocks and herds.

Si Hamick meant to make Alea his wife, and Chippy and Lottie could be the two chief servants of his household.

He seemed to have some doubt about Alea taking kindly to the arrangement, and he wanted Chippy and his mistress to help towards its fulfilment.

"And may I ax what you've really brought us here for?" asked Chippy.

"I was instructed by that hump-headed hyæna, Abdul-ab-Bourad, to sell you for slaves," said Si Hamick.

Chippy was not outwardly startled. He smoked on quietly enough, but he was thinking.

"Oh! that's his idea, is it?" said Chippy. "Well, go on."

Si Hamick knew of a certain chief in the mountains who would buy the Nubians, and that transaction concluded, he could travel on with Alea, Chippy, and Lottie to the land where he would make a paradise.

"Have you said anything to the ladies on this 'ere p'int?" asked Chippy Chunks.

"We do not consult our women, we sons of the prophet," said Si Hamick. "We command, and they obey."

"Oh! indeed," was all Chippy said.

Si Hamick was no longer servile.

Freed from the trammels of his master's presence he rose to the occasion, and played "boss" to perfection.

With the politeness of Eastern rulers, he accompanied the majority of his commands with a curse, and frequently with blows.

He and Chippy slept all night upon the roof, or rather, Si Hamick slept and Chippy Chunks lay awake thinking.

He had shammed acquiescence in the notable scheme, but his blood boiled as he thought of his mistress being servant to such a "Punch-and-Judy image," as he mentally named Si Hamick.

"Let him get rid of the black chaps first," said Chippy to himself, "and then—"

In the morning they started again, and for two days travelled on over level ground. Chippy never got a word with his mistress. He did, however, manage to occasionally exchange a glance with her, and his look was always an effort to assure her that she might rely upon him.

During the march Si Hamick talked a great deal. He told Chippy many strange things of the power of the rulers of the land, and the mighty sway of anyone who could persuade the people that he was a Mahdi.

"And what's a Mardy?" asked Chippy.

"A ruler sent straight from Paradise," replied Si Hamick. "They come poor, almost naked, and the people clothe them; all the warriors of the land gather around them to fight."

"And what's the end on it?" asked Chippy.

"They go back to Paradise," replied Si Hamick, as his lips spread out and his nose came down to meet his chin.

"I should think you'd make a good Mardy," said Chippy.

"If the prophet calls me I will obey him," said Si Hamick, and just for a moment his nose and chin fairly met.

The lower spurs of the mountain range were by this time reached, and Si Hamick, having given some strict command to his Nubian guard, went forward alone.

He was absent an entire day and night, and when he came back he was quite joyful.

Again they moved forward, and journeyed all day along lonesome ways up the mountain-side, through narrow ravines, and around paths that bordered tremendous precipices.

At night they halted by a small cave, in which the women were sent to sleep.

Chippy watched his mistress as she descended from the palanquin, and was glad to see that she bore up bravely.

He avoided catching her eye because he did not wish to commit himself in any way. A conviction that the time for action was near was upon him.

Like a watch-dog he lay down in the mouth of the cave, and soon, under the influence of the soft mountain air, gave way to sleep.

Once in the night he half awoke, and heard somebody moving about near him; but he was too drowsy to pay heed to anything, and was soon off again.

At daylight he was aroused by somebody shaking him, and, opening his eyes, he saw Si Hamick bending over him.

The expression of his face was that of a man who had attained the ambition of a lifetime; but, like all expressions of his face, it was very disagreeable to look at.

"What's the matter with you?" asked Chippy.

"It is dawn," replied Si Hamick. "Lo! in the night I led the guard to their new lord and received the shekels for the same. We are alone with the beautiful. Arise, my brother, and let us speak to them."

"There are the women slaves?" said Chippy.

"Nay," replied Si Hamick; "they too have been delivered to the lord I told ye of. Only thee and I and the two daughters of the moon remain."

Chippy drew a long breath and stared hard at Si Hamick, whose face shone with joy, as if it had been oiled.

He was standing near a sloping precipice, which fringed the path that wound about the mountain.

The cave in which Lottie and Alea were was in the face of the mountain a few yards lower down.

"So we are all by ourselves?" muttered Chippy Chunks, huskily.

He was in a burning fever internally, for dark and desperate thoughts were in his head.

He meditated doing something which, but for the necessities of the case, would be a crime.

Right or wrong he meant to kill Si Hamick.

It could not be done in fair fight, because that wily person was armed with revolver and sword, and Chippy had only his hammer and a two-foot rule available for warlike purposes.

He must, therefore, take the enemy by surprise, and if he waited for a year he would not get a better opportunity than the present afforded him.

Si Hamick stood near the precipice occupied with diverting thoughts, not dreaming that Chippy Chunks could or would assail him.

But it had to be done, and it was done.

Stooping down as if to tie the lace of his shoe, Chippy made a sudden grab at the ankles of Si Hamick, and with a jerk threw him off his balance.

Down he went—too much startled to cry out—rolling, turning, twisting until he came to a point in the slope where the rocks became a precipice.

Over this he shot and disappeared.

Chippy Chunks, with his eyes starting out of his head, waited for the noise of his fall, and presently it came—a soft, dumb sound, and then all was still.

"I've done it," gasped Chippy, wiping his perspiring brow, "and some may say it's murder; but I don't care. If hanging me will save missus they are welcome to do it."

CHAPTER XV.

THE START WITH THE MAHDI—UNDERGROUND TRAVELLING—THE ATTACK IN THE DEFILE.

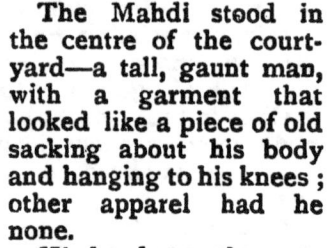

O the Mahdi!"

The Mahdi stood in the centre of the courtyard—a tall, gaunt man, with a garment that looked like a piece of old sacking about his body and hanging to his knees; other apparel had he none.

His head was the most striking thing about him. The crown of it was covered with a thick matting of hair, uncombed and unwashed. He was bearded up to his wild, dark eyes, that flashed the fire of an extraordinary intelligence or madness.

In his hand he held a sword of extra length and very broad in the blade.

On either side of him, in two lines, widening from the base so as to form the letter V, were a number of the Cherif Bouzian's followers, with eyes darting warlike fury and nostrils dilated—all that was bloodthirsty in their natures aroused by the presence of the fanatic.

As Bouzian and the two brothers appeared the Mahdi leaped thrice in the air, whirling the huge sword above his head, crying out—

"The hour of Ozrim, the son of Melshah, is at hand! Ere the moon is at its full the lions shall eat his flesh, and his bones whiten on the sands of the desert. Cry aloud! The avengers are at hand! Abdallah the Mahdi has spoken!"

Neither Tom nor Ned knew exactly what to do under the circumstances, but Abdallah relieved them by taking all the proceedings out of their hands.

At a signal from him a swarthy warrior, who had been standing back a little behind the rest, advanced with two swords in their sheaths, and with leathern belts studded with gold nails, so arranged as to form certain cabalistic figures.

These were buckled about the waists of the two Tartars, and afterwards a pair of revolvers were given to each.

Then Abdallah leapt again into the air, with extraordinary agility, crying—

"To horse and away. Let there be no more setting of the sun until Ozrim, the son of Melshah, is dead, with his face in the dust."

This was followed by a general drawing and waving of swords, which Tom and Ned thought it advisable to take part in, and then a number of horses were brought into the court by a side door.

One was led by the mane, for it had neither bridle nor saddle, and across its back Abdallah the Mahdi leapt at a bound.

Three others, with high-pommelled saddles and heavy, half-shoe stirrups, came next. These were for the Cherif Bouzian, Tom, and Ned.

"Mount!" cried the Mahdi, whose steed was prancing about, controlled, as it seemed, by the knees of its rider.

"We are in for it now," said Ned, as he slipped lightly into the saddle.

"I feel as if a brush with some fierce devil of a Moor would do me good," replied Tom, just loud enough for Ned to hear.

Then came more horses, to the number of two score, which were appropriated by the followers of the Cherif.

The band of musicians, which had formed behind, struck up a wild air, and as the outer gate was thrown open the Mahdi led the way forth.

Tom expected they would go away by the narrow defile he had traversed on his arrival, but he was disappointed. Their road lay in an opposite direction.

The Mahdi rode straight at what looked like an inaccessible mountain, at the foot of which a number of men were gathered together, watching the labours of others who were using levers to turn away large stones from the mouth of a cave.

Some were kneeling down, with flint and steel lighting torches, which, as they one by one flared up, were borne away into the cave.

By the time the Mahdi reached the cavern the mouth of it was wide enough to admit a horse, and he rode in fearlessly at a hand gallop.

The Cherif went next, and Tom and Ned were bound to follow.

As soon as their horses were inside they subsided into a walk, but went on steadily.

Ahead the glare of several torches danced about like will-o'-the-wisps, and the voice of the Mahdi was heard chanting a hymn or song.

The cavern widened gradually from its mouth, so that ere long Tom and Ned could ride side by side.

The Cherif went on a dozen feet ahead of them.

As the warriors marched in they were, in a manner of speaking, interleaved with other torch-bearers, to light them on their way.

The cavern echoed the clang of steel and the thumping of hoofs in every variety of reverberating sound.

Speaking for some time was impossible.

On they went through the wondrous cave, which at every step became wider and higher, until it

THE TWO TARTARS:

Or, Tom and Ned among the Moors.

NED FAVOURED THE MAHDI WITH A VIGOROUS KICK ON A PART OF HIS ANATOMY.

No. 27.

Price One Penny.

terminated in a vast hall, with a roof so high that the glare of the torches failed to relieve it.

Here the Mahdi halted, and the strange host gathered about him, chanting weirdly.

The musicians, it seemed, had been left behind ; but there were a number of men on foot who, in addition to being armed, carried bundles, which Tom judged contained dates and other forms of food.

Of all the experiences of his varied life this was the strangest. As for Ned, he could only sit silent in the saddle staring about him.

For a time both forgot their troubles.

The chant ended with a waving of naked swords, glitteringly blinding to the eye, and once more the Mahdi led the way.

Down through a cavern of great length to yet another hall, which led to a third hall vaster than the rest, and then a halt for another chant—so wild, so fierce, that it stirred the blood like the tumult of battle.

The brothers had nothing in kindred with these swarthy men, but their pulses leaped in their veins, and they thirsted only in a minor degree to the rest for a meeting with some foeman worthy of their steel.

Happily fencing and broadsword practice had been pastimes with them for some time.

It had been taken to as a healthful exercise, little dreaming that a use for it would be found in the land of the Moor.

On once more down a cavern that, unlike the rest, wound about in a strange fashion, and so to the daylight again, which they came upon with startling suddenness.

The underground journey terminated in a defile running right and left between two tremendous mountain walls.

High ahead, about fifty yards away, there was a natural bridge of stone, on which half a dozen men armed with rifles could have dealt death out to all those below.

Tom, as soon as his eyes became used to the stronger light, marked this point of vantage, and wondered, not without some anxiety, if any of the followers of Ozrim, the son of Melshah, were posted there.

The need of caution in advancing was recognised by all, even the Mahdi, notwithstanding his faith—if he possessed such a thing—in his supernatural powers.

If indeed he lacked confidence in himself he seemed to have full belief in the potency of the brothers, for he signalled to them to draw up nearer to him, and they rode on almost abreast.

The defile was long, and every footstep of the horses raised an echo. In stern silence Abdallah rode on, with his drawn sword resting upon his shoulder. The ground was rough, and the horses had to pick their way with great care.

The defile wound about for awhile, until it took an abrupt turn, and this brought them to a view of open ground.

It was a sandy expanse, white and glaring in the sunlight, but dotted with black figures, that were moving rapidly towards the defile.

The Mahdi uttered a shout and whirled his sword over his head. At the same moment his horse sprang forward and broke into a gallop.

Tom was momentarily left behind, but he was soon on the track of the wild leader, impelled by a feeling of excitement it was not in his power to resist.

It was as well that he could not quite overtake Abdallah, for as the wild-eyed fanatic drew near the mouth of the defile some large pieces of rock came tumbling down from above.

The Mahdi, or his horse, or both, were struck and fell in a heap upon the ground.

"Hurry up, Ned," cried Tom, "or they will smash us."

He dug his heels into the sides of his horse and sent it full at the fallen steed of the Mahdi.

The defile was so narrow that a leap over them was necessary, and Tom's horse gallantly performed the feat.

An instant more and he was in the open. Turning, he saw Ned's horse take the jump over, fall almost upon its knees, recover itself, and dash out of the narrow, dangerous way.

A glance above showed a number of half-naked men rolling stones to the edge of the precipice, with the intention of sending them down upon the Mahdi and his followers.

The revolvers were useless, for the men were fully two hundred feet from the level ground, and, in addition, Tom had no shots to spare, for a host of dark-skinned sons of the desert were bearing down upon the brothers in scattered form.

Some had swords, others long muskets and a variety of weapons, which they doubtless knew well how to use.

Within the defile there were sounds of firing and the shouting of men.

Ozrim, the son of Melshah, had evidently done his best to take time by the forelock, and had come half-way to meet his foes.

Tom thought of the bridge, and the whole defensive scheme flashed upon him.

Doubtless some of the enemy were posted there, ready to act as soon as the mouth of the defile had become well nigh impassable with fallen rocks and the dead and dying.

"Ned," said Tom, between his teeth, "we've got one pull over these fellows—we are mounted, and they are not. Let us make a dash at them, and if we have the luck to get through, take our chance of what there is on the other side."

CHAPTER XVI.

FOES AND YET NOT FOES — DEFEAT OF THE KABYLES—RETURN TO THE CHERIF BOUZIAN'S CASTLE.

TOM TARTAR with set teeth rode on, sword in hand, determined to cut his way through or give up his life in the attempt. By him was Ned, sitting well down in the saddle, also bent on setting his mark upon those dark-skinned sons of the desert.

Two hundred at least were before them, at first in open order, but as the brothers galloped into their midst they closed in with wild cries, much brandishing of swords, and a scattered fire from their rifles.

The shots flew harmlessly by the brothers, and the first two men Tom encountered he struck down.

The tribes of the desert are naturally brave to a fault, but they are also superstitious, and the bearing of Tom and Ned had a decidedly depressing effect upon them. The reason for this we shall see by-and-bye.

Ned, being a stride or so behind Tom, found the way cleared for him. The fall of the first of their assailants had a scattering effect upon the others.

They did not flee, but widened out like an eddying ring on water caused by the casting of a stone into it.

And now others appeared upon the scene. Men sprang up all over the plain, from the very ground it seemed, but in reality from behind hillocks of sand, which they had raised for the purpose of concealment.

Finally, from behind a huge rock a number of horsemen, headed by a chief in a robe of scarlet and gold, appeared.

In the defile where the Mahdi had been unhorsed the sounds of combat were increasing in volume. A desperate conflict was going on, and as yet only Tom and Ned had got clear of the narrow way.

The movements of the Fanzuals on the plain were very rapid. In an inconceivably short space of time Tom and Ned found that a complete circle had been formed around them, and they reined up, uncertain what to do.

The idea of breaking through and finding liberty beyond the circle had to be abandoned, for there were other men springing up in every direction, and the body of horsemen just referred to were sweeping round so as to further check their advance.

"Tom," said Ned, breathlessly, "what is to done? Can't we get back again?"

"Where to?" asked Tom. "Into that defile? No—that is certain death. I do not quite understand these fellows. They don't seem to want our lives."

"Rather death than slavery, Tom."

"Tall talk won't do us any good. Keep cool!"

"Here they come!"

The whole circle, guided by some invisible signal, now closed in. Those on foot dashed up fearlessly, and the horsemen, with wild cries, rode round and round at a gallop.

A double movement of this nature had a bewildering, dazzling effect upon Tom and Ned. The flashing of bright swords and the swirl of horsemen in many-coloured robes was like the circling of a string of prisms. It was distracting, blinding.

The horses ridden by the brothers became restive, and plunged here and there—rearing, kicking, turning this way and that, utterly regardless of the reins.

To fight under the circumstances was well nigh impossible. It required pluck and nerve to keep in the saddle alone.

"Allah—Allah!" chorussed the Fanzuals, as they made their final dash, closing in so suddenly that Tom had scarcely raised his arm to strike one more blow for life and liberty when he found himself unhorsed.

He lost sight of Ned, but he heard him utter a cry of defiance ere he too was dragged out of the saddle.

Above the din and confusion of the struggle was heard the voice of the chief horseman giving commands in his native tongue.

Not a sword was raised against the brothers. They were simply seized and their weapons taken from their hands as they lay upon the ground.

The horses they had recently ridden were dragged away, snorting and wildly plunging, mad with fright.

"Why don't they kill us?" was Tom's mental query as the men fell back again a few paces, forming a close, compact circle, leaving the brothers lying on the sand.

Tom sprang up, and Ned followed his example.

"Keep cool," said Tom. "Never show any fear before these fellows."

"All right," replied Ned, as he brushed the sand from his nether garments with his hands; "but I'm hanged if I can make out their little game."

"Wait; it will all be clear by-and-bye."

In their position they could see very little of what was going on, but they could hear the sound of rifles and other indications that the battle still raged in the defile. But it was flagging. On one side or the other the shadow of defeat was descending.

Tom had little doubt which way it was going.

The impassiveness of the circle around him showed that the victory was with the Fanzuals. The swarthy fellows stood at ease, as much at rest as if they had been made of stone; but every eye was on the prisoners, keeping close watch and ward over their movements.

A quarter of an hour or so passed. Tom and Ned stood side by side, keeping up an appearance of indifference equal to that shown by Indians in the hands of their foes. After the first few words exchanged they kept silent.

At length all was quiet, or comparatively so. The fight was over, and the Fanzuals were triumphant.

There could be no doubt of it, for suddenly, as if they had all been one man, they gave vent to a shout—one word only—that echoed among the hills like the report of a mountain gun.

Then there was a forward movement of the circle, and the brothers went with it. What else could they do?

A haughty demeanour always impresses a savage, and the dignified bearing of the brothers was all that could be desired.

They strode along, shoulders well squared, heads up, and eyes ahead, supremely indifferent to the wild warriors around them.

At first Tom did not observe whither they were going, but ere he had gone far he saw that they were returning in the direction of the defile, and presently they entered it.

All doubt, if any could possibly have been entertained, as to the outcome of the struggle was at rest.

The Cherif Bouzian had suffered defeat.

Every step revealed something that showed it.

Like the leaves of the trees in autumn the dead Kabyles lay strewn about.

None showed any signs of life, but some had many wounds, which were evidence of the coup de grace having been given after they had fallen.

It was a terrible, sickening sight, but the Fanzuals impassively passed by their dead enemies, and the brothers steeled their faces to an indifference they did not by any means feel.

Tom watched closely for the bodies of the Mahdi and Cherif Bouzian, but saw neither.

Probably they had been made captives or possibly escaped.

Back by the way they had come through the bowels of the mountain the captive brothers were taken, guarded closely all the way, but never molested or so much as spoken to in any way.

It was very strange.

What was in store for them?

Slavery, perhaps, or it might be torture.

Similar thoughts were in their minds, but neither flinched.

One drop of comfort they had—they still lived; and while there is life the strong heart never abandons all hope.

Boldly the Fanzuals advanced upon the stronghold of the Kabyles.

There was no attempt to hide their coming or to make a sudden descent upon the place.

The way was easy, and they marched into the grand arena among the mountains.

A glance at it showed that some of the Fanzuals had been there before them:

Dead men—all of the Kabyle tribe—lay scattered here and there, but no women or children.

They had doubtless been saved to be the slaves of their conquerors.

Back to the castle, where the gate was wide open, and there, seated upon a horse, ready to receive them, was a man once seen not easily forgotten.

It was Abdallah the Mahdi.

He had cast aside his rags and put on a white turban and a purple robe, changed so far, but still the Mahdi.

He saluted Tom and Ned by placing both hands to his forehead and bowing low in the saddle.

Then he drew aside and motioned for them to go in.

With their escort they entered, to find the evidence of recent slaughter everywhere—in pools of blood upon the mosaic floor, in dreadful dark red splashes on the walls.

Without a word being spoken to them the soulsickened captives were escorted back to the very apartments they had left that morning.

At the door the guard drew back and they were alone.

In the centre of the room, upon the floor, wine and fruit and meat were spread for their refreshment, but there were no slaves in attendance.

Both were worn out with excitement and horror, and neither could at once touch wine or food.

"I have had little to do with the slaughter of to-day," said Tom; "but I cannot touch food until I have bathed. How do you feel, Ned?"

"As if I had been in a country where it rains blood," replied Ned.

Tom pushed aside the curtains and saw that there, as in the other chamber, everything was ready for their use.

Pellucid water filled the bath, and an abundance of thick, soft towels lay on a marble bench above. Open alabaster boxes of ointment and bottles of perfume invited them to anoint their bodies after the manner of the East.

"It is like a story of enchantment," said Ned.

"With a spice of ugly reality in it," replied Tom.

They bathed in the cool water, and it refreshed them, but they were still weary.

Returning to the other apartment, they sat down and poured out some wine.

"Ned," said Tom, "I give you a toast—'Speedy destruction to the Mahdi!'"

"Eh! speedy destruction to him? Why?' ejaculated Ned. "On the whole he has been fairly civil to us!"

"He is a traitor!" said Tom. "Can't you see

through it all? He has betrayed Bouzian, who was at least honest to his enemies. The whole thing was a plan to destroy the Kabyles, and I fear it has been passing successful."

"But they tried to kill him?"

"Yes, Ned, by a premature movement, I fancy. I've been working it out in my mind. The Mahdi and you and I, perhaps, were to be allowed to get out of the defile safely. I noticed that he was in a hurry to get in front, and that we should be with him. The intention was, to my way of thinking, to block up the defile as soon as we had passed, and then finish off Bouzian and his followers."

"You have a clear head of your own, Tom," said Ned; "but for the life of me I can't see why we are spared. Surely the Mahdi doesn't believe in our possessing supernatural power?"

"He may not believe it," said Tom, "but he wrote a prophecy, and we, in a manner, fulfil it. What he is going to do with us remains to be seen; but I promise him one thing, and that is if I get a chance of lodging a fair amount of steel or a bullet under his ribs I shall do so without the least compunction."

"He's got himself up as no end of a swell on short notice," said Ned, "but I think he might have washed himself first."

"Here's confusion to him—washed or unwashed. I am sorry for Bouzian, for, although a bit of a savage, he was a gentleman. I wonder what has become of him?"

"Dead."

"I think not. They didn't appear to have any time to bury the slaughtered men. If he had been among them we should have seen him."

"Here's luck to him, if alive," said Ned, "and dead, of course, I wish him no harm. I say, Tom, I've got an idea."

"Have you? Let us hope it is a good one."

"If the Mahdi has visions why should not I have one now and then?"

"I don't understand you," said Tom, with a puzzled look.

"I am going to have visions," returned Ned, deliberately, "that is, if they will let me live long enough to work them up. It's a brilliant idea, Tom; upon my word it is. Let me do a bit of business on my own account, will you, just for once?"

"Do what you like," said Tom. "Pass the wine. We will try to be merry, old boy, though it's a rough road we are travelling. Once more, confusion to the Mahdi!"

"May the head of his mother be shaved by a halfpenny barber," said Ned, imitating the solemnity of the Eastern potentate, "and Hampstead Heath jackasses caper on his father's grave. May his flesh become meat for a travelling menagerie, and cheap waistcoat-buttons be made out of his bones. There, Tom, I think that's hot enough?"

"Quite," said Tom, with a smile upon his face, brighter than any he had shown since his captivity.

"Hush! what's that?" asked Ned.

They both sat quite still for a moment. The noise that had attracted Ned's attention was a dumb kind of wailing and groaning, like the cries of wounded men muffled by thick walls.

———

CHAPTER XVII.

THE MAHDI'S THREATS AND TOM'S DEFIANCE—
NED TELLS THE STORY OF A VISION—A
STARTLING ANNOUNCEMENT.

A FEW moments only it lasted, and then died away. Ned shivered as he helped himself to another draught of wine.

"More slaughter, I suppose," he said.

Whatever it was remained a mystery for that night at least. Nobody came near them, not even a slave to attend to their possible requirements.

But in reality they needed nothing.

As if a magic wand had been at work on their behalf, everything was ready to hand.

All the food they required—pipes, tobacco, and the old tinder-box—cushions on which to sleep—everything.

It had been a day of excitement and movement, seeming longer than it really was.

Worn out, they slept easily, and did not wake until the morning.

Bright daylight was there, and in the night silent-footed attendants had cleared up the place and laid a breakfast.

There was even a coffee-pot of polished silver—kept warm by the aid of a spirit lamp under it.

"I can't think it is real," said Ned, as they rose up and descended to the bath; "it is almost fairy-like."

Tom said nothing, for he was thinking of his home in England—as it was when he left it.

Should he ever see that home again?

After the bath they returned to the other room, and found no less a person than the Mahdi awaiting them.

His attire was more gorgeous than they had seen on any Moor since they had arrived in Algiers. Nothing like it, off the stage, had ever been seen by mortal man.

His turban was of golden-coloured satin, with a diamond crescent on the front rising above the crown. The coat or jacket he wore was of white velvet, trimmed with scarlet.

A cashmere shawl was about his waist, and in it was stuck many jewel-handled pistols and daggers. It was quite a small armoury.

Neither of the brothers gave him greeting, and Tom in particular showed his aversion to him by first of all frowning and then turning his back upon him.

"Sons of infidels," he said, "it would be well with you if you sought my favour."

He spoke really excellent English, so good that Tom stared at him with wonderment expressed in his eyes.

"In what way would it benefit us?" he asked, sternly.

"I hold the keys of Paradise in my hands," said the Mahdi; "the gates of the infidels' hell are also under my command."

"To speak plainly," said Ned, coolly, "you have our lives in your hands, and if we die the unmentionable place is in store for us?"

The dark, evil eyes of the Mahdi glittered as he bowed assent.

"Well, go on," exclaimed Tom, seeing he paused.

"If you do my bidding and bend your neck to the commands of the faithful," returned the Mahdi, "your lives will be spared; if not, there is torture such as men have only dreamt of awaiting you."

No answer was given him, and as he waited to see what impression his words made the brothers neither spoke nor stirred. Not a muscle of their faces quivered.

"Yesterday," continued Abdallah the Mahdi, "twelve men who were placed on the summit of the rocks at the mouth of the pass sought my life. They were commanded to close the way after I had gone through. They conspired to crush me first and then destroy Bouzian and his host afterwards. They perished, for I am mighty, and the Prophet's blessing is on me."

"I hope you feel the better for it," remarked Ned.

"Those men were punished for their sin. In a chamber yonder they were placed under a mighty stone that pressed slowly down upon them. They cried out for awhile, but their speech was soon stopped, although they lingered on till the sun had risen above the mountain tops."

He paused again, waiting for some sign of fear from them.

It was not vouchsafed him.

"You hear?" he said, savagely.

"Not being deaf," answered Ned, "we do."

"What is it you want of us?" asked Tom.

"Obedience to and reverence for me," was the answer. "You must sit on my right hand and on my left, as the ministers of the Sultan do, listening to the words of wisdom that fall from my lips. You must at all times say that they are good."

"But why?" asked Tom. "Are not your words of wisdom sufficient without our assistance?"

"No."

"Why not?"

"It is written that you were to come and save the people from the accursed invader. From your lips must emanate the guiding power to lead us to victory."

"Who or what you are I know not," said Tom; "but that you are no Moor or of the tribes around I am certain. You have put yourself forward as a Mahdi, led on, I think, by ambition, and, like the dastardly traitor you are, you begin your career by selling one chief to another."

"That is not your affair."

"It is my affair so far that I will not be your tool. You have my answer. Go."

"Get out of it, and, as a preliminary to an inside cleansing," said Ned, "wash yourself."

"I have your answer," said Abdallah, fiercely, "and now I will let loose the whirlwind of my wrath. You are doomed."

He swung upon his heel and strutted towards the door.

Tom's eyes blazed with anger, and Ned felt a regular volcano bubbling within him.

He was young and impetuous.

Self-restraint did not belong to his years, and, for

lack of a fitting weapon to cut short the career of the Mahdi, he rushed forward and favoured him with a kick on that part of his anatomy where this peculiar form of assault is considered permissible.

Ned put all his youthful ardour into the assault, and Abdallah the Mahdi literally skipped several inches from the ground.

Drawing his sword, he wheeled round, and received the coffee-pot, well aimed, between his eyes.

The lid flew off and the remains of the coffee rained over him.

He aimed a blow at Ned but missed him, then, seeing Tom coming for him, he shrieked out, "The torture for you both!" and fled.

As he tore the curtain aside Tom saw that the passage without was full of armed men, and he checked a second rush on the part of Ned.

"Wait," he said; "we can do nothing more."

"I have done something anyhow," replied Ned. "Hang him! I have broken half my toes."

Of the result of their treatment of the Mahdi they were not long left in doubt. Two minutes after Abdallah disappeared a number of the Fanzual tribe rushed into the room.

They were met with such weapons as the brothers had at their command—their fists. Several of the foremost were knocked down, but the others threw themselves upon the gallant pair with the force of a tornado, and, bearing them to the earth, bound them hand and foot. They were then lifted up and borne away by a grim and silent band, down the passage outside into a hall, where Ozrim, the son of Melshah, was awaiting them.

He sat upon a raised throne at one end of the hall, with the Mahdi by his side, disclosing the face and form of the leader of the horsemen they had seen in the desert.

No change had been made in his attire, save that he wore a girdle of gold around his waist, and had twisted a string of pearls about his turban.

Armed men with ferocious faces stood behind the throne and on either side of it. Some wore long robes, and had the look of sheiks, but the majority were sparsely attired in white or coloured tunics and trousers.

Tom and Ned were placed before the chief, their guard falling in behind them.

Ozrim was a handsome man, about as dark as a negro, but with good features. His brows were knitted, half in anger, half in trouble.

"Offspring of the accursed," he said; "let your tongues speak ere you die."

"Of what are we to speak?" demanded Tom.

"Tell me who and what you are," said Ozrim.

"Tom," whispered Ned, under his breath, "it is my turn this time. I feel I can work that Mahdi's business. Give a fellow a chance."

"Go on," replied Tom. "It will not matter much in the end, I fear."

"Ozrim, son of Melshah," said Ned, "mighty father of the desert. We are in this country against our will, being taken prisoners by a band of ruffians in Algiers, and transported here. We have done no harm, and mean none."

"Who and what are you?" demanded Ozrim.

"In our own land we are high priests of the God of Courage. We are brave men, and will prove it against any man who bears a sword. Last night I had a dream—"

He stopped short, and Ozrim, bending forward, gazed at him eagerly.

A dreamer is always an object of interest to the Eastern tribes. In their abounding health they are rarely troubled with night visions.

Ned, who was not a bad actor, looked like one inspired, notwithstanding his humiliating bonds.

"Speak!" said Ozrim.

"I saw a tribe of brave men led to the slaughter by a false Mahdi," commenced Ned. "The enemies prevailed against them, killing all who came within reach of their sword."

"Yes, it was so," assented Ozrim. "The dream was good."

"Among the victors," continued Ned, "I saw YOUR face, oh! chief, and you rejoiced while your enemies were being slain. But lo! while yet the song of mirth was on your lips, and ere the blood of the fallen was dry upon your swords, there was a cry that the true Mahdi was on the way, and in a moment I saw him with a sword of fire slaying all before him. He breathed fire as if his stomach had been a furnace of coal, and you and yours fell away from him as the chaff of corn from the heat of the simoon."

Tom stared hard at Ned.

His words, his manner, the very tone of his voice was so different to what it had ever been before. He spoke like one inspired.

"I had no idea," he thought, "that Ned had anything like this within him. But how will it help us?"

"And the true Mahdi swallowed up the false Mahdi," Ned went on. "All else fell down before him and withered away. There was death in the breathing of his nostrils—his eyes gave out flames of fire. Ozrim, son of Melshah, beware if you harm us, for we alone can save you from the coming ruler of the earth."

Then up sprang Abdallah, and, throwing up both his arms, he cried out—

"Lies—lies! The Frank speaks nothing but lies!"

"Is he not one of the Franks of YOUR vision?" demanded Ozrim. "Truly I have marvelled at your wishing them to be brought before me."

"They are lions in the clothing of the lamb!" cried Abdallah. "Put them to the torture now. If they be true it will not harm them, but if they are false so surely shall they die!"

Ozrim opened his lips to reply, but a commotion at the bottom of the hall checked him.

A tall, swarthy man, with only a cloth about his waist, was trying to push his way through the armed men, who endeavoured to bar his progress.

Ozrim stood up and looked in the direction of the commotion, and his eye singled out the man.

"It is Selim—my messenger," he said; "be still, there. Let him pass!"

Then Selim was allowed to come through, and, rushing up to the feet of his chief, he threw himself upon his knees.

"Oh! my lord," he cried, in Arabic, "I bring you wonderful tidings. I have met the real Mahdi on the mountains. He speaks a strange tongue, and has followed me hither."

Abdallah rose up and would have fled from the room, but Ozrim, the son of Melshah, threw himself upon him and hurled him upon the floor.

"Seize him!" he commanded, "and bind his

arms. The ropes will be as flax if he is not like—"

"Oh! spare me, my lord," cried the Mahdi, "and I will tell you all. It is fitting that you should know, but spare my life."

"Bind him fast, I say," thundered Ozrim, "and you, my good Selim, tell me—where is the true Mahdi?"

"My lord, he is without the gate," answered Selim.

The brothers could not understand what was said, for Arabic was strange as yet to them, but they saw something had transpired in their favour, and their hearts bounded with joy.

Abdallah's sudden deposition was enough in itself to warm their breasts, and they exchanged glances of pleasure, which were suddenly checked when Ozrim drew a dagger from his breast and advanced towards them.

But he came not to kill.

All the use he made of the weapon was to cut their bonds, and this done he bowed himself low before them.

"Oh! rulers of the earth—great prophets! let one sit on my right and the other on my left. The real Mahdi is drawing near."

He backed slowly, turning at every step, while the men clashed their weapons and shouted.

"What does it all mean?" asked Ned, quite bewildered.

"I don't know," answered Tom; "but there is something about a real Mahdi. I have heard that they are always cropping up in this country, but I certainly did not expect one so soon. Ned, you must have known of his coming?"

"I'll vow I didn't," replied Ned; "but luck's with us again. Shall we give three cheers for number two Mahdi?"

"No—no, don't cheer," said Tom. "You have had your chance, made the best of it, and it's a lucky hit. Rest on your laurels, for the time at least."

By this time Ozrim, the son of Melshah, had reached his throne, and was standing there with his hands spread out, inviting the brothers to be seated.

On either side of him was a broad stool of ebony, inlaid with jewels, and, putting as much dignity into the ceremony as they had at their command, Tom and Ned took their seats.

CHAPTER XVIII.

THE REAL MAHDI APPEARS, AND PROVES TO BE THE MOST ASTONISHING OF HIS SPECIES EVER SEEN.

BRIEF pause, and then Selim, who had vanished temporarily from the room, reappeared. He came in backwards, bowing low before the most extraordinary figure Tom and his brother had ever seen. It was that of a man of medium height, spare of form, and just a trifle knock-kneed. Round about his body was one simple garment, made of unprepared sheepskin, and in the place of hair he had upon his head a mass of uncombed wool.

All the visible parts of his body were of reddish-brown, save round the eyes, where the skin was almost black, which gave to his small, dark eyes a very wild appearance.

In his right hand he carried a staff about five feet long, the straight trunk of some small sapling.

As he entered the room he went through several contortions of a most ludicrous nature, knocking his knees together and thrusting his arms down into imaginary trousers-pockets, just as a clown might do.

"Yah! yucco!" he shrieked.

Abdallah, who was standing on one side, with his arms bound, and closely attended by his guard, stared at the new arrival with an expression of face that was equally ludicrous.

And when he cried "Yah! yucco!" the words seemed to go through him like two bullets.

An exclamation also escaped him which sounded familiar in Tom's ears, but in the jubilant shouts which hailed the new Mahdi he could not be certain about it.

Eastern men have a very poor sense of the ludicrous.

They hardly if ever laugh, and strange contortions on the part of dervishes and other fanatics never excite their surprise.

They look upon these things as the workings of the spirit of prophecy.

The real Mahdi, as we must for the present call him, stopped half-way up the hall and gasped out—

"Bi Blimblo!"

That he was short of breath was evident, but he made strenuous efforts to hide it, and went through a dancing performance which bore a slight resemblance to the opening of the British hornpipe.

Ozrim threw himself down upon his knees and spread out his arms to greet the strange creature, who stopped short a few feet from him, and with folded arms signified that he was not as yet prepared to embrace any of the faithful.

"Chick—can—arv," he said.

"Ozrim, son of Melshah," shrieked Abdallah, "hear me!"

"That dog here yet?" thundered Ozrim. "Away with him!"

"I must have your ear," yelled Abdallah. "I will! Know ye not that—"

But the guards gagged him with the end of a scarf thrust into his mouth, and dragged him from the room, apparently on the verge of convulsions.

Then came a strange silence, as if some supernatural power had turned all there to stone.

Ozrim had drawn aside from his throne, and motioned for the real Mahdi to take it.

But that new light for the faithful did not seem to be in a hurry to do so.

He looked at Ned first and then at Tom steadily, and the look thrilled them.

What was the potent power in that glance to move them so?

Neither could tell.

But moved they were, and on Tom's cheek there came a rosy flush of excitement.

All sorts of possible things flashed up before him, but in chaotic form, and he could not detach them from each other or give them form.

Ned felt that he was going wrong.

His recent adventures had been of a bewildering

nature, but here was something that more than amazed him.

The real Mahdi did not accept the proffered seat, but, after standing still for awhile, he motioned Ozrim and his men to retire.

The action was dramatic, but inclined to be of the burlesque order.

At the same time he signified, by looking at Tom and Ned, and shaking his head, that they were to emain.

When a Mahdi commands the faithful have nothing to do but to obey.

Unwillingly enough Ozrim signalled for his men to depart, remaining to the last, with the hope that the order as concerned himself would be rescinded.

But the real Mahdi was inflexible.

Ozrim had to go.

A warning look of the eyes and an extended arm showed that he was not wanted there.

Bowing low three times he went forth, and Tom and Ned were left alone with the real Mahdi.

"You'll excuse me, gentlemen," he said, "but I really didn't like to sit down in your presence without leave, and I daren't ax for it afore them black chaps."

"I'll be hanged," exclaimed Ned, breathlessly, "if it isn't Chippy Chunks !"

CHAPTER XIX.

CHIPPY CHUNKS TELLS AN INTERESTING TALE—NED IS APPOINTED INTERPRETER—BY ORDER OF THE MAHDI.

ES—it was indeed Chippy Chunks in that extraordinary get-up, and Tom was too much overcome with amazement to say anything.

Ned began to laugh in a quiet way. He had been long enough among the Moors to learn that mirth was by them looked upon with contempt, and, if he were overheard, he knew that doubts of the authenticity of the new Mahdi might arise in their minds.

"I hope, gentlemen, you will excuse this get-up," said Chippy, "but it was the only chance I had of getting near you. It was the idea of that dark-eyed minx Alea, who certainly is a rum-'un."

"And who is she ?" asked Tom.

"Wife of that old party who is boss of the castle at Algiers. He sent me and his wife and Mrs. Tartar away to be sold, but we've got away."

"My wife lives and is FREE ?" exclaimed Tom joyfully.

"Not exactly," replied Chippy Chunks, "but I think she's pretty safe for the present. They've food enough for a few days."

"Tell me all about it," said Tom, in a state of nervous agitation, "and be as brief as you can."

Chippy Chunks, with commendable brevity, told him all that had taken place after Tom and Ned were put in the Cabash.

The reader is already acquainted with the facts, and we need not record them here, but simply take up the thread of the narrative from the time we left them in the cave in the mountain.

Chippy Chunks was complimented for his ready disposal, as it was believed for good and all, of Si Hamick, and his mind was relieved upon the question whether it would come under the head of murder.

"Certainly it is nothing of the sort," said Ned "it's dog-slaughter."

"Well, if you think so, it's all right, sir," said Chippy Chunks ; "but I certainly prefer a fair fight, hammer to hammer, as it were. Mrs. Tartar wasn't sorry, and that dark-eyed Alea was glad—and she put it into my head to be a Mahdi. This 'ere sheepskin was found in a cave, and I got a gummy substance off a tree growing near to stick the wool on my head. My skin's coloured with the juice of some berries growing near where they are hidden, and that's my get-up."

"I ought to say," he added, with an indescribable look on his face, "that I made my t'ilet where nobody could see me, and I've put my clothes in a bit of a hole and stopped it up with a stone. I've got my hammer, though."

He showed them the handle by drawing it out from an opening in the breast of his woolly tunic, with all the pride of a warrior exhibiting his trusty sword.

"Missus," he said, "won't go back—if she can get back—until she knows something about your whereabouts, sir, and that's why I got myself up this way. Alea said all I had to do was to kick about if I met anyone, and holler gibberish, and they would take me for a prophet. So I came out and went forward to look about me."

"How far is the cave from here ?" asked Tom.

"About two miles as the crow flies, sir, I should say," replied Chippy. "Well, I come away from the cave, and afore I'd gone far I met a woman with a jar on her head. As soon as she see me I'm blowed if she didn't fall flop—"

"I don't wonder at it," said Ned.

"Flop, sir, forgetting all about the jar, which, I'm sorry to say, was busted to pieces. She got up after a minute and ran away at the rate of ten miles an hour. I didn't know what she might be up to, but I still marched forrard, and presently I saw a lot of other people approaching. I got my hammer ready for action, but it wasn't wanted.

"They all flopped," he went on, gravely, "and I got up a dance which tried my poor old bones, I can tell you, gentlemen. Arterwards they makes signs for me to follow them, and I went with them, bent on taking my chance of what turned up, and, as I'm a livin' sinner, they brought me right on here."

He stopped for a moment to take breath, for he had been talking very fast.

"It's about as wonderful a chance as ever I heard of," said Ned.

"I judge that the route taken to the place for the disposal of prisoners and slaves," replied Tom, "is a general one. At least, it bears in one direction, and, as we were all to be sold, it comes about that we have been brought together. But still, as you say, Ned, it is indeed wonderful."

"You may reckon, gentlemen," resumed Chippy Chunks, "that I was a bit flabbygasted when I saw you here ; but I rose to the occasion and didn't faint away as I felt inclined to. And now I've found you I must leave it to you, gentlemen, to say what is to be done."

"We must be very careful in our movements," said Tom ; "and above all you must keep up your character for the present."

"What am I to do, sir ?"

"Talk any nonsense that comes into your head when speaking to them. Do not for a moment

"HURRY UP, NED, OR THEY WILL SMASH US," CRIED TOM TARTAR.

betray that you speak English, as many of them understand it."

"All right, sir. Hullaby—lullaby—goo wang—bee. How's that, sir?"

"It will do," replied Tom; "and as we have by good luck fitted in with some ridiculous prophecy of the other Mahdi, I think we had better announce ourselves as your interpreters."

"I'll take that post," said Ned.

"Very well," replied Tom; "but don't be more jocular than you can help."

"I wonder why the dancing takes their fancy so?" mused Chippy Chunks.

"Because they are too lazy to go in for it themselves," replied Ned.

"A great many religious rites with Eastern people are mainly dances," said Tom. "Now we have been long enough in secret conclave, so we had better summon Ozrim, son of Melshah, and let him know we are the interpreters of the unknown tongue of the new Mahdi."

"The only real and unadulterated article," returned Ned. "Shall I call him in?"

"Yes; but none of your jokes, Ned."

"I'm as serious as an owl. Chippy, put on a look of wisdom, and as soon as I open the door or curtains begin the performance."

Ned rose up, and was about to cross the chamber, when a further idea occurred to him.

"I shall favour Ozrim with an address," he said, "and when I stop you cut in, Chippy, with something—a bit of dancing or gibberish of some sort won't be thrown away."

"Don't overdo it," warned Tom; "these Moors are sharp in their way, although imposed upon by the fanatics and humbugs of the Abdallah class. Go easy, Ned."

"All right, old man."

Ned raised the curtain at the door of the room, and in a loud voice cried—

"Ozrim, son of Melshah, the Mahdi desires your presence—advance!"

A clashing of swords was heard, and the Fanzual chief with about a score of followers approached.

But Ned waved the latter back.

"It is the Mahdi's wish that you should enter alone."

Ozrim bowed low and strode into the chamber, halting just within it.

"It has pleased the Mahdi, who speaks a new tongue, which shall by-and-bye be the speech of the world," said Ned, "to make me interpreter of his commands."

"He does not understand our tongue?" queried Ozrim.

"Oh! yes," replied Ned, quickly. "He understands all things, but he will only speak his own tongue until all infidels are swept from the face of the earth."

Turning to Chippy Chunks, who had risen and was standing in an attitude like that of Pizarro, as depicted in those remarkable cuts got up for the young to colour and cut out for the model stage, Ned went on—

"Geefor ofor afar lifor efor afor defor."

Chippy Chunks in reply gave out a series of sounds of a most extraordinary nature, being a mixture of choruses attached to our popular negro and music-hall melodies.

"It is the will of the Mahdi," said Ned, addressing Ozrim, "that we have a portion of the castle set aside for ourselves, and that none intrude upon us save by his command."

"It shall be done," replied Ozrim.

Once more Chippy Chunks gave vent to the unknown tongue, his strange speech commencing with—

"Olemotherhubbar wentothecubbar togivepoor doggerbone."

And then running on to the story about those remarkable blackbirds that were baked in a pie, which, when the crust was broken, flew out joyfully singing.

"Your commands, Mahdi, shall be obeyed," said Ned, bowing low. "Ozrim, son of Melshah, it is the Mahdi's wish that the portion of the castle facing the east, and the outer part thereof, be given up to us; and, further, that the whole of that wing be apportioned us, so that we may prepare for the coming struggle with the infidel; that wine and food be placed in the outer chamber, and that no man show his face to the Mahdi for three days."

"So shall it be," replied Ozrim.

"And he further commands," continued Ned, "that the place be at once prepared for our reception, and meanwhile food and wine be sent hither. Ozrim, son of Melshah, you may go."

And Ozrim, son of Melshah, turned and went away.

CHAPTER XX.

PLAYING MAHDI—THE EASTERN WING—ABDALLAH'S DANCE OF DEFIANCE—A PROPHET BOUND.

'M blessed if it isn't as good as a play!" said Chippy Chunks, as he resumed his seat. "Mister Ned, you are a horator."

"What made you select chambers in the East?" asked Tom; "or what put it into your head to go in for a change of quarters?"

"Outside the castle, don't forget," replied Ned, with a knowing wink; "we can then see exactly what we have to run through to get away."

"It's a good idea, Ned," said Tom.

"You may leave him, sir, to—" began Chippy Chunks, but Tom cut him short.

"Hush! I hear footsteps."

They were but the naked feet of Nubian slaves bringing food and wine, but even before them it was necessary to dissemble.

Chippy Chunks resumed a dignified position, and Tom and Ned a dependent one, as the curtains parted and the ebony-skinned children of Africa entered with the food and wine.

They all needed something in the way of refreshment, Chippy Chunks especially, and as soon as the slaves had retired they fell upon the fruit and dried goat's flesh and other things provided for their consumption with the appetites of athletes.

"The wine's good, gentlemen," said Chippy

Chunks," smacking his lips; "but to my thinking nothing comes near good old English porter."

When they had eaten and drank all they required Ned summoned the servants back again, and with them came Ozrim, to show the trio to their new quarters.

With the limited furniture of the castle very little preparation was needed. A few rugs and shawls cast upon the ground, some cushions to sleep upon, and the place was ready.

It was, in an architectural sense, a magnificent set of chambers to which Ozrim ushered them.

To get at this new abode they had to cross the courtyard, which was empty of all living beings—none daring without command to intrude upon the new Mahdi.

What had become of the deposed one was a problem Tom was revolving in his mind as they crossed the courtyard, and glancing upward he saw a face peering over the top of one of the towers and watching their progress with a very evil eye.

In this spy upon their movements Tom recognised the deposed Mahdi, and the ludicrous expression of the fellow's face nearly brought on a fit of laughter.

But gravity is everything among the Eastern people, and he managed to keep an expression of solemnity almost painful upon his face.

The eastern wing was sufficiently like the place recently occupied by Tom and Ned to need no description, save in one respect. There were open windows that commanded a view of the country, and a flight of steps, about a score in number, led to a walk upon the summit of a square tower about sixty feet high.

The latter fact was not discovered at once by our friends, but later on, just before sunset. Tom suggested they should keep quiet for awhile, lest they should be watched by somebody in whose heart suspicion of the genuineness of the new Mahdi might have taken root.

So they lounged about and whispered the ideas that came to them of methods of escaping, or spoke of Lottie and Alea awaiting their coming in the cave upon the mountain.

In this way they killed the time until Tom thought they might safely ascend.

Then they went up the steps and stood side by side with bent heads, but with eyes that took in the country before them.

"Do you see the way you came, Chippy?" said Tom, in a voice scarcely audible.

"Yes, sir," was the answer. "It's that bit o' crack in the hills right forrard."

"I see. You are sure?"

"Quite sure, sir."

"Hi! Tom. The other chap is on a tower to the left. Look at him."

They all turned their eyes in the direction named by Ned, and a most extraordinary sight met their gaze.

On the very summit of a tower, higher by a score feet than that on which they stood, Abdallah was leaping up and down, bounding to the right and left, and exhibiting in a fantastic way the extraordinary agility of which he was possessed.

That these antics were directed against the trio was clear, as he kept his face towards them, and occasionally gesticulated in a challenging manner to Chippy Chunks.

"He wants you to enter into a competition with

him," said Ned, "and I am afraid you are not in it, Chippy."

"No, sir," replied Chunks. "I'm not a born male bally-girl. Yah! yer ole fool!" he bawled out at the top of his voice.

Whether it was the words or whether the dance was done we cannot tell, but Abdallah vanished, and they went down to their chamber.

"The way out," said Tom, "is simple. We must work all to-night and to-morrow making a rope out of the shawls and rugs. Then as soon as the sun has set again we can try to get away. You'll not be afraid, Chunks to slide down a rope?"

"Not me," replied Chippy. "When all is ready, you go down first and clear off for the hill. I'll get down somehow, if it's head first."

So they worked all night as well as they could in the gloom, tearing the shawls and rugs into strips, and twisting the pieces into a rope which they believed would be strong enough to bear them.

Occasionally Ned would steal out in his stockinged feet, and go quietly through the passage and two other chambers which had been set apart for them, but he could find no indication of a spy present.

He had to go more by sound than sight, although his eyes got so used to the gloom that he could have seen moving objects half-way across the darkened chamber.

But he saw nothing—heard nothing.

A dead silence lay on the castle, save on two occasions in the night, when the silence was broken by a wild cry of great intensity, that seemed to come from someone in pain.

They judged it came from the summit of the tower whereon Abdallah danced, and in all probability it was the fanatic bewailing his downfall before a "false prophet."

Strange to say that, though he had been virtually deposed as an impostor, no harm was offered him. He was not even treated as a prisoner.

This leniency, no doubt, arose from the lingering fears of a superstitious people that he might after all be gifted with the powers of a chosen destroyer of the infidel.

At morn, an hour after sunrise, he was seen strolling across the courtyard in the direction of the eastern chambers of the castle, when Ozrim, the son of Melshah, barred his way.

"Whither goest thou, Abdallah?" he asked.

"To strike to ashes this dog who comes here as the Mahdi," replied Abdallah.

"Ah! darest thou do so?" asked Ozrim.

"I have fasted and danced all night," said Abdallah, "and I have prayed for strength to destroy this old liar, who comes here with his toothless mouth to lead our people to death! It is true! I will destroy him as the blazing furnace burns a handful of withered grass!"

"He has commanded that none intrude upon him," said Ozrim.

"I care not for that, oh! Ozrim."

"Go, then, mad fool, to thy death!"

Ozrim stood aside, and Abdallah passed on with the fierce light of the fanatic blazing in his eyes.

His footstep was so soft that our friends were caught laughing together over some jest of Ned's.

Early as it was, breakfast had been brought to the entrance of the chamber, and they had partaken of it. They had just risen to their feet laughing, as we have said, when Abdallah appeared.

"Ha !" he said, "you dogs, have I caught you ? English ASS ! I heard your tongue," pointing his finger at Chippy Chunks ; "you speak as the others do ! Dogs all ! I am here, as I have sworn to Ozrim, the son of Melshah, to make ashes of you."

"Here, you be civil," said Chippy Chunks. "English gentlemen don't want any of your cheek. You make ashes of me ! I'll make mincemeat of you !"

And Chippy Chunks, to show that he meant business, began to spar in a style that would have laid any professor of the "noble art" upon a sick bed who had witnessed it.

Abdallah regarded him with scorn, evidently looking upon the display as a feeble specimen of dancing.

From this false idea he was awakened by a blow between the eyes that laid him on the flat of his back.

Before he could rise, Tom and Ned, who had been laughing at Chippy Chunks' display, were upon him. Instinctively both felt that matters had now entered upon a serious phase.

"Gag him, Ned," said Tom. "Chippy, hold his legs. I've got his arms. Now, all together—turn him over."

Abdallah, having been fasting and capering all night, was not so strong as usual, and moreover the blow he received had half dazed him. Otherwise he had not been made a prisoner so easily.

But in a few moments his sash had been twisted and utilised in binding his arms behind him.

Then with two of the pieces of rope they had made his legs were secured, and some odd pieces of rag bound round his mouth made a good gag.

"What's to be done now ?' asked Ned. "Run for it ?"

"No," said Tom. "He came here to make ashes of us—go and proclaim that Chippy has made ashes of him."

"And suppose they won't believe me ?"

"You must take your chance of that, Ned. To get away in daylight is impossible. Here, Chippy, you go with him. Proclaim that Abdallah, for his temerity in daring to intrude upon your presence without being commanded, has perished."

Ned and Chippy Chunks vanished, and Tom turned Abdallah over again, so that his face lay upwards.

Never before had Tom seen such an expression in the eyes of living creature. Anger, mortification, despair, were all so forcibly expressed that each emotion seemed to be well defined, and have its place in those wild, dark eyes.

A wolf chained and bound would not have had such eyes. Despite the ludicrous nature of his capture and his position there was something terrible in having such a captive near him.

"Better kill him now !" something whispered to Tom, "or ware him by-and-bye."

But Tom could not do that.

He was one of the last in the world to commit cold-blooded murder for fear of a possibly dangerous foe in the future.

"You have brought this on yourself," said Tom, "and if you are quiet no harm will be done to you."

But the eyes changed not if the ears heard. Not

one shade of passion relaxed. If the varied expressions had been BURNT into them they could not have been more fixed. So Tom spoke no more to him, but with the sword of Abdallah drawn, kept watch and ward over him until Ned and Chippy Chunks returned.

CHAPTER XXI.

THE HOUR OF ESCAPE—CHIPPY AND ABDALLAH HAVE ANOTHER ENCOUNTER—FLIGHT—THE PASS LOST.

ED first appeared, and a glance at his face showed that all went well up to the present.

He glanced at Abdallah, whose eyes shifted to him, and remained fixed upon him for the next few minutes.

"Chippy is giving them a dance," he said, "and they are in a howling state of delight. Ozrim, son of Melshah, is prone on his nose with adoration."

"You should not have left Chippy," urged Tom.

"He's all right," replied Ned. "I thought I would run back and tell you how he was. Our friend here seems to be in a queer state."

"Never mind him," said Tom. "You get Chippy back, and, above all, let it be known that the next rash fool who intrudes upon him will die horribly, and be cut off from Paradise."

"I'll lay it on thick," said Ned.

But Ned's services were not needed, as Chippy Chunks was coming along the passage outside the chamber panting, and with his eyes well out of his head.

"I can't do much more o' this, Mister Ned," he said ; "my hamstrings won't stand it. I don't know how the regular Maddeys do it, but they must have lots o' training."

"There is nobody following you ?" said Ned.

"Not they," replied Chippy ; "I left 'em all in a heap on the ground, a-wallowing about and howling. I'm sorry to carry on this imposition, Mister Ned."

"Oh ! don't bother about that," replied Ned. "It will soon be over. Go and join my brother. I'll stop here on sentry duty, for fear some spy should come along."

But none ventured in that direction, and when at noon the slaves brought some additional viands for the use of the real Mahdi and his friends, they came no further than the outer entrance to the eastern wing.

This gave a little extra trouble to Ned, who did waiter's duty, and carried the dishes one by one to the inner chamber.

Meanwhile Tom and Chippy Chunks, seated so as to keep an eye on the prisoner, were working away at the rope-making, knotting and testing its strength by every conceivable means.

Propped up against the wall like a limp doll, Abdallah watched this proceeding with eyes that took in all it meant.

But now his emotions had subsided or been got

under restraint, for he simply gazed at the work like a dispassionate observer.

All the while he was slowly and persistently working at his bound hands, to loose his bonds and set himself free.

"I should like to give him something to eat and drink," said Tom; "but it can't be done. He would not be grateful, and his first act would be to shout out that he was alive. These fanatics know no such thing as fear."

"And they are used to fasting," hinted Ned.

Slowly the day passed away.

At intervals Ned stole down to the chief entrance to see what was going on outside, and he always returned with the same report—

"They are buzzing about like bees, in a state of excitement, but they make no effort to enter here."

Nothing, indeed, occurred during the day to mar the plans of our friends.

The night approached, and they got ready for a move.

The rope was carried up the flight of steps and laid on the topmost one, out of sight of the higher towers, ready for use, and Chippy Chunks took up his position on the summit of their tower to give the signal when the sun was about to dip.

Three minutes after the sun went down it would be dark enough to fasten the rope across one of the embrasures by the simple means of the strong scabbard of Abdallah's sword, which was of extra length, as we have previously stated.

One by one they would glide down, Chippy Chunks going last, as he desired.

"I will go down first," said Tom, "and keep the rope taut, so as to prevent the scabbard slipping."

The eventful moment arrived at last.

A hurried examination of the bonds of Abdallah showed them to be apparently as fast as ever, and then they all quickly ascended the tower.

The rope had been previously knotted over the centre of the scabbard.

It was laid across the embrasure and the free end thrown over.

Tom slipped through the opening and glided down.

On getting to the bottom he found it about ten feet short of the required length, so he had to drop. He did it as quietly as he could, and alighted upon his feet, scarcely making a sound.

When Ned in his turn came down he bade him in a whisper to hang on for a while until Chippy Chunks came in sight.

Barely had he thrown out this hint when an unearthly yell was heard on the summit of the tower, followed by a cry from Chippy Chunks—

"Run, gentlemen, that chap is free!"

Then came a sound of scuffling, and the fall of a heavy body.

"Poor Chunks!" gasped Tom.

"It's too heavy for Chunks," replied Ned. "Here he comes."

And down came Chunks with a run so sharp that he was upon Ned before he could let go, and fairly "shinned" him off the rope.

They fell upon Tom, and all three went down in a heap.

But nobody was much hurt, and they were up again in a twinkling.

"I was obliged to hit out," said Chippy. "I gave him one with the hammer—somewhere 'twixt the eyes."

And now arose a frightful clamour in the interior of the castle. The voice of Abdallah had been heard, and his voice recognised.

In a flash as it were the truth burst upon the deluded Moors, who all at once seemed to recognise the fact that they had been DONE.

There were cries of men calling others to arms, a rush of feet, the clattering of weapons, and, above all, the voice of Ozrim, the son of Melshah, calling upon his men to follow him into the Eastern Tower.

"Away," said Tom, "and don't speak a word. Tread as lightly as you can. I've got the track clear in my mind."

"Go ahead, sir," said Chippy Chunks, "I'll follow as well as I can; but, oh! the chafing them knots gave me. I feel as if I'd been riding donkeys on Hampstead-heath for a month."

"Catch hold of his other arm, Ned," said Tom, seizing his right one. "We must get him along somehow."

"Go and leave me," gasped Chunks. "It don't matter what comes of an old beggar like me. They can kill me, if they've a mind to."

"Not another word," said Tom. "All together or none."

And away they went over the broken ground, Chippy Chunks enduring tortures such as have fallen to the lot of few, with his eyes shut and his teeth clenched.

It was night now, but there were stars shining brightly over the mountain-tops, which were dimly limned against the great arch above.

In the hollow where the castle stood the gloom was fortunately very deep.

On the castle walls the Moorish warriors were rushing to and fro, some firing without aim into the darkness below, others shouting in answer to their chief, whose voice rung out like a clarion upon the night air.

The form of Abdallah had been found.

At first they must have thought him dead, for a great wail of anguish went up to the stars.

Then, when they discovered that he breathed, they called upon him to "awake and lead them to vengeance on the infidel."

That he did soon recover consciousness was clear, for his voice in turn was heard shrieking for lightnings to leap from the sky and destroy those who had dared to lay hands upon one of the chosen of the Prophet.

Tom and Ned, with the agonised Chippy between them, kept steadily on.

No great pace could be attained, because the ground was very rough, and the smaller stone obstacles were not visible until they had stumbled over them.

Not more than half the distance to the narrow mountain pass had been accomplished when the Moors, with torches and glittering spears and swords, were seen to be pouring out of the castle gates.

It was a brilliant, imposing, yet terrifying spectacle, if fear had not been almost a stranger to the brothers.

Chippy Chunks had no thoughts outside those engendered by the anguish arising from a rapid slide with naked legs down a very roughly-made rope.

A coloured fire of some sort was lighted on the summit of the tower they had just left.

It threw a broad glare over the surrounding land.

"Stoop," said Tom, "but keep going. They may not see us. If worst comes to worst, Ned, we'll fight and die. Don't be taken by those fellows alive. They are devils incarnate when they are heated by the fires of vengeance."

"They haven't got us yet," replied Ned.

"Oh! gentlemen," softly moaned Chippy Chunks, "if you would but only leave me and take care of yourself you could get away easy."

"All or none," Tom said again.

Bent almost double, so as to give as little possible chance to their foes, they crept on.

But presently a yell from the tower summit announced that they were seen.

Tom cast a hasty look back, and saw that it was Abdallah who had discovered them.

He was in the act of creeping through the embrasure so as to descend by the rope they had left behind them.

A moment later and the fire had died out.

Once more darkness.

But only for a little while they knew.

On—on, with limbs that ached and with muscles strained. Behind them the fanatic Abdallah, yelling to the Fanzuals to head the fugitives and block the pass.

It now became a race who should be there first.

The majority of the Moors were too heavily clothed and armed to run fast; but many of the tribe wore apparel light enough for indulgence in athletic exercise.

These latter gained ground fast, and they knew the way too well.

Though Tom had laid out the direction to take, he could not, in any case, keep it so well as the men who were accustomed to prowl about at night, and who had the eyes of wild beasts.

"I, Abdallah," shrieked the fanatic, as he tore over the ground, "have been let loose to destroy all infidels. Three of their high priests are here. On —on! and let them die by fire and sword!"

"Ease up a bit," said Tom, with a groan, "I can't see exactly where we are going."

"You've lost the line for the pass," said Ned.

"Only for the moment."

"Then we are lost too."

"Ned, old boy, if you talk in that way I shall think you have lost your pluck."

"Wheel about, Tom! We've nothing to do but to die."

"The sword of the prophet!" shrieked Abdallah from the rear. "It comes like a whirlwind to destroy those who have foully laid their hands on the chosen."

"Oh! for a little light," groaned Tom.

As if in response to his heart's desire, another gleam of fire burst out from the top of the tower—a weird, white light, that cast an uncanny sheen upon the scene.

"The pass!" cried Tom. "I see it. One more effort, Ned. Chippy, rouse yourself, we have another chance for life."

CHAPTER XXII.

THE FLIGHT ALONG THE DEFILE—OUTSIDE THE CAVE—A VAIN CRY.

 HE race to the defile was won by our friends. Tom and Ned were pretty well breathed with the sharp run and the labour of hustling Chippy Chunks along, and the "real Mahdi" was so thoroughly pumped out that when they let him go he dropped into a sitting position on the ground.

Facing about, the brothers drew their revolvers, and Tom, with a sure aim, fired at the foremost of the foe, a tall, spare savage, whose eyes shone like jewels in the light of the fire, which still glared on the summit of the tower.

He was running so fast that when the bullet struck him square in the forehead he plunged forward and tumbled over like a hare at full speed brought down by an expert sportsman.

Another of the Fanzuals immediately behind him tripped over the fallen man, and striking the ground with his head lay stunned and helpless.

Immediately afterwards the glare of light from the tower again died away, and darkness was upon them once more.

For a few moments it seemed blacker than it really was in the open ground. But the defile was truly dark enough for a tomb, and the pursuers came to a halt.

There was a rattling of arms, a movement of feet, and a chorus of hurried voices.

Tom, addressing Ned, bade him assist Chippy Chunks to rise and get away along the narrow road.

"If we go quickly," he whispered, "I do not think they will follow us."

Chippy heard the whisper, and roused himself so as to dispense with assistance.

He got upon his feet somehow, and they all backed slowly, carefully picking their way.

A short distance from the mouth of the defile it bore away to the south-east.

It was so dark where they were that the ground was only seen in the faintest way, but overhead they could see the stars shining between the jagged outline of the summit of the rocks, and these were their guide.

Barely had they got round the first bend when the Fanzuals began to fire into the defile, and the ping ping of the bullets as they struck the rocks showed how narrow had been the escape of the fugitives from death.

Had they not moved on death was inevitable.

"Let them blaze away!" muttered Tom, grimly, "If I know these men they will not venture in until they feel sure they have only dead men to meet."

The path wound slowly upwards, and they toiled on for awhile, the firing going on unceasingly, awaking echoes below and above.

After a time Tom called for a halt, and they sat down to rest—all three had need of it.

"We've made a start, gentlemen," said Chippy Chunks, as he slowly rubbed his aching limbs, "and that's something."

"I think that killing Abdallah would have been justifiable under the circumstances," said Tom; "it would have given us a few hours' clear start, and left them in doubt of what had become of us."

"Never mind, Tom," replied Ned, cheerily. "They haven't got us yet. Just think of the old days in Siberia, and what we went through there."

"I'm not funking, Ned," said Tom; "but not killing that fellow was an error, and yet I CAN'T do that sort of thing. Somehow it goes against the grain."

All this time the enemy was firing into the defile, and it was clear that the pursuit had been carried no further.

Having rested, Tom suggested a move on, and they once more started.

Chippy Chunks declined all further assistance. He declared he never felt "fresher in his life," which may be put down as a slight exaggeration.

"You must be our guide now," said Tom.

"The way ain't easy to miss, sir," replied Chippy Chunks. "I don't think I'm likely to make a mistake."

It was a slow journey, for despite the assumed briskness of the guide he could only just hobble along, but, strange to say, he did gather strength as he proceeded, and when he came to a point where the defile widened he became positively lively in his movements.

"I'm right now," he said; "a little further on we come to a steep path up the mountain, and half way up is the cave."

"Go on," said Tom, drawing a quick, short breath.

On their way thither they had passed two other paths that came from different directions into the defile, and in them lay two chances of safety in case of further pursuit.

The enemy would not be positive which way they had gone, and might possibly make a mistake unless they divided their forces.

There was also the hope that the Fanzuals might not venture to follow them, for the country really belonged to hostile tribes, who might resent their intrusion.

Tom had learnt that much from Cherif Bouzian prior to the fatal attack upon the Fanzuals, whose land lay beyond the Atlas Mountains.

And now the path led out of the defile and up the steep hillside, huge rocks towering on the right and open ground to the left.

"The cave's yonder," said Chippy Chunks, pulling up at a turning of the narrow pathway, "and I think, Mister Tartar, I had better go forward and just prepare the ladies for your coming."

"Do so," said Tom, "I will be near you."

So Chippy Chunks went up to the cave, which looked like a huge mouth in the face of the mountain, and, halting outside, put his fingers in his mouth and whistled.

Then he and Tom stood still listening.

No sound or movement came in response.

"They're asleep, sir," said Chippy Chunks, in a broken voice; "I'm sure of it."

He had an idea of something being wrong, and Tom's heart beat fast with the rising of a dreadful fear of disaster to his wife.

"I'll speak to her," he said. "Sleeping or waking she will hear me."

"Lottie!" he cried aloud.

His voice penetrated into the cave and reverberated back again.

But that was all.

"Lottie!" cried Tom again, and scarce waiting for the answer, which never came, he plunged into the cave.

"Lottie—Lottie!" he shouted as he groped about in the terrible darkness.

No reply was vouchsafed to ease the anguish of his heart, for no Lottie was there.

Nor was there Alea to respond, nor any living thing.

The cave was small, and Tom had soon felt all over it.

"Not here!" he cried.

Then Chippy Chunks and Ned came in, and, like men who seek for a thing they do not expect to find, but fighting against conviction, they searched as they went round and round, examining the ground and the rugged stone walls.

"Gone—gone!" was all Tom could say, and sick with the weight of disappointment, he sank into a sitting position upon the ground and buried his face in his hands.

CHAPTER XXIII.

THE WRITING ON THE FLOOR—TOM'S ANGUISH— A MEETING WITH AN OLD ACQUAINTANCE.

 KEEP up a good heart Tom," said Ned, after a pause. "Perhaps they feared to be disturbed, and are not far away."

"Let us lie down and sleep," replied Tom. "We want rest, for we have work before us on the morrow."

That was all he said, and he spoke calmly enough. By way of example he stretched himself upon the ground, and his companions did the same.

It was not long ere the latter slept, and to Tom's eyes there eventually came the outer darkness of repose.

He slept, with all his weight of care, as commanders of armies sleep on the eve of battle, because he insisted upon it.

Without rest how could he work on the morrow?

The brothers still wore the swords with which Cherif Bouzian had armed them, and they slept with them by their side.

No dreams disturbed Tom, and it was daylight when he was awakened by a hand laid upon his shoulder.

It was Ned, who softly said—

"Get, up Tom—there's something for you to see below."

Tom sprang to his feet and saw Chippy Chunks kneeling by the mouth of the cave staring at the plain beneath them.

There was something worth the attention of them all.

Led by a figure on horseback, easily recognised as Abdallah, was a long line of Fanzuals on the march, wending their way in the direction of Algiers.

They were chanting in monotonous tones some wild song or hymn, occasionally pausing to give vent to the fierce war-cry of the desert—

"Ti Sebih Allah!"

Once heard it is never forgotten.

It is the cry that rang in the ears of Hicks Pasha and his eleven thousand men, on whom the hundred thousand followers of Mohammed Achmet, the Mahdi of Khartoum, fell with irresistible force, and left none to tell the full tale of the disaster.

It is the cry that is heard by the desert warrior who falls to the ground before the fierce onslaught of a foe, and sees the fatal razor-edged sword descending upon his head.

Expressive of implacable ferocity, of rampant fanaticism, of faith in the right to kill, it resounds in the ears with a terrible significance.

Only a few short hours since the episodes in the Moorish castle, and yet the restored Abdallah had gathered his forces and was on the way to "rid the world of the infidel."

Not only were the Fanzuals there, but other men, who had sprung from the watchers knew not where—half naked, with black hair hanging about the face, like a lion's mane, and long rifles or keen swords in their hands.

"Ti Sebih Allah!" from a thousand throats, musical enough as the cry floated up the mountain side to the cave, but still a cry for slaughter—the shriek of those who thirst for blood.

"We should stand very little chance with that lot," said Ned.

"No," said Tom ; "but we are already forgotten. Abdallah has higher prey in view. Still, this march is fatal to us."

"How is that, Tom ? I don't see it."

"Ned, this march of wild men will gather in number as it goes. Our hope of freedom lies in getting to Algiers. That army will for weeks to come—and maybe months—bar the way to home. But that is nought to me. Lottie—" He stopped and spoke to Chippy Chunks, who was still upon his knees—"You have no doubt this is the cave ?"

"None at all, sir," was the reply.

"If you have any doubt," said Ned, "look there."

He pointed to the loose sand upon the floor, on which the word "Lottie," traced by the finger, was clearly discernible.

Tom knelt down to kiss the dear name, written, as he knew, by his darling wife, and in doing so made a heartrending discovery.

Above it on the sands were traces of words, broken up and almost entirely obliterated by their groping about the cave in the darkness of the previous night.

He tried to read what was left, for beyond all doubt it was a message meant for him ; but all he could discern was this—

"D . . . . . . Tom, ... go . . . . Al . . . .
C . . . . . it . . . . . saf . . . . to . . . g . . . . .
m . . . . . . we . . . h . . . . . . onl . . . . . k . . ."

And at the bottom was the dear name, which had escaped being wiped out.

"Oh ! what accursed ill-fortune," moaned Tom. "How am I to know what this message means ? Is it to go here or there ? Has she found friends or fallen among foes ? Oh ! Ned—Ned, it is very hard to bear."

"If I may be so bold, sir," whispered Chippy Chunks, "I'll ask you not to give way, sir, just now. I think I hear somebody coming up the path."

Tom was himself again in a moment.

If careless of his own person he was ever thoughtful of others.

"Back to the bottom of the cave," he said "and stand quite still."

They retreated to the end, about fifty feet down.

Their swords they had instinctively drawn, and by Tom's advice they kept them behind, so that their glitter might not attract the eye.

Chippy Chunks knelt down by Ned's side.

Yes, some of the enemy were coming up the path.

They could hear their voices and the rattle of arms. Presently one appeared, and, halting at the mouth of the cave, he peered into its dark depths.

He was one of the wildest-looking men they had seen in the country—dark-skinned, eagle-eyed, and clothed in ragged garments, but well armed with a long Moorish rifle, a sword, and a broad knife stuck in a leathern belt.

After a moment's hesitation he passed on, but was quickly followed by another as fierce as he, who, in mere wantonness, as it seemed, fired into the cave.

The bullet struck the rock a few inches from Ned's head, and it must be confessed that he did just wink his eyes, but he did not budge an inch.

The smoke from the rifle filled the cave, but it soon cleared to the proportions of a thin mist, and through it they saw the man who had fired talking to another.

After a short, quiet debate, they went away.

Then came a pause, and for a minute it seemed as if all the scouts of Abdallah's hosts, as Tom judged them to be, had gone forward; but it was not so. One yet remained.

He was a grizzled old man, with a cunning, hawk-like face, who, as the others had done, stopped before the cave and peered in.

Some words—a query, doubtless, in a strange tongue—came in guttural sounds from his lips.

Of course no answer was given him, and it was hoped that he would follow the rest.

But the curiosity of old age was in the breast of the hillman. He must needs make sure that nobody was hiding there, and with a cautious step he entered.

His rifle was slung upon his back, but he carried his sword in his right hand, ready to strike. It was broad and keen, and shone like burnished silver.

"It must be done," thought Tom, as he slowly got his sword ready to strike.

Slight as the movement was, the old man heard it, and shrill and clear the cry burst from his lips—

"Ti Sebih Allah!"

He knew an enemy was there, but what sort of enemy he had in his mind will never be known, for as he fearlessly rushed forward Tom thrust out his sword and pierced him to the heart.

He fell heavily on one side ere Tom could withdraw the weapon, bending it like a bow.

Had it not been made of the finest steel it would have been hopelessly bent or broken off at the hilt.

As soon as he was down Tom slowly drew out the sword that had done such good service and replaced it in its scabbard.

"It couldn't be helped, Ned," he said ; "it was either his life or ours."

They undid his leather belt, and Tom handed it to Chippy Chunks.

THE TWO TARTARS:

Or, Tom and Ned among the Moors.

CHIPPY CHUNKS SPARRED UP TO ABDALLAH IN A STYLE THAT MEANT BUSINESS.

No. 28.   Price One Penny.

"Take it," he said; you may find it useful."

"I'll take it, in course," replied Chippy; "but in my opinion, for an all-round tool, there's nothing like a hammer. You give a man a fair knock with either end and he don't want any more."

"Unless he happens to be a Mahdi," suggested Ned.

"Well," replied Chippy Chunks, slightly disconcerted, "I'll own that I didn't make due 'llowance for the thickness of his head. The proper use of a hammer is to hit just as hard as is necessary with it, and NO MORE. You give a tap for a tack, and a whack for a three-inch nail. I'll bet I'm not far off the right strength the next time I gives one to Mister Mardi."

Tom had gone half way up the cave, and was looking out upon the plain. The main host of the Mahdi's followers had disappeared, and only a few stragglers—the camp followers of the East—could be seen. So he went boldly to the mouth of the cave, and scanned the country round.

In the direction of the Moorish castle there was nobody in sight, and in the opposite direction a long line of men was growing faint in the distance.

"Let us leave here now," said Tom.

"Which way are we to go?" asked Ned, when they were all outside.

"Let us follow the Mahdi's army," said Tom, wearily. "It is at least on the road home."

So back by the path which Chippy Chunks had traversed with Si Hamick they went.

As he passed the spot where he had pushed that wily Algerian down into the depths below the precipice Chippy shut his eyes, for he too was sensitive on the point of taking advantage of any man in an unfair way.

"I hope he ain't dead!" he murmured. "I wouldn't mind seeing him hopping about on crutches, but I shouldn't care to see his body. Ugh! but he was a great rascal, and that's my only comfort."

An exclamation from Ned caused him to open his eyes, and there, peering above a rock some distance away, he saw the head of the very man he had been thinking of.

Could it be him in the flesh or was it his ghost?

A creepy sensation came over Chippy Chunks, and he felt as if all the life within him was gliding down to his toes.

But Tom was not troubled with any demoralising sensation.

He had seen the head of Si Hamick, and with a rapid movement covered it with his revolver.

"Attempt to stir," he cried, "and you are a dead man!"

"Oh! son of the Moon, and ruler of the Belt of Orion," replied Si Hamick, "it is my joy to remain here now and for ever, until your lordly voice bids me move."

"Are you alone?" demanded Tom.

"Even as the scapegoat in the wilderness," replied Si Hamick. "Friendless in the land of an enemy, with no brotherly love to ease my aching heart and pour oil on my weary bones."

"Come over here and let me look at you," said Tom. "Ah! yes—it is our slippery friend, Si Hamick."

"Come back to life!" gasped Chippy Chunks, "after being chucked over a precipice as high as Saint Paul's."

"Hush!" whispered Ned. "He doesn't know you. See how he is staring. Keep quiet, and we will mystify him a bit."

CHAPTER XXIV.

SI HAMICK TELLS TWO STORIES, ONE FALSE AND THE OTHER TRUE—SEEKING A FRENCH OUTPOST—THE SLAIN SENTINEL

I HAMICK advanced slowly and painfully, like a man who had travelled far and without too much nourishment on the way. His body was as thin as a rake, his cheeks hollow, and his clothes soiled by nights of sleeping in the open air.

"You remember me?" said Tom.

"Ay! my lord," replied Si Hamick, "and with anguish, for I was then the servant of that son of the hog with the evil eye—Emir Abdul-ab-Bourad. I did as he commanded me, oh! my lord, with my heart weeping tears of blood."

"And how came you here?" Tom asked.

"Ah! my lord, that is a long story," replied Si Hamick, "a story of woe and suffering—for your sake—oh'! son of a golden land, which is on the borders of Paradise."

He addressed Tom, but he looked with amazement, not unmixed with terror, at Chippy Chunks, who was distorting his face and twisting his legs, so as to put up a few more barriers to hide his identity.

It was a waste of energy, for Si Hamick had not the least suspicion that it was Chippy Chunks.

A wink from Ned apprised Tom of this fact, and then all was ready for the drama of mystery that followed.

"Dog!" thundered Ned; "liar—knave! Is it thus you stand in the presence of the Mahdi of the Mountains? Kneel, you newt—you louse of a man!"

Si Hamick fell upon his knees and raised his clasped hands in piteous appeal.

"How should I know, oh! potent ruler?" he cried. "For is not my mind dazed? Have I not wandered here and there, with noises in my head and bruises on every limb, satisfying the cravings of a mighty hunger on berries? Have I not crawled out at night, hearing the lion roar, looking each minute for his coming to pick my bones? Oh! weary feet of mine, that have trodden these mountains and brought me at last to sacred ground?"

"Have you never been here before?" asked Tom

"Never," replied Si Hamick.

"Look around you and make sure," said Ned.

"Never. May my body perish and become dust, mingling with the sands of the desert, if ever these eyes of mine have looked on this spot before."

"You lie!" said Tom, taking him by the throat. "You rat! Where is my wife whom you brought here to sell into slavery? Where is the woman whom you intended to steal and make your wife?

Speak out, or I will choke you, inch by inch, and slowly. Speak, you stoat!"

He cast him heavily to the ground, for Tom's blood was up thinking of his wife, and he was not sorry to be able to vent his wrath on one of the agents of his own and her misery.

Si Hamick lay upon his side, with his knees drawn up to his stomach, in the very depth of abjectness and terror.

"My lord—my lord, at whose voice the ocean is still," he gasped, "spare me. I know not what has become of your queen. She was stolen from me by a withered old man, whose turban was of paper, and whose throat was choked with lies."

"Ah! so he stole my wife from you?" said Tom, grimly.

"Even so, my lord," continued Si Hamick, "while I slept close by keeping guard over the angel from the land of the Peri. He could not have loved her, oh! my lord, for his body was as a withered apple. But he had the lust of the wolf in his heart, and what he did unto her was revealed to me in a dream."

"And what was your dream?" asked Tom.

"I sat beside a stream," said Si Hamick, "on the borders of which the palm and date-tree grew, and lo! on the other side of the water I saw your wife, whose beauty was as honey to the mouth, lying asleep also. Then from across the desert came a hideous beast advancing, with fires leaping from his mouth, and eyeballs like those of the crab-fish after it hath been boiled. On its head was a paper turban, and its many legs were like unto those of the ghoul whom I knew in life as Chippy Chunks."

"Well, what happened?" asked Tom.

"Oh! my lord, and shall my tongue speak it?" moaned Si Hamick, writhing about in anguish.

"You had better," said Ned, "and be sharp about it."

"Be it so, then," replied Si Hamick, rubbing his eyes with his hands. "MY LORD—HE ATE HER!"

This indirect accusation of cannibalism was almost too much for the implicated Chippy, who thrust his hand into his bosom in search of his favourite weapon, but fortunately he did not draw it forth. Tom looked down at Si Hamick for a few moments with a strange smile upon his face.

Then he lightly spurned him with his foot.

"Get up," he said, "you living incarnation of Eastern veracity. Have you any weapons about you?"

"My lord, a poor thing of a pistol, and a rusty strip of iron that serves as a knife."

"Give them to me."

With great reluctance Si Hamick produced a loaded revolver and a broad dagger, keen as a razor.

"And now," said Tom, as he disposed them about his clothes, "tell me how it was you did not break your neck when you were pitched over the precipice. And, mind you, the TRUTH this time, or I will flay you!"

"My lord, shall I lie when you ask for truth?" said Si Hamick. "When cast over the precipice I fell down and down and gave up my spirit. All was darkness until I awoke and found myself hanging from a tree like overripe fruit. Upon my haunches sat a vulture, who used his beak with severity, and made incisions in my flesh which I shall bear marks of while I live. Oh! my lord, since then I have not sat at ease."

"Well?"

"The tree grew near the plain below," answered Si Hamick. "It was not far to fall, and in the act of kicking at the vulture, whose beak I trust will one day be thrust into his own vitals, I released myself and fell. Soft sand received me, and I lived, sore as to buttocks, but with my bones entire."

He was speaking the truth now—anyone could see that—for, as Ned said, "he looked so sneaky—not being used to it."

"Sore and weak," he went on, "I have crawled about, even like a worm, fearing to meet man, for here they kill the ailing, as it has not pleased the prophet to send any doctors into the mountains."

Tom had scarcely listened to his last words—he was occupied with thinking. When Si Hamick ceased he looked at him with ill-concealed scorn, and said—

"You are a liar and a scoundrel, and the correct thing to do with you would be to shoot you over the precipice again, and leave you to the chance of another lucky escape, but I will spare your life on one condition."

"My lord is more than gracious," returned Si Hamick; "he is like a bounteous spring with his mercy."

"I want to get to one of the French outposts," said Tom. "Which is the nearest?"

"My lord, there is one about five miles, to the east—it lies on the spur of Mount Fubla."

"Well, you will please lead us straight to that post, as I presume it to be. No tricks. You see this?"

Tom held the muzzle of a revolver close to Si Hamick's nose, and, fascinated by terror, he gazed squint-eyed down into its depths.

"I am a good shot," continued Tom, "and I can make sure of bringing you down. Show us the least treachery and I will leave you to die."

"I am joyful in being able to serve my lord," said Si Hamick, screwing up a sickly smile, "for he is as sunlight on the mountain and his voice is as the lute."

"Having rolled off that bit of florid bosh," said Ned, "perhaps you will start."

The French outpost, one of several which Tom had read of, seemed to be the only place of refuge open to them.

There they might get help, and possibly learn something about Lottie's fate.

So Si Hamick, with much wriggling and many protestations of truth and fidelity, led them along.

At length he came to a narrow track that led again into the higher land, and here he paused.

"This is the way, my lord," he said, "but it is not good to travel unless you have the word to pass, for it is written by the accurs— by the great man of Algiers that whoever being a native sets foot here without leave shall die."

"In other words," said Tom, "you would rather we went on without you?"

"My lord has been so kind that he would not of a verity see his faithful servant slain," hinted Si Hamick.

"I am not so sure about being concerned in that matter," said Tom.

Here Chippy Chunks took the matter in hand, and having dug Si Hamick in the ribs, motioned for him to go on.

Si Hamick groaned and rubbed his eyes, but

Chippy Chunks, taking him by the arm, led him forward. So they proceeded together.

The path was so narrow that there was little more room than was needed by one, and two together were sure to blunder, so Chippy gave Si Hamick a kick and pushed him to the front.

In and out, among huge lumps of rock, they wound for awhile, and then began to ascend, still in Indian file, until Si Hamick, with a stifled shriek, stopped short.

"There—see!" he said.

And, looking, they saw a French soldier lying on his back, with a dreadful gash in his throat, from which the blood had not yet ceased to flow.

Whoever had done this ghastly deed had robbed him of his arms and disappeared.

This was an ominous discovery, and they all lingered for a few moments, considering what had better be done in their minds, but none speaking.

"Where is the outpost?" suddenly demanded Tom; "how far from here? Know you not the exact direction?"

"If my lord will walk on a few paces more his eyes will be gladdened by the sight of it, looking like a big bird's nest on the mountain spur."

"Let us go forward," said Tom. "I don't like the look of this affair, but what can we do?"

As he moved on the silence ahead was suddenly broken by a shout, followed by the report of a rifle. Then arose a clamour of arms and fierce cries of men in combat, mingled with the booming of mountain guns.

"The outpost has been attacked," said Tom. "Come on, Ned! We may be of service here."

Si Hamick endeavoured to slip behind, but a push from Tom and a kick from Ned sent him to the front again.

"Oh! my lord," he whined, piteously, "I am but as a sheep going to the slaughter. I have no arms wherewith to defend myself from the ravening wolves."

"Look after him, Chippy," said Tom, as he seized Si Hamick by the collar and swung him backward. "Ned, follow me. Warm work is going on up there."

So it seemed, for the firing of small arms and the clash of swords was continuous, and above all raged a storm of voices of men possessed with the passion of war.

CHAPTER XXV.

A SKIRMISH—GOING TO THE RESCUE—THE FIGHT OUTSIDE THE FORT—A DEEP AND SOMBRE GRAVEYARD.

NDER the stimulating influence of Tom's threatening air, Si Hamick kept up with the party for the next half dozen yards or so. Then he suddenly tripped over a stone and fell apparently with great force to the ground.

As he lay quite still, with his eyes shut and his mouth open, he presented a very unwholesome appearance. A dead fox would have been quite as pleasant to the eye.

"He has stunned himself," said Ned.

"Let him be until we return," replied Tom; "we are losing our chance of giving help yonder."

The noise of the firing had very much increased in volume. There was inspiration in these sounds, which had on Tom an effect similar to that which a blast of a trumpet has upon an old war-horse.

Ned, too, felt he wanted to be "in it," as his recent experiences among the Moors had rather embittered him against the swarthy race.

As they bounded round a bend in the path they came upon some Moors, with swords in their hands, retreating from above.

Ned and Tom had their weapons drawn ready for action, and they each went for one of the foe with all the energy and fire of youth.

Chippy Chunks, with an abounding faith in his favourite article of use and weapon, whipped out his hammer and stood on the defensive against the third.

Whether it was his remarkable appearance, or surprise at the temerity of a man daring to oppose him with no better means of protection, the Moor remained for a few moments staring at him with his dark, fiery eyes.

Meanwhile Ned's man, after making two or three wild passes at him with his sword, wheeled round with lightning celerity and darted down the path.

Tom at the same moment laid his man low with a dexterous thrust of the sword, after having received a prick of no moment in his right shoulder.

It was all quickly over as far as the two brothers were concerned, and it would have been almost as soon over with Chippy Chunks had not Ned come to his assistance.

The best of hammers would not have shielded him from the broad, keen sword raised at last to strike him down, and it was fortunate for him that Ned, wheeling about, saw his peril.

He had no time to rush forward and use his sword, but he had his revolver, and an instant sufficed for him to draw it and fire.

At the distance it was hardly possible he could fail to kill the man, and the Moor, with the pellet of lead between his shoulders, threw up his arms and tumbled down in a heap.

Fast and furious raged the fight above, and Tom, casting his eye upwards, saw the outpost where the attack and defence raged furiously.

A small fort, erected on a flat, jutting rock, and commanding a view of a wide tract of country around, was the scene of action.

About a dozen Frenchmen were gallantly defending themselves against double the number of Moors and Nubians, who were endeavouring to force their way over the breastworks.

Now when a Britisher is called upon to go to the aid of his own people he never thinks twice about himself, and he does not stand thinking long when it is a neighbour who is in trouble.

Tom had no great reason for being in love with Frenchmen in general, but anyway he liked them better than the Moors, and on he went, with the idea of falling upon the attacking party in the rear.

"When you get near them, Ned," he said, "shout as if you had a hundred men behind you, then do your level best to cut your way through. Chippy, you MUST use a sword."

"All right," replied Chunks. "I'll make a 'speriment with it. Go ahead, sir."

There was rather a steep ascent of about fifty yards to make ere the scene of the struggle could be reached, but to the younger men it was nothing.

They bounded up like mountain sheep, and fell upon the startled Moors like wolves.

"Hurrah for the old country!" shrieked Ned. "At 'em, boys!"

The "boys" were, of course, the imaginary hundred men behind him.

Tom at the same moment uttered a shout that rang out high above the din of war, and plunged into the swarthy body, cutting right and left with his sword so furiously that it appalled them.

Inside the fort this advent of help was speedily seen, and whoever was in command acted with considerable promptitude.

The word was given, and the defenders, boldly leaping over the breastwork, became in turn the assailants.

Some desperate hand-to-hand fighting took place, but the original attacking party, startled and daunted, soon lost heart.

Leaving half their number dead or writhing on the ground, the rest fled, the majority by the path, the remainder blindly blundering over the precipitous side of the mountain, to find death in the sombre bottom below.

Possibly three or four minutes sufficed to bring matters to this sudden termination, but how long or how short it was Ned at least never knew.

He remembered afterwards being mixed up with waving arms, glittering swords, and demoniacal faces for a time, while doing his "level best," as Tom suggested, to scatter the enemy.

That he must have done something in this direction was certain, for when the brief but terrible fight was over he found himself leaning against the breastwork panting, with a bloody sword in his hand and several dark bodies lying at his feet.

Two men were quite still, while three others with staring eyes and foam-flecked lips were futilely endeavouring to stop the flow of blood from gaping wounds.

He took in, as it seemed to him, every detail of the scene at a glance.

The state of tension to which his mind had been raised was almost unendurable, and yet, as he stood there regaining his breath, he observed something which made him laugh.

It was nothing more nor less than seeing a young French officer pounce upon Tom and kiss him on both cheeks.

Tom appeared to be startled, but he had the good sense to recognise that it was a Frenchman's way of expressing gratitude.

"Ah! mon ami," said the officer, "it is for your help thanks. We salute you, brothers."

The French soldiers were already busy attending to such wounds as they had, and seeing to the proper disposal of three of their number who had fallen in the fight, never to rise again.

"Say—how come you, so—so opportune?" asked the officer.

"We were coming to you for assistance," said Tom, as he drew off a sash from a dead Moor and proceeded to wipe his sword with it.

"Ah! so Anglais like," replied the officer, smiling, "to come for help and give it. But your story vill do anoder time. It is enough, you are

here, we are saved, all France will be grateful. I introduce myself to you, Lieutenant Carmean—Louis to his friends and you."

"I am simply Tom Tartar, and this is my brother Ned."

"So—two Tartars—very much so," Carmean said, smiling. "A little while ago I sleep—I rest—not dream of danger; but lo! the canaille come quick—sudden, and shriek in our ears. We were almost surprised. It was a narrow escape."

He turned to Ned and held out both his hands, which Ned grasped.

But the smiling young Frenchman did not attempt to kiss him. With ready tact he had alread remembered that Englishmen do not cultivate that form of salute.

"You are young," said Carmean, "and you are brave. You fight well enough for—" he was going to say "a Frenchman," but he changed it to—"a general."

"We did our best, of course," replied Ned; "but what we did I cannot clearly remember. It is all mixed up in my head."

"It is as well," said Carmean, more gravely, "dat ve do not alvays remember vat ve do in battle."

"I say!" exclaimed Ned, "where's Chippy Chunks?"

"Here sir," replied a doleful voice from where the slain had fallen thickest.

And there he was, with five or six dead Moors piled upon him, leaving just his head visible.

"This is a friend of ours," said Tom; "you must not be surprised at his remarkable appearance. We will explain it to you by-and-bye."

"He is your friend," said Carmean, "and of his looks vhat are dey to me?—noting."

Chippy Chunks was drawn out and got upon his feet. He had the appearance of a man who had gone through a mangle.

"Blessed if it wasn't a scrimmage!" he said. "I was a little behind you, gentlemen, and, being a bit pumped out, I was bowled over by one of these niggers running agin me. The tothers were put on top of me by somebody, and there I was."

"Come into the fort," said Carmean, "it is better there. I have a place where we shall not see dese tings."

He swept his hand round, indicating the signs of the recent struggle.

The sight was not a pretty one, and they all scaled the sloping breastwork of the fort, glad to get away from the scene.

Inside there were arrangements for the comfort of the occupants which rather surprised Tom.

There were two long wooden huts for the private soldiers, quite a commodious one for the officer in charge, as well as a store house and a magazine.

Carmean took Ned and Tom into the living roo in his quarters, and first gave them what they both needed—a little eau-de-vie.

"It is not good in dis climate," he said, "to drink mooch of him, but as a medicine—yes—a little is all right."

He showed them where they could wash, and presently they were all seated at the table talking about the cause of their meeting.

Suddenly a pistol shot was heard and Tom sprang to his feet.

"Do not arise," said Carmean, laying a hand upon his arm; "it is noting. It is ze wounded Moors."

"Are they being shot?" exclaimed Tom, startled.

"Mon ami! what shall be done?" asked Carmean, sadly. "Can we doctare zem? No. Zey rise as soon as vell and stab us. Zey have no notion of ze honare of men—no gratitude—no noting. We kill, or shall we let zem lingare on in prison, to die slowly—inches by inches, as you say? No, it is kinder to kill."

"I suppose so," said Tom; "but it seems a horrible alternative. And where will you bury them?"

"Outside ze fort," said Carmean. "It is steep and deep—so deep zat you cannot see ze bottom. No living man go down, for dere is no path. If you go down—no return, for you fall smash! It is a good graveyard, and vild birds see zat zere is noting to nose. It is all vell."

"And your own dead?" asked Ned.

"All go," replied Carmean, bitterly. "Who shall help us? Solid rock here and dere, and den de sun. It commands us to hurry quick, so de grave is all for one."

"What an awful place to finish life in!" said Ned, in a hushed voice.

"It is," answered Carmean, "and sometimes how I grieve—I grieve for my home in de south of sunny France. But it vill not do; duty—duty! Still it vould, as you say, be awful to have to lie dere. May ve be spared dat fate."

"Amen," said Tom.

And as he spoke the voices of the French soldiers were heard singing a lively song. He looked at Carmean for an explanation.

"All buried," said the Frenchman, "and zey sing lively! Vy not? Vhen you bury your soldier at home do not ze band come back from ze grave playing ze tune 'Go to ze devil and shake yourself?' Ah! yes, it is so. Come."

"Quite true," said Tom, "and, after all, it may be it is right to try and forget."

"If we can," returned Ned.

"Anyway," replied Tom, "it is a pity to let grief hinder us in the work of our lives."

"And your work?" asked Carmean.

"To find my dear wife," said Tom. "If living, to bear her away from this accursed land—if dead, to avenge her!"

CHAPTER XXVI.

NO LEAVING HERE—THE BATTLE ON THE PLAIN —BLOCKING THE PASS—GATHERING OF THE FOE.

ERE is no leaving here vithout relief." This was what Carmean said when he heard the whole of Tom's story.

Evening had come, and they were sitting without his quarters smoking a cigar prior to turning in for the night.

Before them lay a magnificent panorama. To the right and left rocky mountains, ahead a vast plain, with here and there a village or a cluster of palm-trees dotted about it.

Far away on the horizon a dark, misty line, which Carmean told them was Algiers.

"Of course," he said, "there is no leaving for me; but you can, if you vill. But it is to go to die."

"You know why I wish to leave?" said Tom, uneasily.

"Ah! yes; but den vhat can you do?" said Carmean. "Vich vay you go? You not know. All ze plain swarming with zese mad fools, who get up a Mahdi every year or so that lead dem to death. It is anoder rebellion—it is noting. Ve are use to dem, and know vhat to do. It vill all be ovare in a day or two; in a veek at most. A few fights—a slaughter—a dead Mahdi—and it is all done. Ze fools vill go back to zere hills and villages to vork in peace until anoder fanatic arrives."

"I am sure Lieutenant Carmean is right, Tom," returned Ned. "We are helpless."

"As soon as dis last Mahdi get vat you English call de knock," said Carmean, "den de relief come. My time is up here—I get leave, I go vith you. I find men to help—but it no good now."

"I will try to be patient," replied Tom. "Perhaps you are right. I am sure you mean to give me the best of advice."

At the other end of the mountain fort the French soldiers, some of them on duty as sentinels, were enjoying themselves in their usual lively fashion.

Towards this end they were assisted by Chippy Chunks, who had discarded the sheepskin and put himself into a mixed uniform.

He was wearing the coat and trousers of a Zouave, a Moor's turban was on his head, and a gorgeous sash round his waist, in which he had stuck a number of pistols, knives, and his favourite hammer.

Altogether he was a very formidable-looking personage.

Refreshed and invigorated by food, and cheered by a pipe of tobacco, his spirits had risen until he was almost festive.

In consideration for the feelings of the Frenchmen, and with the idea of making himself understood, he talked broken English to them, which of course was a great advantage to men who understood little or nothing of the language in its purer form.

We will give one specimen, leaving the reader to imagine the rest.

"Ah! Mossoo, I varee please to know oo. Me nevare took to Frenchmen as rule—too much shruggy shoulders; but now me do—comprenny? So den ve all are brave camaradoes. It was friendly to lend me dem ere clothes. I feel more like one goot man in them. Ze Mahdi business good to dem as like it. Ah! you see—understandy? No more on it if I know it. You laugh—oh! you so funny."

They laughed more at the expression on his face than his words, which were all three quarter Dutch to them.

But whenever he paused they chorused "Oui—oui!" and started him on again.

But what had become of Si Hamick?

Tom remembered him when the fight was done,

and took the trouble to go down and see if he were still alive.

Alive or dead, he was gone, and the French soldiers who had made a clearance of the two Moors slain by Tom and Ned, could not remember whether they had picked up a third man or not.

"It was all so confusing," they said, "and one is glad to forget. We do not try to remember what we have seen."

This was a feeling Tom could well understand. It was as well for their peace of mind that the memory of the dead should lie as lightly as possible upon them.

The sun went down and darkness came. In the fort all was still, for Carmean had forbidden lights and commanded silence to be kept.

For who so cunning as the sons of the desert?

They will steal into the tent of a foe and silently stab the inmates—one after the other—to death, creeping away—unseen and unheard—leaving no record of their visit beyond the still, sightless victims they leave behind them.

The night was hot, and not a breath of wind fanned the cheeks of the motionless sentries who guarded the approach to the fort.

In the deep gully where the dead lay the darkness was like ebony, gruesome and impenetrable, but on the plain the light of the stars shimmered on the sand, and afar off there was a reddish line, indicating the position of the Moorish capital.

As the hours stole on the roar of the lions on the plain faintly boomed up the mountain side, and the chirrup of some nocturnal insect feebly pierced the ear. But that was all until the morning was creeping along the east, and then there was a clamour, yet afar off, of men engaged in deadly combat.

In a moment, as it were, the inhabitants of the fort were up and stirring.

Lieutenant Carmean and Tom first, then Ned, and after him the men who had been off duty.

As yet they could see nothing, for the brooding gloom of night hung upon the plain.

But ere long the sun's herald, "the ooska," as the Persians call it, shot up in the sky.

A bright ray of light, that came and went in a few moments, leaving gloom once more behind it.

That brief ray showed contending hosts about a mile and a half from the mountains, and when the sun peeped up above the horizon shortly after, the panorama of a battle lay before the spectators' view.

It was not a matter of vast armies, but the number was sufficient to make the scene impressive.

About two thousand Moors and five hundred Frenchmen were engaged in a conflict that for the greater part was hand to hand.

Louis Carmean brought out a field glass, with which he eagerly scanned the plain.

Tom, watching him, saw deep lines of anxiety gradually form upon his brow.

"Wrong—wrong!" he muttered, in his native tongue. "Why does he not keep his men closer? Ah! fool."

He handed the glass to Tom, who sighted it so that he could see the combatants, and so good was it that he could presently make out Abdallah riding here and there on horseback, with a banner in one hand and a sword in the other.

He was urging his men on with gestures and probably wild cries.

As for the Frenchmen, they were fighting gallantly, but the men were in open order, so that the mad fanatics could pierce their ranks.

It was easy to see that the day was going against the sons of France.

"The savages are winning, I fear," said Ned.

"There will be wholesale slaughter ere long," replied Tom. "There they go! Don't run, men; it's fatal. Oh! Ned, I can look no more."

He turned to speak to Carmean, but he was gone.

With half-a-dozen men he had left the fort, and they were busy doing something with the rocks fifty feet below, where the pass was narrowest.

A minute later and they were all running upward as if for their lives, and, indeed, if they had remained where they were they might have lost them.

For soon, with a sharp, cracking sound, the rocks began to split up and topple over, so that huge masses tumbled into the pathway, blocking it, while here and there little puffs of smoke-like dust rose into the breathless air to settle slowly down again.

What could that mean?

Tom was not kept long surmising on the subject, for Carmean climbed into the fort and advanced towards him, pale but cool.

"You are surprised?" he said.

"I understand," replied Tom, "that for some reason you have blocked up the pathway."

"Whoever commands dere," said Carmean, pointing to the plain, "is beaten. He shall fly, he must, and with a few men get back to Algiers. Around here," he motioned towards the mountains, "spies look to see how it goes. Ah! now dey see, and in a little time how many tousand vill come forth burning for slaughter?"

"And they will come here, you think?" said Tom.

"Yes, here, and to oder parts," replied Carmean, "to kill. Ve are few, and dey shall be great in numbers. But dey am not here yet."

"I know the fellow commanding the Moors yonder," said Tom. "It is Abdallah, the Mahdi I told you of."

"Yes," replied Carmean, "and de sun have risen on his first victory. He vill go on to Algiers and be eaten up."

"Then we have no cause to fear," said Ned.

"He is tough," said Carmean, "and vill take much eating—days, a week, more; and in de time all round here vill swarm with dem who THIRST for our blood. It vill be defend, defend, day and night until relief come."

"And if Abdallah takes Algiers?"

"It is hardly possible. But if it should be so, no hope for you, for me. No. Better for us to jomp over ze precipice and go down to de dead lying dere, for if dese devils get us—ah! vhat vill dey not do?"

While talking they were all watching the battle, which was going hopelessly against the French.

Little groups of men in dozens or scores were defending themselves, back to back, against the onslaught of treble their number.

Many, pursued by the wild fanatics, were running across the plain.

Some were smitten down as they ran, others faced about until numbers prevailed, and the gleaming swords deprived them of life.

A few—a very few—had got out of immediate danger, and were heading for Algiers.

"It is no use talking," said Carmean, in an agony

" I say, others say, keep close when you fight de ark skins. If you do dat you are safe, if not you ie. See dere—de whole plain is red with ze lood of France."

He covered his face with his hands, shivering. But he soon looked up again with a calm, white ace, and tearless eyes.

"To us it is to defend ourselves to de last," he said.

"Have you plenty of ammunition?" asked Tom.

"Oh, yes. Enough if dey can be kept on de oder side. But dey swarm. You kill one, he is but as a locust, and oders come ovare him. It is no matter —for dem death leads to Paradise."

It was not pleasant work watching that scene below.

What had happened was quite clear.

The French authorities had got an inkling of the coming of Abdallah and his hosts, and had sent out five hundred men to meet them.

The Mahdi, camped on the plain, had been attacked just before dawn, and had not been found unprepared.

Bad generalship and a foe too numerous ended in the Frenchmen's defeat.

Perhaps a hundred in all got away, but the rest lay upon the plain.

It was horrible—maddening—to witness the work that was done when the battle was over.

No quarter was given to the wounded.

Wildly rushing to and fro, the Moors of various tribes were seen stabbing and hacking the fallen. More than one wounded man made an effort to rise up and defend himself, but he was soon cut down.

Limbs were struck off—heads severed from bodies. Every form of mutilation that the promptings of a savage nature could suggest was done.

"De ground blood-stained cries out for vengeance!" said Carmean.

He looked at Tom and saw a thoughtful, troubled expression in his eyes.

"I see," he said, quickly, "you have on your mind, in your heart, de men ve kill last night. But no; it is not de same. Dey vill not live. If you spare dem dey get up and kill. Dey run amuck. You canny spare such men."

He turned away and called to one of his men to bring him some eau-de-vie.

"I am sick," he said, "and must have my medicine."

Then there came up to Tom and Ned, both grave and heavy of eye with the weight of horror that was upon them, Chippy Chunks in a scared state.

"Gentlemen," he said, "tell me if I'm awake or dreaming?"

"Awake," replied Tom.

"You are sure, sir?"

"Yes."

"I can't feel that I am myself," said Chippy. "I ain't used to these things. I once saw the battle o' Waterloo played at Astley's, and I thought that bad enough, but it was less than child's play to this."

"You must bear up," said Tom. "We shall want all our nerves to defend ourselves. We are fixed up here and may have a week's fighting before us."

"I feel as if I could do it," replied Chunks. "The life I've led among these murderous thieves has nerved me up. I want to get at a few more of 'em. Is it all over down yonder, sir? I daren't look myself."

"All over," replied Ned.

"And all dead?"

"No; some have got away, to bear the story home—sad messengers of a nation's humiliation."

"You von't hear much of this at home," said Carmean, who now reappeared, with a bottle and glass in his hand. "Ve Frenchmen are not so open as you are. If you are defeated in ever so small a fight you speak out, you magnify it; but ve —oh! no, bottle up—bottle up—say noting is vhat our people do at home. Take a little of dis, and den to breakfast, for ve must eat if to-morrow ve die!"

He gave them all a sip, and Chippy Chunks betook himself to the privates' quarters, where breakfast was already in the course of preparation.

Down where the blasting operations had been performed three men were busy building up a rough platform for riflemen to stand upon and with their weapons command the pass.

None too soon, as they discovered ere long.

The news of the Mahdi's victory had flashed over the mountains and far beyond ere the sun was a third high in the heavens.

From rock to rock and from peak to peak swarthy watchers had signalled the—to them— joyful intelligence of the defeat of the interlopers in their land.

Ten thousand sluggards of war caught the fever of the fight, and from every quarter armed savages were gathering.

Long before noon their voices were heard upon the mountains, drawing nearer and nearer, and once dark heads were seen peering over distant rocks taking note of the defensive preparations in the fort.

"Ve shall be attacked to-day," said Louis Carmean.

"But surely your men can defend this place against a host," observed Tom.

"Ve vill see," said Carmean; "but hear me. If dey swarm ovare who shall help us? Do not vait to fight needlessly, but go ovare dere."

And with a significance that for a moment turned Ned cold he pointed down in the direction where the dead of the previous day's fight were lying.

CHAPTER XXVII.

CHIPPY CHUNKS MAKES A MESS OF IT.

HE position of the little body of men in the mountain outpost may be described as very precarious, but there was nothing in the demeanour of any of them to show they felt any paramount fear.

Ned was the youngest there, and was as buoyant as any of them. He would have sang if Lieutenant Carmean had not suggested that silence as far as possible ought to be kept.

"Our foe," he said, "is secret. He steal up—so —silent as a mist of the marsh, and he makes his rush when you are sure he is far away."

"I should like to know what are our chances here?" Ned asked. "Of course these Mahdi fellows will get a licking?"

"It is not possible to say," replied Carmean shrugging his shoulders. "Victory comes to them at first—often. It is because of their mob. Anon dey are beaten."

"How long, on an average, does it take to do it ?" asked Ned.

"A day—a week—a month—more. Who shall say ?" answered Carmean. "As I tell you yesterday, it is you English who are so candid vhen you are in trouble. It is for us to hide it. Ve say noting."

"In case of the worst," asked Ned, "how long can we hold out ?"

"Four days," said Carmean.

"No more ?"

"Then our store of vater vill be gone. De vater-carriers cannot bring us more. A native may lif vithout for a time, but not a European. The thirst here is dreadful."

Ned said no more, but took a short stroll round the fort, with his hands in his pockets, whistling softly.

He called to mind an episode of his schooldays when playing at hare and hounds—he and a chum holding the former position. After a long run they pulled up in the middle of a level stretch of common land.

Both were very thirsty, for it was a hot summer's day, and they looked about them for a pond or a stream.

They could find neither, and fagged out by the heat and thirst they wandered here and there with the longing for water growing rapidly upon them.

In a very short time it became overpowering—almost unbearable.

The experience lasted an hour—a short and sharp example of the agonies of thirst—ere it was relieved by a draught of milk at a farm-house.

It made a deep impression on Ned's mind, and his present position brought it back to his memory.

"Here, of course, it will be worse," he thought, "for instead of one hour we may have a day or two of it, and then— Whew ! it will be an ugly business."

Chippy Chunks, in all the glory of his new uniform, came out of the soldiers' quarters.

The men in a body were keeping in the shade, so as to ward off the inevitable thirst as much as possible, for the sun was now high up in the Heavens, pouring down its rays upon the rocky fort.

"Master Ned," he said, in a whisper, "I'm inclined to think that my Mahdi's dress was more suitable for this 'ere climate. It kept my legs cool any way ; but now I've a sensation of being boiled all over."

He carried a rifle, which he kept shifting about after the way of men unused to firearms, moving it from shoulder to shoulder, then bringing it to the trail and turning the muzzle about like a weather-cock.

"Chippy," said Ned, "you have not had much to do with firearms in your life."

"No, sir," replied Chippy, meditating ; "but I went sparrer shooting once on Hackney Marshes with a cousin of mine."

"Did you shoot any sparrows ?" asked Ned.

"No," returned Chippy, "nor him either, and it was all his fault. We went down by the Fenchurch-street line on a Sunday morning, and on the way Ezra—that's my cousin—showed the t'other chaps in the carriage how to load the wepping. He didn't know much about it, as far as I could see."

"And after that ?"

"As he was getting out at Hackney-wick-station, sir, that 'ere gun went off and blowed a hanging lamp to pieces. The station-master was standing under it at the time and he went for Ezra. They took his gun away and put down his name and address for to summons him, which he gave 'em false, and he let 'em keep the gun."

"And that is all your shooting experience ?" said Ned.

"Every bit on it, sir, previously to coming into this mortiful country."

"So I should think. Well, mind, Chippy, what you do with THAT gun, or you may blow off the top of the mountain or somebody's head."

"I'll be careful, sir," answered Chippy. "It's a easy thing to handle. There's no loading to speak of, like Ezra's gun. You simply put in a thing like a bit o' iron-piping and keep it there till it's wanted."

Carmean now softly called to Ned, and bade him come out of the sunlight. All but the two sentries down by the barrier that had been made kept under shelter until the noon had passed.

The day dragged slowly on, and nothing disturbed the fort.

Below, on the plain, dark masses of the native tribes were seen hurrying to and fro, and from afar off the sounds of firing were occasionally heard.

Matters looked ominous without a doubt.

The great emeute had taken place, and all sorts of possibilities might arise from it.

"Ve have not enough men here," said Carmean, with sudden passion, as he and his two guests in the evening went to the breastwork of the fort to scan the ground below. "It is because at home dey zey 'Algeria cost too much money and men.' It is true, but why not send enough or leave it ?"

From this it was clear that he was anticipating the worst, but nothing more was said about it.

As the sun went down Carmean posted two of the best men to keep watch over the path, and all the rest were commanded to lie down with their arms beside them.

A small quantity of water was served out to each, night being the best time to drink, and then the stillness of the tomb fell upon the place.

Silence above, around, and below.

Now and then it was feebly broken by a slight clicking of arms as the watchful sentries cautiously shifted at their posts, or a whisper was exchanged within the huts, but that was all.

Sleep came to none save in fitful dozings, and slowly the hours crawled along with leaden feet.

"It gives a fellow time to think," Ned softly said once in the night.

To which Tom replied—

"Yes, old fellow. I wonder how the little ones are at home."

They did not speak of Lottie, for both now believed they would never see her again. Tom's most fervent hope was that she might be dead.

It would be a comfort, although a poor one, to know that she was not in the power of any swarthy chief with a heart blacker than his skin.

It must have been near the dawn when he and Ned dozed off together to briefly dream of being at home among friends.

All sorts of odds and ends of their past experiences obtruded, of course, but that is the way of dreams. Taking things all round they were, however, satisfied at finding themselves at home.

Ned was just saying to his father, "We had a rough time up in that mountain, but we—" when he awoke with a start, and found Carmean standing near with a hand upon his shoulder.

"Get up," he said. "Someting has happened in de night."

Tom was already on his feet, and they went outside together to scan the scene below.

As they took up a position near one of the embrasures, through which a small mountain gun ready loaded protruded, Chippy Chunks, armed as a full-blown warrior, came out of the soldiers' quarters and walked softly towards them.

On the plain below was a huge circle of black dots, with a small space in the centre, where a man on horseback sat alone.

Carmean explained that they were going through some religious service, returning thanks for a victory achieved, he believed.

"Ve all tink ve are right," he said, bitterly, "and so are grateful vhen ve kill oder men."

By-and-bye the circle changed its form, one side of it breaking away like a stream of water pouring out of a gap in a reservoir, and running towards the mountains.

In a little while it was separated from the main body, and came on in a detached form.

"A number of dem told off to take de supports," explained Carmean ; "all de rest go to Algiers."

So it seemed.

The greater mass moved off, and the chant of thousands of voices floated up the mountain side in sonorous cadence, that was like the tapping of a distant drum.

"Is it necessary for us to remain locked up here?" asked Tom, with sudden vehemence. "It is a thing I don't quite take to."

"Vhere shall ve go?" asked Carmean.

"Out to meet them," answered Tom ; "to fight and die"

"No," said Carmean, shaking his head ; "it is giving ALL avay. It is casting off our only hope. Soldiers have to endure as vell as fight. No—ve must vait here silently for dere coming."

Bang !

They all started and turned round, to see Chippy in an agony of terror and remorse.

While fidgeting about with his rifle he had accidentally fired it off.

Nobody was hurt, for the bullet went up to the sky and, as far as they knew, never came down again.

But the firing of the rifle was, nevertheless, a very serious matter.

"Our friend," said Carmean, quietly, "is not used to arms."

All the soldiers had come out to see what was the matter, but they came no further than just outside their quarters.

"Masters !" gasped Chippy, "I'm a born fool, and I shall be glad if you will just knock off my useless head. I haven't got any right to go prancing about with this sort of thing."

"Give it to me," said Ned, and he took it away from him.

"I ought to have stuck to my hammer," moaned Chippy Chunks. "I'm used to it, and it don't blow itself inside out when you least expect it. Oh ! how I wish one of you would kick me."

"It is our fault for allowing you to have the rifle" said Tom. "Go back to your hut. I daresay we shall find you useful in some other way."

Chippy Chunks, wagging and jerking his head under the influence of the spirit of mortification, passed between the soldiers, who made way for him, and disappeared in the hut.

"It is a good thing," said Ned, "that he did not shoot anybody."

"Oh ! yes," replied Carmean ; "but it is an unlucky shot for all of it."

"How is that ?" asked Ned.

"Our friends below," said Carmean, with a significant movement of his hand, "did not mean to come here first. I say so, for I judge from de vay dey take ; but now at once dey make a rush."

"I see—they have found out we are here."

"Not so much of dat. Dey know it, but it vas possible dey leave us to de last without de firing. Is not de smell of blood a magnet to de lion or tiger, and as for de report of rifle or clash of sword, shall it not be a draw to our foes ? Ah ! yes ; here dey vill come first And now hasten to eat vell, so dat ve fight well. One cannot do much on de empty stomach."

A few sharp commands were given to the men, and breakfast, without any preparation of tea or coffee—there was no time for either—was served out.

The sentries were not forgotten, for Carmean with his own hands took down to them their morning meal.

He lingered with them for awhile, climbing to the top of the barricade and scanning the ground below.

Presently he jumped down, and with a motion of his arm beckoned Tom and Ned to come to him.

They joined him with all speed. Pointing over the barrier, he said—

"Dey are coming up, and in five minutes vill be here."

CHAPTER XXVIII.

THE FIGHT AT THE BARRIER—NED'S EXPEDIENT —VICTORY—TOM AND NED LEAVE THE FORT— CHIPPY ON THE TRAIL.

DVANCING were a horde of fanatics, thirsting for the lives of the infidels perched in their mountain fort. It was daylight, and the fires of a wild fury burned in their breasts ; but they came on steadily, led by a gigantic Moor, who carried a huge sword, which he at intervals flourished over his head.

Beside him was a dervish, covered with linen up to his eyes, and bearing aloft a rag of a banner, on which was some mysterious inscription which no man could decipher, not even himself.

It was not meant to be deciphered.

For was it not written by a spirit in the night,

when the dervish spread it on the earth in the darkness, after having by public prayer asked for a message?

In the morning was found an inscription in needle-work, such as no two women could have put upon it under a week.

Here was a miracle indeed, which a sceptical Englishman would have explained by pointing out that there were TWO sides to the banner, one plain and the other emblazoned with the message.

"Therefore," he would argue, "it would be easy to put the message upon it at your leisure beforehand, lay it down upon the earth, turn the whole thing over quietly in the dark, and, hey! presto, there we have a message from spirit-land."

But fanatical men of the desert are above such suspicions.

They take the thing as they find it, believe in it, and follow it with faith, even to death.

Grimly silent, they advanced until they came to the very narrowest part of the path, in sight of the barrier.

Then the huge Moor paused to look back and encourage his followers.

But the words of fire on his lips were never uttered, for a shot—it came from Carmean—toppled him over dead.

The bearer of the mystic banner, with a shriek, leapt over his dead body and rushed forward.

Tom Tartar—he and Ned and Carmean had taken up the position of leading defenders—covered him with his rifle, but he could not at first pull the trigger.

"The miserable brute has no arms," he muttered.

But as the dervish, screaming like a tortured vulture, climbed up the barrier, something had to be done, and, clubbing his rifle, Tom struck him with the butt of it, and sent him headlong backwards to the ground.

Then the others came on, glorying in the opportunity given them to find Paradise through the gates of death.

The defenders' rifles in turn belched forth their fire, and were handed back to be exchanged for others.

Men in the rear loaded and passed them up. Shot after shot added to the number of the blessed believers who had found rest at last.

Down they fell one upon another, mute as foxes at the hour when "mangling hounds" lay hold of them, piling up in quick succession a heap that threatened to top the barricade.

And the living still came on, climbing over the fallen, spattering shots against the impenetrable rocks, firing in the air, brandishing their swords, and doing anything and everything but injure the small but gallant band defending the fort.

Such a fight could only end in one way unless some diversion was made. Numbers would win.

It was now that an idea occurred to Ned, who hastily signed to one of the French soldiers, eager to shoot and kill, to take his place, and then ran back to the fort.

There were some there who thought the boy was showing fear, and were not astonished at it.

Such awful scenes, of course, would be strange to him.

But it was not fear that sent Ned back.

It flashed upon him that beside the mountain guns there were small, but terribly dangerous

shells, to be used as a last extremity, for firing into the thick of a foe.

He could carry one down, light the fuse, and dash it into the thick of the seething horde of swarthy men, packed so close in their efforts to advance that none but the foremost could do more than fire in the air.

As he conceived it so he carried it out.

The men saw him coming back with the conical shell in his hands, and they made way for him.

Tom and Carmean were too busy to observe what he was doing.

Placing the shell upon the summit of the barrier, he drew out a box of fusees, borrowed of Carmean the night before for another purpose, and lighted the fuse.

As it began to sputter he seized it again, sprang right up to the top of the barrier, and hurled it into the thick of the enemy.

All saw it done, and a fierce shout of admiration and approval burst from the Frenchmen.

Tom and Carmean ceased to fire, and instinctively lowered their heads a little, as if to escape the results of the explosion.

A few moments later, with a fierce, snappy sound the shell burst, ripping, rending, and tossing into the air the men who were around it.

Fragments of that shell also burst, cutting their way through bone and flesh, to explode yet again as they struck against the rocks.

All between it and the barrier went down dead or fearfully wounded. Those in the rear lost heart at last, and as the sea breaking through a weak bank of sand rushes over flat land on the other side, so terror spread among them.

They turned and fled, fighting among themselves for their lives, killing and maiming brethren and kinsmen, and spreading panic down to the hindermost.

For the present the victory remained with the defenders, and with cries of exultation they sprang upon the barrier, tossing their caps in the air and firing their rifles, as if to celebrate this all-victorious deed.

As for Ned, the strain of excitement was for a few minutes too much for him.

He staggered, and would have fallen but for Tom, who caught him in his arms.

"I'm all right," gasped Ned. "I only slipped."

He made an effort and kept upon his feet, white as the lily with emotion, but with eyes filled with a light that was not fear.

"I'm all right," he said again. "Let me alone a moment, and then we will follow them up."

"My dear, brave young friend," replied Carmean, taking him by the arms and gazing in his face, "you have done well. You will never do better; but we cannot follow them up."

"Why not?" asked Ned. "Surely we need not fear them?"

"No; but we are not swift enough of foot to catch dem, and we should be weak to try it. Dey would skulk round and break us up, scatter us, if dey saw us follow. But now dey will fly on—ah! so far dat some shall not return to-day—to-morrow —or for ever."

He was right. Tom saw it was so, and said—

"Come, old fellow, we will get back into the fort and rest a bit. It has been a short affair, but it was hard work."

Ned allowed himself to be led away, feeling a little rocky about the knees with excitement, and when Chippy Chunks, with the homage he would have shown to Alexander the Great, offered to assist him up the face of the fort, he did not refuse him.

"Oh! Master Ned," Chippy could not help saying, "what would you have said if it had gone off too soon and blowed your head off?"

"Not much—most likely nothing," replied Ned, with a smile.

Tom took him into Carmean's hut, and they sat down there awhile.

Outside the Frenchmen were talking and buzzing about like so many bees.

They were very busy, clearing the pathway of the dead and—ah! well, it must be written—the dying.

No mercy could be shown to the foe, because they would not have appreciated it.

Underneath the heap of slain they found the dervish—dead. His life had been crushed out by the trampling of his followers.

He still grasped the banner, so soaked in blood that the supposed miraculous inscription was blotted out, as if it had been an ordinary lie erased from a book.

The huge Moor had been dead from the moment Carmean fired his well-aimed shot, but apart from that, he had been trampled upon so fiercely that his face was scarcely human.

Down into the strange burial-ground they were cast—one and all—fanatical leaders and deluded followers, away from all human ken upon the mountains, to lie in the narrow depths of the gorge until they rotted away to dust.

By-and-bye the work was done, and quietude once more fell upon the fort.

Again two men were posted on guard, and the rest went back to their quarters, to lie about, smoke, and discuss the fight.

"Bravo—bravo!" was the comment on Ned's work.

Carmean brought out a bottle of wine—he had but a few left—to drink to their success and to the coming of a party of relief.

"But for you," he said to Ned, "ve should all now be—"

He turned his thumb over in the direction of the precipice and raised his glass to his lips.

"To de country dat gave you birth!" he said.

"I don't see there is anything to make a fuss about," Ned replied. "Anybody would have done it if they had thought of it."

"I do not know," said Carmean, significantly. "To tink, to act—ah! it is difficult."

As Carmean said, the Moors did not return that day, nor the next—nor the next.

Life in the fort became very monotonous, and Tom chafed under it.

But for the strong insistence of Carmean he would have gone away with Ned and taken his chance of meeting the enemy.

Apparently all the Moors had vanished.

During the time specified none appeared on the plains below, nor was there anything save occasional clouds of dust in the far distance to mark the movements of human beings.

Carmean said these were the result of large bodies of men moving to and fro, and as no relief came he concluded that the Moors had not yet suffered any great defeat.

"As soon as it takes place," he said, "relief will come. It is always so. De outposts are never forgotten."

It might be so, but to remain cooped up there was unendurable.

Even Chippy Chunks moped and went about like an old magpie moulting his feathers.

The water was giving out too. The cistern was almost dry. One day more and they would have nothing to drink.

"Where is the nearest well or spring?" asked Ned, in the evening of the third day.

"Four miles from here," replied Carmean.

"Surely then some of us could go for water," he said.

"I cannot," answered Carmean; "it is my duty to stay here. As for the men, they know the danger, and vill not go. Dey will ask to be shot. It is one ting to die fighting and anoder ting to fall into de hands of de Moor at war time. Torture—torture is vhat to expect."

"How is the water brought?" asked Tom.

"In skins."

"Have you any here?"

"Oh! yes—many."

"Then I will go for water," said Tom, resolutely. "Tell me where to find it?"

"My friend, pause," said Carmean. "It is death so sure dat you may better die here. You see no Moor, but dey are here—anywhere—cowed but not gone. Dey vatch and vatch until de time shall come for us to say 'Ve can bear no more, and must go.'"

"Where is the well?" asked Tom.

Carmean took him out, and, pointing towards the west, showed him a small spot—a mere speck at the base of the mountains.

"It is dere," he said.

"As soon as it is dark," replied Tom, "I will start."

"And I too," returned Ned, standing quietly behind him. "We go together everywhere."

"It will be better so perhaps," said Tom.

Carmean did his best to persuade them against the project, but the brothers were firm, and by-and-bye all in the fort heard of it.

Water was of such immense importance to the party that the men did not demur.

They said it was very brave, and chanted praises of the brothers—fitting extemporary words into an old Normandy tune, such as the peasants of that country sing when returning from labour in the fields.

Chippy Chunks did not know what was up. He alone had been kept from a knowledge of the proposed expedition.

The reason for this was the expedition was only spoken of in French, as Tom had expressed a desire that he should be kept in ignorance of the affair.

"He will be safe here," he said to Carmean.

Thus it happened that when the night had come, Tom and Ned—each with a pair of empty skins, made into the form of Eastern "bottles," slung across the shoulder—stole softly out of the fort and went their way.

Both went armed with sword and pistols, but they did not take rifles as they would be an incumbrance, especially when the bags were filled—if they had the good luck to get s____ ____ from the well.

Now it so happened that Chippy Chunks was very restless that night.

He was fully aware of the perilous nature of their position, but he was not thinking of his own safety—his mind was troubled on account of Tom and Ned.

"It don't matter what comes to me," he muttered. "I'm pretty well worn, and whether I get knocked on the head here or die a year or two hence at home don't matter much; but for two such young fellows, handsome as paint and brave as lions, to die HERE! —well, I can't abear the thoughts of it."

He could not sleep, and when the place had quieted down for the night, he stole out and walked to the edge of the fort, over which he peered into the dark depths below.

Chippy was not very imaginative, but he could not help thinking what a gruesome place it looked—

"Too bad to throw a dead dog into," he muttered.

Turning away, he saw a light in Carmean's hut—shining through a small window.

There was no curtain to it, and he stole up just to peep at his "young masters," the sight of whom had always a refreshing effect upon him.

But of course he saw them not.

Carmean was alone, reading and arranging some papers by the light of an ordinary candle.

Behind him were the three little couches which had been put up for the use of himself and his visitors.

"All empty!" gasped Chippy Chunks. "How's that?"

He could make neither head nor tail of it, and his was not the mind to reason out things.

He wondered, that was all, and while he wondered he found himself knocking at the door.

Carmean got up and came and opened it. When he saw the white face of Chippy Chunks he shrank back.

"You vant something," he said. "What shall it be?"

"Where's Mister Tartar and his brother?" asked Chippy, breathlessly.

"Dey leave for a little while," was the answer.

"Gone! Where?"

"Oh! my dear friend, dat is not vat you must ask. To-morrow you will see dem again—perhaps."

"They can't ha' gone and left me behind sure—ly!" gasped Chippy Chunks, trembling in every limb.

"Not—no," answered Carmean; "not to leave you if dey can get back again."

"Tell me what it all means?" growled Chippy. "I can't see why they should go at all. I'm ready to follow 'em anywhere—to die for 'em."

"My friend," said Carmean, "you must not be agitate. You must be calm."

"I must know where they are gone," retorted Chippy; "in kindness, sir, tell me. You don't know how near they are to my heart. I don't look up to much, but I'm a man with a man's feelin's. For the love of Heaven tell me where they are."

"Come in," said Carmean.

So Chippy went in, and Carmean told him what had become of Ned and Tom. He listened quietly, and apparently settled down into complete indifference.

"Oh! that's all right then, sir," he said. "I'm

much obliged to you. Thanky, sir, and good night."

He went away with a relieved face, exhibiting a restfulness he did not feel, for the old man was shamming.

As soon as he was outside and the door of the hut was closed he walked straight away over the side of the fort, passed the sentries—who had no orders to stop anyone going out—climbed the barrier, and with resolute steps went upon the trail of Tom and Ned.

"They'll want me—sure to want me," he muttered, "and when the right moment comes—I'M THERE."

CHAPTER XXIX.

THE GUARDED WELL—A DISAPPOINTMENT—BACK TO THE FORT—A STEALTHY FOE—A FEW SHOTS IN THE DARK.

LONG the mountain side, in the darkness, travelled the two brothers—side by side.

Conscious of possible peril from lurking foes, they walked as lightly as they could, speaking only at rare intervals, and then in whispers.

They talked not of themselves, but of the lost Lottie.

"Where was she?" was the question asked for the hundredth time, and no mental exercise brought forth a satisfactory answer to the problem.

To wish anyone dead is, in the ordinary way, a sin, but there are times when we feel it would be better for a loved one to be out of this world of care and misery.

To see one who is dear to us in the agonies of death is very terrible, but to feel assured they are suffering keenly when no aid can be sent to save them is more terrible still.

If Tom could only have been certain of the fate of his dear wife he might have rested, in a measure, contented, but there was an impenetrable veil drawn between him and her, and the agony of doubt and apprehension was well nigh insupportable.

It seemed a long journey going down to the level plain, longer than it really was, but they reached it at last, without sign of foe by the way.

After carefully marking the spot where they stood, Tom asked Ned if he could point out the direction of the well.

Ned did so to the best of his ability, but he was not by any means sure of the way.

The plain was not so dark as the mountain path, but the little light that existed was deceiving.

Strange shapes and forms rose up before their eyes, only to vanish as they drew near.

Sometimes it was a wall, at another time a jumble of men, and then a camel with a rider, or perchance it was a lion.

But they were all illusions, and as they melted away one by one the brothers gathered hope.

Their mission promised to be a successful one.

But by-and-bye there rose out of the gloom a dark, uneven mass, which, in an indefinite way, conveyed an impression that here, at least, there was no illusion.

Tom took hold of Ned's arm, and, pressing it, checked his steady marching on.

"What is it you see, Ned?" he softly whispered.

"Something like a low wall," replied Ned, "and around it men lying on the ground."

"It appears the same to me," said Tom; "and hereabouts we ought to find the well."

They walked on, still hoping the vision would sink into nothingness, as the figures of fancy had done before, but there was no change.

Hope faded away, and received its death-blow when a portion of the shadowy mass moved slightly, giving out the rattle of a shifting sword.

"It is the well," sighed Tom, "and the brutes are guarding it."

"I was just thinking of the pleasure a good, hearty drink would give me," said Ned.

"It cannot be obtained here. We must return."

"To go back and die of thirst, Tom?"

"To go forward is certain death. What could we do against so many?"

"There are lots of these things in the fort," said Ned, taking the leathern bottles from his shoulders. "We need not carry them any further."

Tom took off his burden also, and together they softly placed them on the ground.

Darkness had brought no cool wind, and the night was very close and stuffy.

In silence they returned a short way, and then Ned stopped.

"Tom," he said, "let us lie down to rest and think a bit."

"No good will come of either."

"At least rest a little while. I feel as if I wanted it."

Tom complied just to please Ned.

There were many hours of darkness between then and the dawn. Besides, the task of going back with such miserable tidings was not a pleasant one.

They lay down side by side, leaning on their elbows, with their eyes in the direction of the well and its dusky guard.

It was within the bounds of possibility that a forward movement might be made by the body, or scouts sent to look around.

But no dusky forms appeared, and a complete and oppressive silence reigned on the plain.

It was not even broken by the too-familiar lion's roar—no sound of footsteps, no clash of arms, no sign of movement.

"Ready, Ned?" said Tom, after awhile.

"In a moment, Tom," was the reply. "I was thinking that going back would do no good, and if we could strike out a fresh route for ourselves—"

"Ned, think of the anxiety of those awaiting us."

"They have been anxious through all."

"We left Chippy Chunks behind us too."

"Ah! yes, I had forgotten him," said Ned, "but only for the moment—Chippy is faithful, and we must go back for his sake if nothing else. I'm ready, Tom."

They rose up and resumed their backward journey, walking wearily enough, their minds busy with troublous thoughts.

Without a suspicion of further danger they drew near the mountain path, and could just see its dark line, like a huge crack among the rocks, when both stopped short.

"Tom!"

"Ned!"

It was all they could say, and that only in whispers.

Ahead, between them and the mountain, was a dark, moving line, approaching from the south, and disappearing in the shadow of the path.

Silently as a flowing river it pursued its way, requiring no very keen intellect to guess what it was.

The enemy again.

"They are going to attack the fort," said Tom, in tones so low that his voice could not have been heard twenty feet away.

"Can't we give them a warning," suggested Ned.

"How?"

"We could fire into the thick of them."

"And then?"

"Bolt."

"It isn't fair to let our friends perish without doing what we can to assist them," said Tom. "Now both together. Two shots each, and then follow me."

They drew their revolvers, and Tom gave the signal by muttering—

"One—two—THREE."

They fired together, so that the four shots sounded more like two. The sharp, crashing sound went echoing up the mountain side, accompanied by the fierce yells of the surprised Arabs.

Whether any of them were hit or not they could not tell, nor did they stay to enquire. It would have been scarcely politic.

Still they did not run.

The foe were surprised, but no immediate rush was made in the direction of the firing. A few seconds elapsed, and then a dozen rifles sent out their answering fire. The bullets sped ineffectually on, whistling overhead, and finally falling into the sand, to lie buried there until some future era should discover them.

"They won't follow us," said Tom; "they don't like the dark."

But he did not know the cunning of the natives.

A rush in the dark was not to their taste, but they were accustomed to creep stealthily upon a foe, and a dozen or more of the body were stealing towards the direction of the firing-point to inspect the hidden enemy.

Fortunately Tom and Ned walked slowly backwards, keeping their face to the foe, so it happened that presently they saw several dusky forms coming towards them.

"We must run now," whispered Tom; "but I feel I must bowl another over."

"Ditto," muttered Ned.

Their dark jackets prevented their being seen by the enemy, but the white blouses of the latter gave the brothers sufficient mark to aim at. Steadily covering the two nearest men they fired.

One of them, with a scream, jumped in the air; the other fell forward upon his face—dead.

It was time to be on the move. Prudence dictated it, and Tom, seizing Ned's arm, they ran swiftly away.

The soft sand stifled the sound of their footsteps, and little was left to guide the foe upon their trail.

It is probable that no attempt was made to follow them further, for Tom, looking back at intervals, could see no trace of them, and finally they came to a halt.

He and Ned both arrived at the conclusion that they were not being pursued, so they took matters easy for awhile, resting and keeping their eyes about them.

"And now what is to be done?" asked Ned, after a long silence.

"It wants working out," said Tom, sadly enough.

"There is no shelter on the plain."

"Not much. But there are villages scattered here and there. Don't you remember seeing them from the fort?"

"Inhabited by no friends of ours."

"We can do nothing by going back, Ned. We might find a hiding-place in the mountains and starve. We can do no more than that wherever we may be."

"I say, Tom," queried Ned, softly, "suppose we should be taken prisoners again? Might we not fall into the hands of brutes who would *torture us?*"

"I've thought of that, Ned," replied Tom, "and if ever it comes to it we've got to bear it. Anyway, we can fight if we are attacked, and if beaten let us hope they will, in the excitement of the moment, kill us outright."

Boom!

"Hark!" said Ned, "that's one of the mountain guns. There's another. Warm work going on. Oh! Tom, I wish we had not come on this fool's errand for water."

Beyond the sound of the guns they could hear no more of the fighting, but in a little while a reddish glare was seen upon the mountain.

"That's Greek fire to give them light," said Tom; "it isn't all up with Carmean yet."

Again they heard the boom of the mountain gun, and yet again. Light after light flared up—a sure sign the fighting was not yet over.

The brothers, standing silently side by side, prayed for the success of their friends and the confusion of their enemies.

After a while the noises ceased, and no more lights were seen.

The fight was finished, but which side had won?

Ah! there was the rub.

It certainly looked ominous for Carmean and his followers, and, of course, the latter included Chippy Chunks.

"I'm afraid it's all up!" sighed Tom. "Numbers have prevailed. These fellows are like locusts—they do not count their slain."

He turned round and walked slowly away.

Neither spoke now, for their hearts were too full for words.

—————

CHAPTER XXX.

CHIPPY CHUNKS GETS INTO QUEER QUARTERS.

HIPPY CHUNKS, on leaving the fort, hurried down the path with all the speed his aged limbs were capable of.

He was inclined to be angry with his young masters for not having asked him to join in the night's adventure.

They might have known by this time that a man of his stamp could be very useful at a pinch, and it was a mistake to leave him at home.

He had given up carrying a rifle, but he had a revolver.

His idea was that it would be better to shoot with, because it was such a very little thing and easy to handle.

"If I let a bit of a thing like this get over me," he said, "I ought to be whipped."

Of course he had his favourite hammer in one trousers' pocket, and, in case they might be wanted, he had a handful of French nails, borrowed from the fort, in the other.

Without these things about him he would have felt ill at ease, but having them his feeling was that he was triply armed.

He had traversed about two-thirds of the path when he saw a dusky figure crouching on the ground, like some wild beast in the act of springing upon him.

The man was alone, but he was armed, and Chippy saw the bright sword he carried in his hand flash in the starlight.

Instinctively he dodged it as it descended, and felt for the revolver he carried inside the breast of his coat.

It could not be got out in a moment, but after a wrench he freed it, and, grasping it by the muzzle, dealt the Arab a blow on the head with it which caused it to explode.

A sensation of a hot iron grazing his elbow was experienced by Chippy, but no great injury was done to him, as he used the same hand and arm, after dropping his revolver, to draw out his favourite weapon—the hammer.

He had no need to use it, for the butt end of the revolver had dazed the native, and he lay on the ground in a stupefied condition, staring with fixed eyes at the sky overhead.

Chippy did not know what to do with the man.

It was against his principles to kill one in a helpless condition, and he had nothing handy with which he could be bound. Finally he decided to leave him where he was and pass on.

But ere he had gone far he heard the faint shuffling of the feet of half a score others. His recent experience had quickened his wits, or he might have mistaken the sound for the rustling of a garment.

Alarmed, he climbed up the rocks by the side of the path, with the object of hiding.

He obtained good foothold, and scaled the pass a dozen feet or so, where he observed a likely-looking opening between two huge boulders.

So he dropped down, expecting to find solid ground between them, but instead of it he found himself rapidly sliding down an almost perpendicular shaft.

Short and swift was the journey, and eventually he struck level ground with a force that projected him forward and turned him over twice before he lay upon his back in a half-dazed condition.

Around him was complete silence. He could see absolutely nothing, not even when he recovered his wits sufficiently to look about him.

Instinctively he carefully felt himself all over, to see if he had any bones broken. In two or three places he felt they were a bit rocky, but none were materially damaged, and so far he felt thankful.

"But where have I got to?" he asked himself.

It was a question he could not answer, and when

he began to grope about it grew more puzzling still.

Working his way round in circles of increasing size each time, he endeavoured to find a side or wall to the place, but failed to do so.

Apparently he was in some underground cavern of vast size, and the thought was overwhelming.

"Oh! my poor young masters," he groaned, "your Chippy has seen the last of you."

Unable to do anything else, he thought he would lie down and try to sleep. It would be a good thing if forgetfulness would come to him until daylight arrived.

Stretching himself out, with his hands under his head for a pillow, he sought repose.

And what is more he found it.

Chippy Chunks was no longer a young man, and fatigue or excitement easily overcame him. The air of the subterranean place was also somewhat close, and he slept profoundly.

To awake suddenly, with the booming of a gun in his ears.

The report roused him, and starting up he stared about him wildly, seeing nothing, but hearing reverberating echoes of the detonation dying away apparently in the very bowels of the earth.

It took him some time to recall recent events, for his mind was further disordered by the sounds of a fierce fight, the rattle of rifles, and the clash of steel.

The warfare was going on outside, of course, but the echoing cave or caves produced the effect of a battle being waged around and close to him. It was bewildering, awe-inspiring, overwhelming.

He made no attempt to stir—there was nothing to guide his movements—but stood stock-still, listening to the chaotic noises above, below, and on every side of him.

It came to an end at last with a mighty crash, as if the very mountain had been rent in twain.

A more awful sound never fell upon mortal ears, and Chippy Chunks, with a cry of very natural terror, fell forward on his face insensible.

CHAPTER XXXI.

IN A FOG—THE LIFTING AT DAWN—A SURPRISE—AN OLD FOE IN THE GUISE OF A FRIEND.

HERE are occasional fogs in the desert—fleecy, impalpable imitations of the moist productions we are so well acquainted with at home—and one of these rare visitations descended that night upon Tom and Ned as they wandered on in search of a place of safety. We are told that rain always follows a great battle, and the assumption is that it is caused by the firing of the big guns. The repetition of effect following the assumed cause leaves very little doubt in the matter.

Granting the assumption to be correct, the mist of that evening may be accounted for by the fight upon the mountain between the beleagured Frenchmen and their savage foes.

The result of this affair we shall see anon. For the present we must follow the fortunes of Ned and Tom.

When the mist settled down a sense of helplessness came over both. It was not exactly fear, but rather can be classed under the head of apprehension. Both understood the impossibilty of being certain whither they were going.

In the streets of a town a man in a fog can, at least, keep straight on, for he has the walls and the houses to guide him, but in an open space he has nothing but his judgment, and that is sure to mislead him.

The natural inclination of a wanderer in a forest, or on a plain, in the dark, is to bear to the left. Travellers lost in a trackless region have often unconsciously traversed a complete circle, and found themselves, after many hours of weary journeying, very near the spot from where they started.

Tom had a knowledge of this curious fact, and his first thought was to make an effort to battle against the natural tendency to swerve from a straight line.

"Ned," he said, "step as evenly as you can, and keep your shoulders well squared. We must keep straight on, if we can."

"We shall remember this, if ever we get away alive," replied Ned, grimly.

To dwell upon the next few hours would be a waste of space. The time was spent in going as straight as they could, resting at times, and always, as they thought, with their faces to the sea.

The fog kept by them until the dawn, when it lifted with the rapidity of a curtain rising at a theatre, and they found themselves within fifty yards of a band of men, a portion of one of the mountain tribes, bivouacking on the ground.

The natives were awake and in the act of preparing to resume their journey. Their keen eyes, ever watchful for a foe, immediately espied the brothers, and a fierce shout of exultation burst from their throats.

So sudden was the lifting of the fog and immediate the espying of each other that neither party cast a glance beyond.

"Stand steady, Ned," cried Tom. "Give as good an account as you can of yourself—fight to the last!"

"Ready," replied Ned.

It was useless to attempt to retreat.

Their fleet-footed foes, inspired by the signs of fear, would have speedily overtaken and cut them down. A dauntless bearing, on the other hand, always influences them and checks their ardour.

But they came on with a rush, their fierce eyes glittering and their white teeth gleaming between their snarling lips—devils in the form of men.

With revolver in the left hand and sword in the right the brothers stood awaiting the onslaught.

When the foremost of the foe was within ten feet of them they began to fire.

Down went two men, gasping and tearing with their hands at the sand in their frenzy, one with a bullet through his lungs, the other shot in the knee-cap.

As fast as they could fire the gallant pair emptied their revolvers, some of the shots in their haste being ineffectual, and then their swords were their only means of defence.

Dauntlessly they received the foe, slashing right and left with the desperation of those who fight for their lives, and keeping the yelling fiends, armed with sword and spear, at bay for awhile.

THE TWO TARTARS:

Or, Tom and Ned among the Moors.

IT WOULD HAVE BEEN ALL OVER WITH CHIPPY CHUNKS HAD NOT NED COME TO HIS ASSISTANCE.

No. 29.

Price One Penny

But only for a little time, they knew, for what were two against so many?

The prick of a spear—the point just reached him—warned Tom of the coming end.

"At 'em, Ned!" he cried, with a wild outburst of fury that surged up from his heart like the spouting of a geyser. "For the honour of our country die game."

Ned's answer was lost in a sudden accession to the chorus of the fight, in the form of the thud of horses' hoofs upon the sand, and a yelling of many voices in the Arab tongue.

Another band was coming up behind the desperate brothers.

To turn to see who or what it was could only end in their immediate despatch by those in front of them.

"It's got to come," thought Ned, grimly, and with set teeth he bade a hasty adieu to all he loved in the world.

On came the horsemen with a rush, and the foe in front, instead of gathering courage from this apparent accession to their numbers, immediately began to melt away.

Ned, amazed beyond all powers of description, saw them bounding over the sandy plain, uttering cries of lamentation and distress.

Then came thundering by a score of mounted men, on steeds that flew over the ground like the wind.

Moorish costumes fluttered in the air, and Moorish swords shone in the light of the rising sun.

In vain the men on foot sought safety in flight. Man and horse were too much for them.

One by one the screaming wretches were overtaken and cut down.

A few turned and desperately endeavoured to defend themselves, but vain were their efforts. The swift sword or pointed spear laid them low in death.

As for Tom and Ned, they could only stand side by side and look on this startling scene with unqualified amazement.

What did it mean?

How came it to pass that two bodies of men, both in outward appearance friends, should be thus at warfare with each other?

Tom looked around him and saw that although he and Ned had walked to the right and taken every precaution to avoid the fate of travellers lost in the desert, they had not got many miles from the mountain range, but seemed to have been travelling parallel with it in an easterly direction.

This was disheartening to an extent, but his thoughts were taken up by the phenomenon of one body of men he accounted as his enemies attacking the other.

"Can you understand this?" Ned asked him, in a subdued, breathless way.

"No—it is all a mystery to me," replied Tom. "All we can do is to remain here and await the issue."

"Perhaps it is a case of rival robbers and murderers, Tom?"

"I can't say. Wait."

The slaughter of the men on foot was soon complete, and the Arab horsemen, gathering together, came riding back with their chief in front, mounted on a milk-white horse.

As he drew nearer, Tom recognised the face of one whom he had for some time counted with the dead.

It was Cherif Bouzian, head of the Kabyle tribe, which had suffered so heavily from the Fanzuals through the treachery of the Mahdi Abdullah.

As he drew near his friendly intentions were evident, for his sword was sheathed and there was a smile upon his face.

Riding up to Tom and Ned he checked his steed, leaped from the saddle, and extended a hand to each.

"English brothers," he said, "I rejoice that it has been my lot to save you."

They grasped his hand hard, and for a moment neither spoke. Emotion choked them. It was Tom who broke the silence.

"Cherif," he replied, "words fail to express our thanks to you. We rejoice in our good fortune and in finding you are spared."

"I was wounded, but escaped," the Cherif returned, "and with the remnant of my people, some of whom are here, sought safety in a secret place, to which we will gladly bear you, not only for your sakes but for that of others."

"Others?" said Tom.

The Cherif smiled.

"Aye! others," he replied. "But enough for the present. You must mount and ride with me." He motioned to two of his men, who instantly dismounted. "Nay, do not hesitate. You are weary and my followers are fleet of foot—they will run beside you."

Hospitality or gifts from such people must not be lightly refused, so Tom and Ned, both worn out or nearly so with their exertions, climbed into the saddle.

"One on either side," said the Cherif, "that I may talk with you."

"I cannot understand your noble kindness," observed Tom; "your generosity overwhelms me. I have unfortunately considered you in the light of an enemy."

"I am no enemy to the English—nor are my people," replied the Cherif, proudly. "Why should we be? You are not our foes here. You may fight with some of our tribes in other parts, but that is nought to us. You have never attacked the Kabyles. It is otherwise with the French—they only seek to destroy us."

"Who were the men from whom you saved us?" asked Ned. "Of what tribe?"

"Fanzuals," replied the Cherif. "A treacherous race, with whom I have a long account to settle. It shall be paid—every shekel of it. At present I can do no more than go forth with such a following as this, seeking them here and there. We have found many Fanzuals in twos and threes and tens and scores. They are all dead."

There was a dreadful simplicity in his words and manner, which told more than any passionate speech would have done.

He lived to carry death and destruction to the Fanzuals. Whatever might happen to him he would go on with *that*.

There must be no hesitation or turning aside.

You could see the set resolution written on his face as he spoke. But it presently died away, and a genial smile took its place.

"To you and your race," he said, "I am a friend. When first I held you captive it was not to kill you. Your lives were safe."

"I gave the credit of your kindness to the Mahdi's prophecy," said Tom.

"It had something to do with it," replied the Cherif, thoughtfully, "but not all. I hoped, and still hope, to see my country free of the invaders. It may never be, but I at least shall not rest while a Frenchman is here."

"You are fighting against them now?" hinted Ned.

"No," replied Bouzian; "this rising is but a flash in the pan. It is a larger flash than usual, but it will die out as others have done. Thousands will be slain. Abdullah will fall, for he is a prophet of lies, and no true servant of Allah."

He touched his horse with the spur, and it broke into an even, gliding gallop.

The example set was followed by the others, and a long ride ensued without another word being spoken.

The course taken was parallel with the mountains, but in an hour or so the Cherif turned the head of his horse towards them.

Slowly a narrow pass came into view, and this he entered, the rough ground necessitating the pace of the horses being reduced to a walk.

Still nothing was said, and they rode on and on through a gloomy, winding gorge, the well-bred animals finding their way with the sure-footedness of mules.

Anon the gorge grew narrower and narrower, until the force had to travel in single file.

The Cherif went first, and when at length a turning brought them in sight of a tunnel some distance ahead he reined up, and, addressing the brothers, said—

"I have here a great surprise for you. Be strong, for it will tax you in your weary state to bear it. If I thought it right to delay the denouement for awhile I would, but I feel that it ought not to be. Dismount and follow me."

CHAPTER XXXII.

THE GREAT SURPRISE IN STORE FOR TOM—NED OFFENDS A SWEET LADY—THE SONG OF TRIUMPH.

WONDER what he has to show us?" thought Ned.

Tom hardly thought at all, for his mind was in a state of semi-chaos, arising out of a wild hope that sprang into his breast.

It was so wild, indeed, that he could not think of its possibly being realised, and with a slight unsteadiness of gait he followed the Cherif Bouzian into the cavern.

It looked very dark from the outside, but once within the gloom, in a measure, was dispersed. A short distance inside suspended lamps were burning with sufficient brilliancy to guide the footsteps of the brothers.

Cherif Bouzian walked on ahead at a swift pace, as if he were anxious to avoid any questioning on the matter. Not one of the trio spoke until the cavern suddenly terminated in a flight of steps, cut out of the solid rock.

"You will go up here," said the Cherif. "At the top there is a door—open it and you will find a chamber. Beyond that there are other chambers—to the right, left, and in front of you. Unfasten the door of the one in front and you will proceed no further."

"Are we both to go?" asked Ned.

"Both," was the answer. "I have to attend to some personal matters. By and bye I will see you again."

With a courteous wave of his hand he glided away, and the two brothers stood at the foot of the steps, looking at each other with doubt and hope written on their faces.

"Ned," said Tom, "it CAN'T be!"

"Perhaps it is Chippy Chunks he has up there," replied Ned.

"Heaven forbid!" said Tom. "I wish the faithful old fellow well out of all trouble, but the disappointment would be too great."

The word "Lottie" remained unspoken, and yet it was her alone both hoped to see. It was a hope against all reason and calculation, or appeared so to them, but there it was in their breasts, setting their hearts beating with double power.

"Come on, Ned," said Tom; "let us know the best—or worst."

So they went up the steps, which they expected would soon come to an end, but it was a long, winding way they had to traverse, with here and there a lamp hanging, like the others below, from the roof.

Mechanically Tom counted the steps—he did it more to steady his surging thoughts than to find how many there were, and he counted exactly a hundred.

At the top was a broad landing with a massive door.

It was handsomely ornamented with a yellow metal—brass or gold. Which it was neither cared to stay and find out. The door had a handle of the same metal, which Tom turned, and they entered the the chamber the Cherif had spoken of.

A noble room with an arched roof, rich with carved stone, exquisitely gilt and painted. The walls were like a flower garden in the profuseness of decoration—all the work of cunning master hands.

The furniture was of the class they had been made familiar with in the Cherif's other home, where the brothers had stayed as prisoners.

On either side there were two doors, and one ahead.

It was the latter they had to open, and Tom, with every fibre of his body quivering, stepped forward and drew it back.

One glance within sufficed.

He had no eyes for the splendid work of the builder, or for the Eastern comforts in a furnishing direction, for there, resting on a pair of cushions, were two women, and one was Lottie—his wife.

He called to her by name, and she looked up with startled eyes and quivering lips.

"Oh! Tom—is it you?"

She rose, and would have fallen but for the strong arm he put around her. Held tight to his breast she lay speechless with joy.

The other lady was Alea—the "woman with the eye"—with both her optics now fully revealed—in fact, the whole of her really pretty face was visible.

She, too, was considerably astonished, and rose to her feet—but not to faint, or in any way show so much emotion as Lottie.

There was no need for it on her part.

Ned was a little off his head with excitement or he would never have done what he did.

In the exuberance of his joy he put his arm around Alea and kissed her.

She did not mind, but simply smiled, and looked as if she would not object to the salute being repeated.

But Lottie had now recovered so far as to see that another besides Tom was there, and to give him her hand.

"Both of you—BOTH!" she said. "Oh! my heart is too full to speak."

"Let us sit down awhile," said Tom; "it will take a little time for us to get over our meeting. First, dearest—is all well with you?"

"All."

"The Cherif Bouzian—"

"He is a true friend. We found him outside our cave—wounded—and we helped him as well as we could. I did all I could for him, Tom. You don't mind?"

"Not a bit, dearest. So you bound up his wounds?"

"Yes—and he told us our lives were not safe in the cave, for the whole country would soon be up. By his advice I wrote a message to you—in the sand—we had no note-paper, dear—to come down to the plain and bear towards the east. There men would be set to watch for you and bring you here. But, dearest, I hardly hoped to see you again."

"It was chance, after all, that brought us together," said Tom.

"No—the Cherif. After he brought us here, and had gathered some of his people together, he would not rest. He has been out day and night in search of you. 'It is not written,' he has told me more than once, 'that he should die.' By 'he' he meant you, Tom, of course, and perhaps included Ned. There must be something in the belief of these people, for you are here."

"They have faith," said Tom, "which we have too little of at home. The Cherif rescued us when all appeared lost. We were attacked by a savage lot, and it was touch and go. He dashed up just in time to save us. Strange he did not say he was in search of us."

"He meant to give you a pleasant surprise."

"He has done more. He has given me a new life."

Meanwhile Ned felt it incumbent on himself, with due reserve, to make himself agreeable to Alea, and she, on her part, was disposed to be very amiable.

Dropping down upon a cushion she patted another by her side with her hand.

"Sit," she said, showing all her teeth with a true Eastern smile.

"With pleasure," replied Ned.

And down he sat, with his legs tucked under him and his back as upright as a wall.

"Me talk Englisch," said Alea; "me learn. Speak much to me."

"About what?" asked Ned, who had no idea of love-making, and could not quite grasp what sort of conversation would suit her.

"Anyting," she replied; "you have sweet voice."

"I had when a boy," said Ned, "and used to sing, but it cracked two years ago."

"It sweet if crack," sighed Alea, looking at him out of the corner of her eyes.

"Well, never mind my voice," said Ned; "you must tell me how you find yourself. Don't you miss your husband, Old Cheerful—the Emir Abdul ab Bourad?"

"Yes, miss him," replied Alea—"good miss, want always miss; see him no more."

"Is that so?" returned Ned, opening his eyes. "Of course, he wasn't a model husband, but you took him for better or worse."

"He much worse," said Alea, emphatically. "Old rascal, have him hang."

Ned laughed. The hanging of the Emir would be a spectacle he could have regarded with complacency.

"Hang him, by all means, if you can," he returned. "Of course, he doesn't want to live now, separated from you."

Alea made a grimace.

"He buy anoder wife," she said; "hope she scratch him."

"A very good wish," observed Ned. "By the way, what do you think of Chippy Chunks?"

"Good old man," she answered—"kind but old, and so—"

She finished with an indescribable grimace that set Ned off laughing.

Tom here woke up from sweet whispering with Lottie and asked what was the matter.

"No chance for Chippy Chunks," said Ned. "Mrs. Ab Bourad will never give him her hand."

"You must not talk nonsense, Ned," said Lottie, rather severely; "you have no ground for associating Chunks with Alea."

"I thought they might have grown fond of each other," replied Ned, apologetically.

"You bad boy," said Alea, rather sullenly, and with a petulant shrug of her shoulders.

"I'm awfully sorry," returned Ned. "I did not mean to offend you."

But Alea was huffed, and would talk to him no more just then.

So Ned got up and walked about the room, with a sense of being rather in the way than otherwise upon him.

After awhile—an hour or so—a swarthy native appeared at the door, and made a low bow, as a sign that he wished for permission to speak.

Lottie, with a motion of her hand, gave him leave to do so.

"My lord," he said, in Arabic, "is here. He awaits you in the eating chamber."

Alea interpreted, and they all rose. Tom and Ned were much in want of food. The former, with Lottie, went first, and Ned politely offered Alea his arm.

"Go away—no like you, You not like me."

"Oh! don't I," returned Ned. "If you could only read my heart—"

"Pooh—puff!" said Alea; "not got one. You a boy."

It was Ned's turn to be huffed.

He was just the age when a boy prefers being considered a man and the contempt of a pretty woman hits home.

But there was no time for wrangling, and in silence the pair followed Tom and Lottie, who were preceded by the native servant.

They returned to the outer chamber, and from there diverged to a side door, which led them into a small but exceedingly magnificent chamber.

Here there were narrow, unglazed windows, through which glimpses of the bright blue sky could be obtained.

The Cherif Bouzian was there, splendidly attired in a cashmere tunic, held round the waist by a jewelled belt; on his head was a turban of grey silk, studded with diamonds and emeralds, which flashed with every movement he made.

In the centre of the room, spread out upon the floor, was a truly Eastern repast of fruit, rice, biscuits, and sweetmeats.

There was also a flask of wine for the European guests.

"I have not been robbed of all," he said, with hospitable grace; "there is something left for me to entertain my friends with. Sit and eat."

It was a cheery meal—the best, by far, our friends had known in the country.

As soon as it was begun soft music from some concealed source floated about the room. It was of the nature the brothers had heard in the castle, but ten times as melodious to the ears of Ned and Tom.

They were happy now, and our appreciation certainly depends in a great measure upon the state of the mind.

But little was said while the music was going on, and when it ceased an Arab girl, also concealed from view, began to sing.

How weird the strain!

It was more of a chant than a song, rising and swelling like an Æolian harp.

When it ceased the Cherif said it was the Song of Hope of his people. "In your language it would be very beautiful. In our tongue it is more beautiful still. Let me try my hand at a translation for you."

And then, in a rich, clear voice, he sang—

"The dawn is at hand! The strong men have come to our aid! Our people shall be free!

"Even as the light grows brighter with the day so shall the hearts of our people rise. They will go forth to the fight, and our enemies shall be strewn about as the sands of the desert.

"Those of whom the Prophet spake are here—the great white man and his bride, and the other, who is as the young lion of the desert. When they raise their hands who shall stand before them?

"Strike the harp, clash the cymbals, let our voices be heard. Our foes shall fly before us as dust before the wind."

The Cherif stopped and looked at his guests with a somewhat sad smile upon his face.

"We live—we hope," he said. "If you fail us, then the last of the Kabyles will soon leave his bones whitening on the mountain side."

"You saved our lives," said Tom, "and it is right we should do something in return. But do not forget that we have home, friends, and children across the sea."

"They will wait," said the Cherif, simply. "As for you, it is impossible that you should be harmed. As for your home, you cannot return until the subsiding of the great uprising. When that has come to pass you will be free to go."

CHAPTER XXXIII.

CHIPPY'S LITTLE ADVENTURE RESUMED—A PEEP AT THE OPEN AIR—SI HAMICK AGAIN.

CHIPPY CHUNKS, on recovering consciousness, found himself in what appeared to be the twilight of an evening. But in reality it was high noon-day.

The feeble light was the result of his being underground—a fact he did not realise until he had lain for awhile on his back and recalled recent events.

When all was clear as it could be under the circumstances he got upon his feet and made his way to the source of light, which proved to be an almost perpendicular shaft, down which he had been shot the previous evening.

It was too steep to ascend in the ordinary way, and much too wide for him to emulate the ancient order of chimney-sweeps.

A very little inspection pointed out to him there was no road to the outer air that way.

No sound without gave a clue to the upshot of the fight of the previous night.

Whether the French or the natives had been victorious he could not tell. His position all round was far from agreeable.

"I've often heard people brag about having gone to foreign parts," muttered Chippy, "but give me the old country. Here's a nice place to end your days in. Blow it!"

He uttered the last two words with considerable emphasis, and the cave, by means of its echoing power, hurled them back into his teeth—

"Blow it!"

"I can't spare the time to fool around," muttered Chippy Chunks. "Perhaps there is another way out of this dog's hole."

The "dog's hole" proved to be of considerable size.

The cave in which he found himself turned out to be a tunnel, sloping down at first and then upward again.

The light got dimmer for awhile, but presently increased in strength, and at length he came to a huge underground hall, as big as the interior of St. Paul's and in the matter of roof almost as high.

Light came from above through crevices that were mere cracks from below, and on one side there was what appeared to be a doorway—dark as pitch.

The weary Chippy Chunks crawled over to it, and discovered, to his great joy, a flight of steps, as narrow and dark as those found in old belfry towers.

This was promising, and with renewed heart he began the ascent. Half a dozen seconds landed him in complete darkness.

But the steps were there, and he crawled on—up—up—the narrow way, gradually getting into a stuffy state of atmosphere that taxed his respiratory powers.

"I had better go on and get choked, then I shall be out of my misery," he muttered, as he stopped to wipe the perspiration that streamed down his cheeks.

Happily, he had got over the worst part of the journey.

The staircase did not widen, but it grew more airy, and presently lighter. Finally he saw a small hole, about the size of the crown of a man's hat, overhead.

"That's the way out," he said: "but can I do it?"

Part of the way the steps had wound about, but now they went straight up to the open air, the length of the last part of the flight being about sixty feet.

The hole above widened out as he drew near it, until he saw to his joy that a bigger man than he was could easily emerge thereby.

He discovered also that it was jagged, and, furthermore, the steps assumed irregular proportions, until they became mere lumps of rock, an arrangement obviously meant to conceal from the observer outside that there was a way down there.

Chippy was not particular about the style of work so long as he could get out, and with all the haste he could make he ascended to the top and thrust his head out.

To his horror he saw two savage-looking natives there, and, what was worse, they saw him too. One held a gun in his hand, the other a naked sword.

A good round curse in Arabic from the man with the gun followed his surprise, and he brought his weapon to the shoulder.

At so short a distance very little aiming sufficed, and before Chippy could quite make up his mind that he was looking down the barrel of a gun the trigger was pulled.

Snap!

No more—it had missed fire.

Then came more curses, and the man with the sword rushed at Chippy and aimed a blow at him.

Chippy immediately ducked his head, and in the act of doing so lost his foothold on the narrow, ill-constructed part of the stairs, and down he went, sliding on his stomach for half the length of the shaft.

It was a terrible experience, and all the available knobs of his anatomy were knocked about, cut, or bruised. But that swift descent saved his life.

The man with the gun put it right and fired down the opening, the bullet flattening itself against the rocks immediately overhead.

After that Chippy decided to descend to the bottom without loss of time, and there he was to all intents and purposes safe.

But it was a safety of a sort that was of little service to him. He was getting too weary, through thirst and want of food, to go further in search of a road to safety.

Luck was against him, and once more he thought it would be the shortest way out of the miserable business to lie down and die.

"If my young masters were alive," he muttered, "I could bear up; but I reckon they are gone. Chippy, you have done your duty like a man—now die like one."

He sat down upon the lowest stair of the straight line, and, folding his arms, doggedly determined to sit there and have it out with Nature.

"Another hour or two," he said, "will, I think, finish me. Chippy, you are as hollow as a drum. You can't last—all your life you've never showed that you was fit for a fasting man. Good-bye, everybody."

He really felt so horribly faint that he verily believed his last hour had come. At his time of life weakness soon gathers on a man, and further movement on his part was almost impossible.

What little life there might have been in him was shaken out by his fall.

So he sat and tried to sleep, hoping that he would never wake again; but his eyes were as wide open as they could be, and sleep had apparently gone to the other end of the world.

By and bye he fancied the light was growing dimmer, and attributed it to his failing physical state, but a little later he heard whispering and the sound of a soft footfall.

Casting his eyes upwards he saw a man coming quietly down with a gun under his arm and a sword in his hand.

A second glance showed that it was a familiar form—being no other than Si Hamick.

CHAPTER XXXIV.

A WONDERFUL STRONGHOLD — A MARVELLOUS ARMOURY — TOM'S PRESENTIMENTS — THE CHERIF RETURNS WITH STARTLING NEWS.

"IT is a very marvellous place, Cherif," said Tom. "Built many years ago, I judge, by its solidity."

"So long ago," replied the Cherif, "that we have no record of when the foundations were laid. Some of the interior decorations were done by Suleiman, who lived at the time your Crusaders invaded the Holy Land."

They stood on the summit of a square tower, built on the edge of a tremendous precipice a thousand feet high.

No human being could scale it, for it was in parts as upright and smooth as a wall. On either side of the tower were battlements and other towers, extending all round an ample square, with a small courtyard in the centre.

On every side of the majestic building there were inaccessible precipices, like that beneath where Tom and the Cherif stood. It was a castle on one of Nature's huge pinnacles.

"Do you marvel that I feel secure here," asked the Cherif, "for who could assail me with a chance of success?"

"Could they not besiege and starve you out?" asked Tom.

"They might," replied the Cherif, with a smile; "but it is not in the Arab nature to sit down patiently and wait. He makes his dash, and if it is successful he will show no mercy. If he fails he is ready to die—but he has not the slow persistence of your conquering race.

"And again," he went on, after a pause, "outside the Kabyle tribe all believe this castle is the home of a spirit, for there is, to all appearance, no means of access to it. Nor can they conceive how mortal man built it."

"Nor can I," said Tom.

"*It is cut out of the solid rock,*" said the Cherif. "Look closely at it and you will see that what appears to be stones and mortar and cement laid together is one piece. The cunning craftsmen who made this place, cutting their way down from above, formed it so that it has the appearance of an ordinary building. But it is not so. It is a part of the rock on which it stands."

Tom looked closely at the stonework and saw that it was true. Lines to imitate layers of mortar and cement were cut out of the rock.

"But the rooms below," he said, "those magnificent chambers—that courtyard—"

"All scooped out of the solid limestone," interposed the Cherif. "The labour must have been great—so great that it is difficult for the mind to conceive it."

"Wonderful," was all Tom could for the moment say.

It was early in the morning, shortly after the dawn of the second day since Tom's arrival at the castle.

The Cherif had awakened him at that early hour so that he might accompany him on his rounds to see that all was well.

From the elevated position of the building they could scan a large tract of country round, and for the present it was clear of friend or foe.

"There is one thing," said Tom, as they descended the steps in the interior of the tower, "treachery might sell the castle to an enemy."

"To what enemy?" asked the Cherif. "Could a Kabyle sell to a Fanzual when he knows too surely that immediately the bargain was fulfilled he would receive his final payment from the edge of a sword? No—we hate each other too much to turn traitors to our own people."

It was all very interesting, but Tom felt that a short stay in the castle would suffice.

Notwithstanding its magnificence, he was already beginning to feel cooped up, and for Lottie's sake he hoped to get away from that land of fierce fanaticism and constant turbulence.

But when would it be safe for him to make the attempt to get to the coast?

The Cherif could not tell.

It all depended upon how long Abdullah, the Mahdi, would be able to hold the intervening ground against the French.

"He will fail," said the Cherif; "but after him will come a greater man to rid our land of the oppressor."

Fire flashed from his eyes, showing whom he considered that man would be.

At the bottom of the tower was a small open doorway, leading into the courtyard. Here the Cherif paused, and said—

"I have much to do alone to-day, and you will not see me again until eve—perhaps not then. Always in my absence you are master. Command and you will be obeyed, save in one thing—you must not attempt to leave until I tell you the land is clear. For the present farewell. Allah be with you!"

He turned aside to another door, a few feet away on the left, and Tom, crossing the courtyard, entered the wing of the building where Lottie was. A passage, every inch of the walls of carved stone-

work, led to the chamber they were to occupy by day, and there he found his wife and Ned.

Alea had not yet arisen. She was rather a luxurious and decidedly lazy person, like most of the wives of great men in the East.

It was the hour for the morning meal, which was being prepared by two swarthy attendants in their peculiar fashion.

They moved to and fro like shadows, making no sound. Everything required was put into position in a silent way, in harmony with the stealthy movements of their slippered feet.

Talking over what Tom had heard, and discussing their prospects of finally getting away from the castle, occupied the next hour or so, and then they went into the courtyard to enjoy the air before the sun rose high enough to cast its burning rays into that well-like place.

They found it quite deserted save by one old man, who was weaving mats from a species of long grass.

The moment they appeared he arose, gathered his materials together, bowed low, and made his exit.

After that the castle had a deserted look.

No sound of moving men, no clatter of arms, not a voice save their own broke the stillness.

"It seems like the castle of a magician," said Lottie.

"It is a land of enchantment," responded Tom.

"Capital place to read about," said Ned, "but give me the old country. What would I give to be on the Thames in a boat, up Richmond way, lying near some willow tree with a book? Here, Tom, let us have a smoke."

"I don't think I have any left," replied Tom.

"Murder!" exclaimed Ned.

"Stop a moment," said Tom. "I am master here. If I could only summon a servant—"

"By clapping your hands," suggested Lottie. "It is the way in the East."

Tom struck his palms together thrice, the noise he made echoing strangely around. A moment later and a dark-eyed attendant was at one of the doorways, of which there were at least a dozen around.

Tom put his fingers to his lips and went through the action of smoking. The attendant disappeared, to return almost immediately with a cedar-box, inlaid with pearl, in either hand.

One was filled with choice cigars, the other with Egyptian cigarettes.

Tom took one of the former, and Ned half a dozen of the latter.

"Let us go up somewhere, Tom, and lie down," Ned suggested.

Tom escorted them to the top of the tower, where he had been that morning. The scene was new to Lottie, and sufficed to engage her delighted attention for the time.

Ned took a seat on the parapet, at the imminent risk of falling backwards down the precipice. Youths of his age are fond of risking their necks. Tom stood by Lottie's side, discussing the points of interest in the landscape.

Husband and wife had much to talk about—their little ones at home and of themselves—and Ned, not having anyone to talk to, soon began to feel lonely

By the time he had got through his second cigarette he thought he would go and have a look round the castle.

So, quietly slipping down from his perilous seat, he descended the stairs to the courtyard, and debated which of the many doorways he should enter.

Finally he selected the one which the Cherif, at an earlier hour, had passed through. Tom had previously pointed it out to him as the place where he had last seen the Kabyle chief.

Inside was a small chamber, barren of everything but the ornamental work upon the ceiling and the walls. On the left hung a curtain, which Ned raised, and beyond it was a long room, evidently the armoury of the castle.

It was filled with a collection of armour that excited Ned's unbounded admiration and amazement.

Not only were there specimens of all the arms of the country he had seen or heard of, or read about, but there were suits of mail evidently of ancient English or at least European make.

"How came they here?" asked Ned.

He stood before a suit of mail, inlaid with gold, which would have required a man of six feet three inches to fit it.

It was posed upon the bare floor with the visor down, and attached to the closed right-hand iron glove was a huge battle-axe.

It was the finest specimen of old armour in a collection numbering fifty suits.

Suddenly the probable truth flashed upon Ned.

"This is some of the armour worn by the Crusaders who fell in battle," he said, breathlessly.

What ardent thoughts this supposition awoke in his romantic breast!

Here he had evidence of what mighty men lived in those days, and filled with dreams of past valour and grandeur of battle array he passed slowly down the armoury to the other end.

Here he found a number of chests ranged side by side. He tried the lid of one, and found it was not locked.

Inside, in careless profusion, lay a collection of daggers, keen-edged and, for the most part, jewel-hilted. All were bright and clean.

Not one of the chests was locked.

He opened them all in turn, and in each found something to wonder and admire.

In one were swords of every known make and shape; in another rings, bracelets, and many Eastern ornaments; in a third gold coins, the like of which he had never seen before.

All left open to anyone, and yet secure in the honesty of the Cherif's followers.

The time passed so rapidly inspecting these marvels that he did not know it was high noon until an attendant suddenly appeared at his side.

So sudden was his appearance that he might have risen through the floor.

Ned was startled, but he had the presence of mind not to show it. He had learnt that composure, under any circumstances, was expected of great men in that country.

The attendant bowed, and with a sweeping motion of his hand indicated that Ned was wanted outside.

"Dinner time, I suppose," thought Ned. "I have an indicator inside me that tells me it is so. Heigho! if I could only shift this place home."

The sun was high overhead in the courtyard, and the place was like an oven. Ned, as he crossed it behind the attendant, felt half stifled until he got into the shade of the castle again.

It was dinner time, and they were awaiting him. Alea was there, looking as radiant as a tropical flower.

"Ah! you naughty boy," she said, "hide away. Eh!—so?"

"I have been in the armoury," replied Ned, "and, I say, Tom, if you want a final staggerer, just pop in after dinner."

The rest of the day passed pleasantly in conversation, roaming about, and general idling.

Alea was very gracious, and sang songs in her native tongue to Ned, which he listened to with the interest one feels in seeing a play in a language we do not understand.

Lottie did not exactly approve of Alea, but Tom laughed, and told her Ned was not going to fall in love and marry just yet.

"It's a way the women have out here," he said; "they must cast eyes at somebody or die."

"I like Alea," replied Lottie; "she has been good and kind to me, but Ned is too young for flirting."

The evening came, but the Cherif did not return. Darkness fell, and he was still away.

The attendants lighted the lamps in the chambers and passages, brought in coffee and sweetmeats, and retired.

Alea had got hold of some sort of instrument like a guitar, and once more burst into song.

Lottie liked it, and Ned was amused, but somehow it jarred upon Tom's nerves.

"I think, dear," he said, to his wife, "that I will go into the courtyard and have a cigar."

"Don't be long away," said Lottie.

He kissed her and went out, seeing no one on his way to the courtyard.

The stillness of the place was impressive by day At night it was more so.

In the open air there was silence also. Above the dark sky was strewn with stars of every magnitude, casting that curious, indefinable shadow which arises from their light alone.

Tom felt sad, much sadder than he had been for many days, and not even the joyous fact that he had recovered his lost Lottie could drive it away.

A presentiment of coming evil was upon him.

He lit a cigar and smoked it, walking slowly to and fro, the soft echo of his footsteps sounding in his ear like a far-off voice calling him away.

He fell into deep thought for awhile, but he was awakened by a heavy footstep and the rattle of steel.

It came from behind, and turning sharply he saw the Cherif approaching him with rapid strides.

"Allah be praised, oh friend!" he said. "Abdullah is slain."

"Slain!" echoed Tom.

"The sword of the oppressor," answered the Cherif Bouzian, "has laid the liar low. So shall all false Mahdis perish."

"Then the way is free for us?" cried Tom.

"No," answered the Cherif; "the plains and hills are filled with the hosts of France, who are slaying and killing all to whom Allah has given a skin that is darker than theirs. The sands of the desert are red with blood. There are cascades of it upon the mountains. Each hour sees a host of the deluded followers of Abdullah enter Paradise."

"But this slaughter cannot go on for ever," urged Tom. "In a few days—"

"Nay—there will be no more for weeks," interposed the Cherif.

"And we?"

"Ah! you must remain here. Abdullah is down —another has arisen to avenge the slain. I, Bouzian, of the Kabyle tribe, will sweep our foes into the sea. When that is done you will be free to leave me."

Tom stood dumb with this new phase of trouble before him.

The Cherif, with blazing eyes, raised his right hand Heavenward, as if invoking the stars to bear witness to his words, and continued, in passionate tones—

"At last—at last my hour has come. My followers have scattered to bring in the broken remnants of the tribes to a spot I have chosen. A mighty host will be gathered together, and you and I will lead them to victory."

"Your followers are gone?" said Tom.

"Yes, I have returned alone," replied the Cherif; "yet not quite alone, for I gathered two men by the way. It is given to me to bring all who can aid me together. Come, it is right you should see who has returned with me. One of them is of your race. Follow me!"

CHAPTER XXXV.

CHIPPY CHUNKS AND SI HAMICK—THE CHERIF'S RAGE— A YARN WHICH EXPLAINS HOW CHIPPY WAS SAVED.

OU have brought more friends to me?" said Tom.

"One at least," replied the Cherif Bouzian; "a quaint old man who wears the uniform of the oppressor. I should have slain him but for his crying out in your tongue."

"It's Chippy Chunks!" exclaimed Tom, delighted to find that his faithful follower was alive.

The next moment Chippy was coming through the doorway into the courtyard. Tom stepped forward and held out his hand.

"Mister Tartar," said Chippy, overcome with emotion, "I'm glad to see you."

He did not take Tom's hand until he had given his own a rub upon the side of his trousers, just as men accustomed to grimy hands are apt to do when called upon to greet one they consider socially above them.

Tom recognised the nature of the action.

"Ah! Chunks," he said, "there is little on the hand of a honest man that needs rubbing off. But who is that behind you?"

"A nice party, sir," replied Chippy, "him as you know as Si Hamick. Come out there, you warmint."

And the "warmint" came sneaking out, with a whipped expression on his face.

"Come out further," said Tom, sternly, "and let me have a look at you. How did you come to be in his company, Chunks."

"I'll tell that 'ere story by and bye, sir," replied Chippy. "Oh! he's a beauty. But I've got him in hand. If ever he tries any more of his tricks I'll nail him up somewhere, as keepers do the stoats and weazels they catches."

The Cherif Bouzian stood quietly watching the

trio, but there was a gleam of anger in his eyes as he fixed them on the creeping Si Hamick.

"Who is this dog?" he asked, abruptly.

"He was a servant of the Emir Abdul-ab-Bourad."

"Ah! I know him," said the Cherif, with a frown. "A false Moor, who takes a pension of the French. And this man served him?"

"I am but a worm," groaned Si Hamick. "It was given to me to be a slave. I am my lord's most obedient servant."

"You will be none of mine," said the Cherif, "but, being a dog of Abdul-ab-Bourad, how is it you are here?"

Si Hamick clasped his hands and, shivering, cast his eyes upon the ground.

"I did but obey my lord," he muttered.

"This creature," said Tom, "was sent to sell my wife as a slave. You have heard her story, Cherif."

"Ha! is this the dog that would sell a queen of the noble race?" said the Cherif, drawing his sword.

Si Hamick fell upon the ground and laid at full length, his dark eyes rolling in abject terror.

Tom stepped up and laid a hand upon the shoulder of the Cherif.

"I beg of you not to harm him," he said; "he is not worth it."

"I despise these time-servers of the city," answered the Cherif; "it is to them that our country owes its degradation. But it shall be as you will, only let him beware of meeting me alone. Friend Tartar, I will see you on the morrow. For the present adieu, and good sleep be with you to-night."

He replaced his sword in its scabbard, and with a bow to Tom and Chippy Chunks strode away, his noble head erect and his eyes flashing fire.

Si Hamick kept quiet on the ground, making no attempt to rise. His dark eyes watched each movement made by Tom, and his ears drank in every word that followed.

"Tell me, Chunks," said Tom, "how you came to be in the company of this man."

"I'll do it as well as I can, sir," replied Chunks, "although I'm a poor hand at yarn-spinning. And don't you"—to Si Hamick—"attempt to get up until I've finished."

"I am your nobleness's servant," softly replied Si Hamick.

Chippy, with a terseness that was highly creditable to him as an inexperienced story-teller, then related his adventures after leaving the fort until he came to the point where Si Hamick and he were brought together again.

That much of his narrative we have given elsewhere, and from there we will now follow him.

"This 'ere warmint," he said, "comes a-sneaking down that chimbley with steps in it, expectin' to find me dead. He said as much. Two other warmints had told him that they had killed a Frenchman, and I reckon he was coming to see what he could find on the body. The first thing he found was a crack on the toes with my hammer, and then, before he could guess what o'clock it was, he gets another on the head, which brought him down similar to what he is now."

"You are noble—you are great. Your father was a king among the wielders of iron," said Si Hamick—"you are greater than he."

"He's the biggest groveller goin'," said Chippy Chunks. "Well, when he's down I relieves him of a few weppins he was carrying, which I chucked away, bar the knife—that may come in useful for wood-chopping. Then I says to him—

"'Si Hamick, you are a scoundrel, and have got to die!'—not as I'd perlute my hammer by knocking a hole in his head with it, but I felt he ought to be skeered.

"'Oh! my lud,' says he, 'I'm a poor man and your servant—I am a dog.'

"I said he was a poor sort of dog, anyway, but if he behaved hisself I'd see if I couldn't spare him a bit."

"'Si Hamick,' says I, 'how many ways are there out of this place?'

"'My lud, I know not,' he says.

"So to stimerlate his memmery I ups with my hammer, and 'mediately he begins to howl.

"'Oh! my lud, there is one way—two ways—three.'

"He rose in numbers as I wagged the hammer, and he finished off with four.

"'Now,' says I, 'you've got to take me out by one of the ways where we are not likely to meet your friends, and I'll keep close behind you a-holding on to your sash. The moment you tries any trick on me I'll make a oaryfice in your 'ed with this,' says I, a-tapping him with the pointed end o' this 'ere instrement.

"Well, to cut it short, he led me to the outer world by a way that was as much like a chimbley as the other, and he was careful to act straight, for we didn't tumble across any of his friends. But I was mortiful hungry, and I wanted something to eat. Under pressure of a tap or two he takes me to a place where some pervisions was hid away under stones—a sort o' rough store-house. The grub, from an English point o' view, wasn't up to much, but it was welcome."

"My lord ate as one who had hungered. It was as water from a pure well to see him eat."

"Arter breakfasting," continued Chippy Chunks, "as I am bound to say coporously, I axed him if he'd seen you, sir, and he admitted he and his friends had observed you riding with the Sheriff in these parts—that gentleman as just left us. So I axed him if he'd take me to him, and he did so, for we fell in with the Sheriff, who was going to skewer me, but, I hollers out 'What yer doing of? It aint a fair fight!' and then he bursts into smiles and grasps me by the hand, saying, 'I'm glad to see you, old chap,' or summat as was quivalent to it. But he didn't hardly look at this 'ere dog—which it's a libel on the noble animal to call him one.

"It was late in the day when we met, sir, and the Sheriff was waiting for somebody to bring him a message. Meanwhile I told him who I was and all about it.

"Just as it was getting dark," continued Chippy Chunks, "the messenger comes up—a fine, wild-eyed chap—who pitched a yarn into the Sheriff that made 'em both wild with excitement. Then the messenger goes off, and we comes along here. That's all, sir."

"You have not seen Mrs. Tartar yet?" said Tom.

"No, sir—nobody but you, although it will do my old eyes good to see her pretty face again."

"Then come with me," said Tom. "If she has not retired to rest she will be more than glad to see you. By the way, you can tell me nothing of the fate of our friends at the fort?"

"No, sir—but I'm afraid it's all over with them."

"I hope not. Come along."

"Si Hamick," said Chippy Chunks.

"Yes—oh! noble Emir Chunks."

"Go and lie in that 'ere corner, and don't you come out again until you get leave from me."

"If my lord returns a year hence he will find me there," replied Si Hamick.

CHAPTER XXXVI.

A DEEPER FIX THAN EVER—IN NED'S CHAMBER—THE DEVOTED CHERIF—A DOG IN A CORNER ALL THE NIGHT THROUGH.

LOTTIE had not retired to rest, nor Alea either, and from both Chippy Chunks had a warmer greeting than old men generally get from young and pretty women. As for Ned, he shook hands with him again and again, and slapped him on the back until he brought on a fit of coughing that nearly choked the recipient of these friendly attentions.

"Which," he said, "it's pleasant, because friendly, but ill-convenient on account of a leaning towards asthma."

Alea had not seen Chippy in his uniform before, and she appeared to be quite struck with his gallant appearance.

"You quite pretty," she said to him. "Great man to fight—French general."

"I reckon I'm worth half a dozen French generals, ma'am," replied Chippy, "but I take it as a compliment, for you mean well."

The party soon afterwards broke up, the ladies retiring first, and a slave was sent by the hospitable Cherif to guide Chippy to his chamber.

It was evident that the Kabyle chief intended to treat Chippy Chunks as an honoured guest.

"You and I, Ned," said Tom, "must sit up awhile—I have something serious to talk about."

"Anything wrong, Tom?"

"Wrong and not wrong, Ned—it is more a misfortune than anything else."

It was a very serious subject the brothers had to discuss—their position with the Cherif Bouzian.

"He does not understand our relations with Frenchmen, whom he hates so bitterly," said Tom.

"It's awkward," said Ned.

"Men like the Cherif," continued Tom, "are behind with history. They know that in the old days the English practically drove the French out of Egypt, and that there is some friction about our occupation now, but they do not grasp that notwithstanding this the two nations are at peace with each other."

"He expects us to fight for him."

"He does—and blindly assumes we shall be glad to do so."

"It is a pity, Tom, you can't undeceive him."

"I don't see my way to do it. He is a splendid fellow and has done us great service, and I feel we owe him something in return. I would not mind having a brush with any of his other enemies."

"Could you not leave Lottie to explain the situation?"

"Nothing will explain it," said Tom, with a groan. "I can see that. It is impossible to know how he will take the truth. Abdullah is dead, and Bouzian thinks that he is to be the man to sweep the French into the sea."

"He can't know the power he has to contend against."

"He does not, Ned, and, to add to the misfortunes of our position, he believes we have been sent to him to lead his hosts on to victory. Nothing could be more unfortunate."

"I advise you to do one thing, Tom."

"What is that?"

"Don't bother about it, but take whatever turns up, and make the best of it."

"We may be able to make only the worst of it one day, Ned. I could follow your philosophy if you and I were alone."

"Come, Tom," said Ned, "don't you, of all men, despond. We shall come out of it. There's Chippy—a host in himself—and the chances of the thing are you and I— Oh! it is all right."

"Well, Ned! you, as usual, take a hopeful view," said Tom, rising, "and I will try to do the same. But it's a queer business altogether."

"Suppose the Cherif manages to smuggle Lottie back to Algiers?"

"She won't go, Ned. She will never consent to our being again parted."

"All right," said Ned, serenely. "It complicates matters, of course, but we shall get out of it."

Further discussion would not serve them, and so they parted.

Ned had a chamber set apart for him now—adjoining the room in which he was—a grim, silent attendant standing by the door awaiting his coming.

He opened the door, and Ned passed through to a small room, so elegantly constructed and ornamented that a monarch might have been contented with it.

A swinging lamp, giving a fairish light, hung from the ceiling, but the far-off corners were wrapt in gloom.

The attendant waited to see if he could be of service, but a wave of the hand dismissed him, and Ned, before undressing, paced slowly up and down.

He was troubled on behalf of those who were near and dear to him. As Tom had pointed out, the position was full of peril. They were, in a sense, between two fires.

If they were rash enough to fight with the Cherif against the French, they had a choice of dying on the battle-field or being taken prisoners and shot.

Scant mercy would be shown to any European found fighting in the ranks of the so-called rebels.

And, if they refused to fight, might not the passionate, fanatical Cherif turn and rend them in the anger of disappointment?

"Hang it all," muttered Ned, "it is a blessed fix."

There was the hope that the Cherif would not be able to get an army together, and so be compelled to abandon the idea of fighting the French, but it was not a very strong one.

Weary with thinking, Ned at last threw off his clothing, and, wrapping himself in a sort of linen toga, provided by the Cherif's people in the place of our English nightdress, he threw himself down among the cushions on the floor, which served as a bed, and tried to sleep.

But sleep would not come.

Closed eyes did not bring it, and he was meditating on getting up and walking about to tire himself, when the door of his room was softly opened.

Ned unclosed his eyelids, so as to be able to see who it was, but otherwise he showed no sign of being awake.

He did not suspect evil intentions on the part of anyone in the castle, unless it were Si Hamick and he doubted if he would have the courage to attempt violence.

Nevertheless his heart beat a little faster as he heard the rustle of a garment, produced by somebody stealing softly into the room.

It was not Si Hamick, but the Cherif Bouzian, and even in that dim light Ned could see that he looked like a man transformed.

His eyes, always bright, now blazed with light, and above the darkness of his beard his lips could be seen quivering and showing two white rows of teeth.

He had no ill intent, for he was not armed. He wore his turban, as he invariably did, but there was no covering on his feet. As the Cherif drew up to Ned he raised his hands above his head.

And then Ned knew why he had come thither.

In the fullness of his faith in having found those who were to give strength to his arms and victory to his sword he had come thither to pray.

A pang shot through Ned's breast.

He almost loathed himself as an impostor, and yet he was not to blame. Neither he nor Tom had ever hinted or suggested that they were more than ordinary mortals. The error of the Cherif was not founded on anything they had promised.

For a little while the Cherif stood there, wrapt in his meditations. On behalf of his country he prayed for a relief from the hand of the oppressors.

It was a pathetic spectacle and moved Ned deeply. He was glad when the Cherif had ceased his devotions and had stolen from the chamber as softly as he came.

Shortly after Ned fell asleep, and he remained in the land of oblivion until the first light of the morning was stealing through the windows of his room.

Always an early riser, he got up at once, and took advantage of a small bath attached to the chamber.

Water must have been valuable up there, and how it was obtained he could not tell, but there it was for his use, and its cool and refreshing influence was welcome.

Opening the door he went out, and, early as it was, found a number of attendants softly stealing to and fro.

What a strange, silent body they were. But for an occasional murmur they exchanged among themselves he would have put them down as mutes.

"I wonder where Chippy is?" thought Ned. "And can any of these fellows understand me if I put a question to them by signs?"

He tried them—first by feigning sleep with his eyes, and then pointing around. They comprehended him more quickly than he hoped.

And yet it was no marvel they comprehended him, for, of course, they knew he would not be asking after any who had been there the night before.

One of their number immediately beckoned him to follow, and led the way through a passage to the upper end of that wing of the castle.

There, in a quiet corner, in a room beautifully decorated, although not to be compared with his own, he found Chippy Chunks in the act of dressing.

"Good-morning," he said. "I hope you have slept well."

"Yes," replied Chippy, slowly, "but I do dream frightful; it's all such a mixed-up job, sir—like a fairy tale. Why, only think—" He stopped short and began to rub his head. "Dash it! how stupid of me—"

"What's the matter?" asked Ned.

"Well, sir, I told Si Hamick last night to lie down in the yard outside and wait until I came, and I'm blessed if I did not forget him!"

"Oh! he has made himself comfortable, Chippy."

"I'd like to see, sir. I gave him orders not to move, and he aint got any right to do it. I'm going to break that fellow in. If he's shifted ground I'll tan him."

Having by this time finished dressing, he and Ned went out together, and, the latter leading the way, they were soon in the courtyard.

There, in the corner where he had been told to lie, was Si Hamick, without any signs of having budged an inch during the night.

"Good-day," said Chippy, with approval; "I'm glad you've learnt to be obedient to your master."

The eyes of Si Hamick twinkled in a peculiar manner, but his tongue was very soft and oily as he replied—

"My lord says, 'Lie here,' and I lie."

"Yes," remarked Ned, quietly, "you DO lie, like Ananias. The courtyard is covered with dew, and it is damp where you are lying, which proves that you have not been there long. You lie—because you are a born liar."

"When I was a boy," said Chippy Chunks, "and I told a whacker, as boys will do sometimes—more's the pity—my father used to say to me—'Chippy, when the truth slides inside a chap it's got to be drawn out of him,' and then he used to draw it out of me—with a rope's-end. Next to rope there's nothing like leather. Si Hamick, there's one for you."

Chippy raised his foot and Si Hamick skipped into the air.

"Now then, do you feel the truth a-rising?"—another kick—"out with it."

"Oh! my lord," gasped Si Hamick, "who has feet of brass and the strength of the young ox, bear with me while I speak. It has been given me to walk in my sleep, and perchance I rose in the night and sought my lord"—here was introduced another stimulant—"peradventure I was half awake"—another application—"nay, I feel that I was awake, and sinned. The dew was heavy, and that I might live to serve my lord with bones that did not ache I did venture to lie in yonder passage until I heard his footsteps, as soft and springy as the lion upon the mountain, and then I lay me down here again and waited for his coming."

Ned could hardly keep his countenance, especially as Chippy looked so very wrathful and preternaturally grave, so he walked away and re-entered the castle.

"There," he said, "I think I've brought him to his senses at last."

"I hope you have," was the reply.

In the courtyard Si Hamick, brought to his senses, was rubbing himself where necessary, his face expressive of satanical malignity.

"May the night dews screw him up," he groaned, "and the winds drive the blinding sands of the sea into his eyes, so that he may see no more. May a mountain fall upon him and make food for hungry vultures of his flesh."

Having worked off a bit of steam this way he composed his features, and sneaked away into the servants' quarters of the castle, to see if he could get anything to eat.

CHAPTER XXXVII.

THE GATHERING OF THE MEN—CHIPPY GOES INTO POETRY—THE CHERIF BOUZIAN ANNOUNCES THE HOUR HAS COME.

NE fire of fanaticism was extinct, and the ashes of it scattered far away o'er desert and mountain, but in its place another flame was rising.

East, west, north, and south swift-footed and weird messengers were speeding, bearing with them tidings that, though the false Mahdi had fallen, the true one yet lived. Cherif Bouzian himself—raised from the dead—was arming for battle with the infidel. Fugitives, wearily wending their way back to their mountain homes, were overtaken and caught up in the whirlwind and brought together.

Drop a little quicksilver upon an even surface and it will scatter in a hundred particles. Walk round, blowing gently, and these particles will soon gather together again—in small drops, then in large drops—and finally become one. So it was with the tribesmen of the hills.

Defeated and deceived one day, they were ready the next to give up all, aye! their very lives, to the leading of a new light.

They longed, they thirsted for the hour of their country's release, and believed, with all the strength of their patriotic souls, that one day the true leader must arise.

So first the men got together in twos and threes, and as they wended their way to an appointed spot they picked up other small bodies, until at last they gathered together in the huge hollow formed by the hill where stood the castle in which Tom and Ned had first been confined.

The Fanzuals, who had seized it when they defeated the Cherif Bouzian, were all dead, or had forsworn their old enmity to join the new movement.

Fragments of a score of tribes gathered there, each carrying some distinctive mark of dress or arms, but all one in purpose.

"Bouzian, the chosen, lives! We will follow him!"

That was their battle-cry.

It took but three days to gather the host together. In number they were about three thousand—as wild and motley a crowd as ever assembled to fight for freedom.

These three days were days of dread anxiety to Tom, who saw but little of the Cherif, and when he did see him he heard of nothing but the coming descent upon the French.

From the summit of the tower Tom and Ned often quietly scanned the country around, seeing signs of activity everywhere—men running stealthily to and fro, some with burdens of food, others with arms, and each hour showed them how futile, with women to take care of, would be any effort to escape.

Ned, on his own account, tried the way he knew, through the cave, but found the great door at the top of the steps secured.

It was the only apparent outlet, but they were assured that there must be another.

"No man, even in the darkest ages," said Tom, "ever yet was fool enough to make a trap of his own castle, but for all that I do not think the Cherif knows of any other."

"If we find one, Tom, we must get away,"

"True," replied Tom, sadly, "but it makes me feel mean to have to repay the hospitality of such a noble host by running away from him."

"We don't run away from the man, but from his fanatical idea."

"And we haven't got away yet, Ned."

As far as they could, without exciting attention, they examined the various parts of the castle, hoping to find an outlet, but there was none.

In company they visited the splendid armoury which Ned had discovered, but, although there was an open window, the sheer descent of the rock outside effectually barred the way.

"I'll find the way out," said Ned, desperately. "I feel it is here. If I can get only another day or two I shall be able to drop upon it."

Not a word was said to Alea about their anxiety. Lottie, however, understood it, and in her quiet way she went about the castle, examining walls and floors with the hope of finding an outlet.

Alea meanwhile devoted herself to Chippy Chunks, and that dry old chip, acting up to instructions, endured his martyrdom bravely.

"We are doing something she must not understand," was all Tom said; "these women of the East cannot keep from chattering."

"Her tongue goes like a penderlum all day," said Chippy—"wag-wag."

For all that Chippy felt flattered.

He was long past the bloom of youth, but he had a bit of an eye for beauty still. Alea was more than passable, and she was very vivacious.

It was a sight to see Chippy sitting Turk fashion, listening to Alea tinkling a little musical instrument and singing songs in a language that was Dutch to him.

One day—it was the third after Ned expressed his determination to find an outlet from the castle—Alea asked Chippy if *he* could sing.

"I used to tip 'em a tune at the ware'us in dinner hours," he replied, modestly; "some of the good old 'uns. Did you ever hear 'My Lodgings is on the Bare, Cold Ground?'"

Alea had never heard that song.

"Then suppose I try it," said Chippy.

Anything more mournful than this tune, when in good hands, it is impossible to conceive. Sung by Chippy, in a voice that was like a penny whistle with a pea in it, it was slow torture and prospective death.

Most men and women would have preferred being boiled in oil.

Alea stood it as long as she could, trying to think it was music she was listening to, but at last she put her hand over his mouth and stopped him.

"It is too sweet—so good—so much," she said, with Eastern veracity. "I die of joy. Stop."

"I don't want to kill nobody," cried Chippy, very much flattered. "I say, that's a nice little hand of yours."

He took it up, looked at it, then at Alea, who dropped her eyes and sighed.

"Dashed if I aint got a good mind to," said Chippy. "Yes—I'll have a kiss."

He advanced his head cautiously, with the idea of stealing a sweet salute, and had got within two inches of her blooming cheek when he heard a shuffling noise near him.

Looking up, he saw Si Hamick standing before him, with a keen expression of knowing nothing—seeing nothing.

"You thief, you miserable hound!" cried Chippy; "what do you mean by sneaking in here?"

"My lord of Tartar sent me," replied Si Hamick, quaking all over.

"Did he?" said Chippy, rising. "And is that any reason why you should come in on tip-toe, as if you wanted to see—to see—as if—you wanted to— Hang you—you damson, plum-eyed villain—take that!"

He aimed a blow at Si Hamick, who dodged it and backed towards the door.

"Blame my lord—he of Tartar," he cried. "He say to me, 'Go to your lord and tell him to come hither in the armoury.' And shall I rush like a wild beast into so great a presence?"

"Get out with you," returned Chippy, "or there'll be murder done."

Si Hamick vanished, and Chippy, turning to Alea, coughed twice, and then said—

"I'm called away—my—my love—but I will return anon to—*thee*."

Having rolled this touching farewell off his lips he got out of the room with all speed.

"Chippy," he said, when he was outside and the curtains were closed, "at your age to rush into poetry! You ought to know better. You'll be writing a walentine next."

He hurried away to get rid of the remorseful thoughts that laid hold of him, but ere he had gone far the Cherif Bouzian suddenly stood before him.

Where he came from Chippy did not exactly know—he was not looking for him, in fact—but there he was, with his sword in his hand and the light of war in his eyes.

"Where are the brothers?" he asked.

"I aint quite sure," stammered Chippy. "Shall I go and look for 'em?"

"Aye! do," replied the Cherif. "The hour is come, the men are ready—they only await the presence of their leaders. Hasten—say there is not a moment to be lost. The French are camped upon the plain. We must fall upon them to-night."

CHAPTER XXXVIII.

THE APPROACHING HOUR—SI HAMICK ASKS FOR LEAVE OF ABSENCE— CHIPPY CHUNKS AGAIN TO THE FORE.

CLANGING of arms and the weird music of the Moors resounded throughout the castle. On every side there was a hurrying to and fro of feet.

The Cherif Bouzian, having made the triumphant announcement that the hour to march was at hand, disappeared for awhile. All were armed now, and a council of war was held by the brothers and Lottie.

A council of war we have called it, and it truly was one, for, against their will, they must sooner or later be at variance with one who had been a true friend to them.

Chippy Chunks was told off to watch for Alea and keep her engaged if she appeared.

"She cannot help us," Tom said, "and might mar a possible chance of escape."

There was no better place for a consultation than the armoury, in Ned's opinion, but they found themselves shut out from it by a number of men who were engaged in removing the weapons it contained.

Everything save the suits of armour was to be brought into use. The Cherif had need of every pike, sword, axe, or any other weapon. The armour, of course, would be useless.

Who could wear it in such a climate? The marvel was how knights of old had ever endured it.

Driven from this place of resort, Tom, Ned, and Lottie again sought the summit of the tower, and sat down wearily enough.

They had not as yet broken their fast, but they had no appetite for food—the dread anxieties of the hour had taken it away.

Again they looked around, and saw an increased number of men upon the mountains—arms were being distributed and banners unfurled. Here and there, standing on some elevated place, a wild-looking dervish could be seen gesticulating to a knot of men gathered about him.

They could not hear what he said, but they knew the purport of his utterances.

The final effort to oust the infidel was about to be made, and the dervishes taught the doctrine of their race—Heaven for him who fell upon the battle-field.

"It is hopeless to try and find a way out of our fix," said Tom; "our only course is to say 'No' to the Cherif, and take the consequences."

"Think of Lottie," said Ned.

"I wish I were a man," Lottie said, "and then I should not be a stumbling-block to you."

"There *must* be another way out of the castle," groaned Ned.

"That's an old story," returned Tom, gloomily. "Of course there is. But how are we to find it?"

Another clash of arms in the courtyard below drew their eyes in that direction. The Cherif had returned with a number of his minor chiefs.

Quick as an eagle's sight, he espied the heads of the brothers peering over the rocky embrasure, and beckoned them to come down.

They had no resource but to go.

"Lottie," said Tom, "you remain here."

"No," she said; "we go together. Why, Tom, if the worst comes to the worst, I can die as bravely as you."

They all went down, and their coming was hailed by a shout and the raising of swords in the air.

The Cherif came forward and knelt at the brothers' feet.

"Mighty saviours of our people," he said, "when the sun is a third high we leave here for the battle-field, for the movements of the foe enable us to move at an earlier hour. The fair women will remain until we return victorious from the fight."

"Cherif," returned Tom, "you have endowed me with powers I do not possess. In case of failure it may be visited on my head."

"All that comes be on mine if we fail—I will not return alive."

"Give me your sacred word that whatever happens you will not harm our women."

"Brother always," said the Cherif, "I could not harm them; they are honoured in my eyes."

"Our hearts may fail us," rejoined Tom. "My brother and I may yield to fear at the last moment."

"All things are in the hands of Allah," said the Cherif. "Go, break your fast, and I will send a messenger to you anon. For my place is outside—among my people; there I will await you."

He waved his sword, and his followers did the same, uttering wild cries. Then at a signal from him they vanished.

"Farewell for the time," the Cherif said. "Brothers, I will await you."

And then he, too, was gone, with a heart rich in hope of victory.

"Once more a respite," said Tom, drawing a deep breath. "Any moment may bring us a chance of release."

"It seems to get smaller by degrees and beautifully less," muttered Ned.

They went to the chamber where the breakfast was spread. Alea was there, but not Chippy Chunks. Si Hamick was standing at the door.

"What do you want here?" asked Tom.

"I seek my lord's protection," replied Si Hamick. "The Cherif—a mighty man of the sword—hath rafused to take me with him. He says I am a dog, and will bring a curse upon his cause."

"Well?" said Tom, inquiringly.

"Everyone will go—even the slaves," replied Si Hamick. "Even now they are departing. Of all here none will remain save a leper and myself."

"Again—well?" queried Tom.

"The Cherif is gone," said Si Hamick, dropping his eyes, "and I am but a burden to my lord—he of the hammer—who but now, when I would have followed him into the armoury, did raise his foot—blessed be it through all time—and strike me therewith."

"Come to the point, man," said Tom, impatiently.

"It is this," said Si Hamick. "The Cherif gone—all gone save a guard at the cavern, who will escort you and your celestial brother to the Cherif—would you leave a leper and a dog like me in the castle with two houris? If ill befall them—"

Tom raised his hand, and Si Hamick shrank away.

"Give me leave to go, my lord," he whined. "Let me be your messenger to the chief of the guard that I and the leper shall go forth to hide on the mountains until the war is over."

Tom saw at once the advantage that would accrue from the absence of the wretch, and he certainly would never have left him alone with Lottie.

If all else were gone, and he and his could be left in the fortress by themselves, even for a brief time, the hoped-for escape might be attempted.

"Go—bring the chief here," he said.

Si Hamick disappeared, and in a few minutes returned with a swarthy son of the desert armed to the teeth.

"He speaks French, my lord," said Si Hamick.

"Let this man and a companion pass," said Tom, in that language; "he is not wanted here."

"My lord's commands will be obeyed."

The chief departed, and Si Hamick bowed his thanks.

"To my lord a word," he said. "Why do fools go struggling with the sea? The Cherif and his hosts will perish, and a flood of maddened French soldiers will come hither, for the secret of the castle entrance is known. Let my lord take his lady with him or slay her."

And then, ere Tom could realise the full import of his warning, he was gone.

"Where is Chunks?" he asked, addressing Alea.

"No see him," replied Alea, shaking her head.

"A nice sort of fellow to give a commission to," returned Ned. "Well, Tom, we have a little time to ourselves. At least we shall get a chance to run over the castle—"

"Eat, and in haste," said Tom. "As for Chunks, he must take his chance of a breakfast. I wonder where he is and what he is doing?"

"Gone wrong somehow," replied Ned. "Lottie, you *must* eat. We may feel the want of food by and bye—"

As he spoke the curtains at the end of the room were pushed aside, and Chippy Chunks appeared in a wild-eyed condition.

He came forward, and, saluting Lottie in the old respectful way, sat down.

"Excuse me," he said, "for coming in a bit rumpled. It's more in mind than body. Please let me have a cup of corfee, as I'm a bit faint. I think I've found out a way to dodge the Sheriff."

CHAPTER XXXIX.

CHIPPY CHUNKS CONCEIVES A BOLD IDEA—TWO MODERN MEN IN ARMOUR—SI HAMICK AND THE LION.

HIPPY CHUNKS was in such an agitated state of mind that when Lottie handed him a cup of coffee he could not hold it steadily, but shook as if he had the ague.

"I'll be better in a minute," he said, apologetically. "It flashed on me all in minute, and it almost floored me."

"What did?" asked Ned.

"The way to dodge him," said Chunks. "All I'm fixed about is the ladies; myself don't count. They may chop my head off, and it wouldn't matter a brass button."

Chippy Chunks drank his cup of coffee, ate a piece of bread and a little fruit, and then arose.

"I'm ready now, gentlemen," he said, "and if the ladies will excuse us a minute—"

"You had better confide in us all," said Tom. "What have you found?"

"Not a way out, sir, but a place to hide in."

Tom shook his head.

"We should be searched for and found," he said.

"I don't think so, sir," said Chunks. "I heard the Sheriff talk about going, while I know the castle is as good as clear of 'em, and I can stow you

away so that nobody will find you. Besides, I've got a yarn for 'em," he added, reflectively. "It's a bit of a lie, but I think it will be excusable under the circumstances."

"Well, tell us what your plan is."

"We can all be trusted, I suppose?" asked Chunks, with a meaning glance at Alea, who was toying with her scarf.

"She is one of us," said Ned.

Alea looked up quickly, with a smile upon her face.

"I hear—I know," she said. "Trust me much."

"I'm at your service, sir," said Chunks. "Will you all please follow me?"

They went out together, Alea and Lottie last. The castle was quite deserted, save—as Tom knew—by the guard at the top of the cavern awaiting the message from the Cherif Bouzian to escort Tom and Ned to lead the wild mountain horde.

Down the passage, across the courtyard to the armoury, went Chippy Chunks. Ned's face lighted up like one who finds his prophecy fulfilled.

"I knew we should find a way out," he said, exultingly.

"There's no way out here, sir," quickly answered Chunks, "only, as I told you, something to hide in."

They entered the armoury, now denuded of everything in the form of a weapon. Only the armour remained, and several suits, in pieces, lay upon the floor.

"There you are, gentlemen," said Chippy, pointing to the latter; "there's your hiding-place."

"Gone right off his head!" gasped Ned.

"No, sir," said Chippy. "I've been looking at these things for some time this morning, just to see how they could be put together and took to pieces. A tap of the hammer here and a little unbuckling there does it. Now don't you see?"

"No," replied Tom.

"Why, sir, all you and your brother has got to do is to let me fix one of these suits on each of you, and when they come for you you'll stand up amongst the rest of 'em. They'll look everywhere and never find you."

Tom looked at Ned, who drew a deep breath; then both looked at Lottie and Alea.

"The ladies will be safe enough, gentlemen," said Chippy; "I'll take care of that. Trust 'em to me. It's you these mad people want, and they will find you gone."

"But what will they think?" asked Ned.

"You leave it to me, gentlemen," replied Chippy Chunks. "Here, let me put this ironmongery about you. Mrs. Tartar, you take my word for it, these things will be the saving of us all."

"Tom," said Lottie, with a sudden light of hope in her eyes, "do as Mr. Chunks asks you. Never mind us—we are not in danger."

"It seems so cowardly to hide," said Ned.

"It is foolish to needlessly throw away your life," urged Lottie.

"She is right, Ned," agreed Tom; "there is no time to lose. Chunks, you have our best thanks; put the armour on me."

"It'll be sweltering hot in it," said Chunks, "but it will be better to perspire a little rather than lose your lives."

Like a true workman, he had got all the bearings of the task he was about to perform, and piece by piece he built up the armour about Tom until he was completely cased in it.

As everything had been kept in perfect order Tom was able to raise his vizor.

"Oh! Tom," exclaimed Lottie, "what a handsome knight you would have made."

"Thanks, my dear," he replied, laughing, "but I don't know that I should care to do much fighting work in this suit."

Ned was soon fitted up, and here again Chunks showed the workman's mastery of detail by having selected smaller armour for him than for his brother Tom.

He could not have done the work better had he been an expert—accustomed to arming knights in the old tournament days.

The buckles, springs, and rivets he fitted and fastened with the aid of his ever-useful hammer, and in less than half an hour Ned and Tom were both fully accoutred.

"And now, gentlemen," Chippy Chunks said, "the ladies will have to say adieu to you for the present. We had better not be seen near you."

"Good-bye, Tom," said Lottie, standing on tip-toe to kiss him. "Oh! how I wish we had lived in the old days."

"We should be dead men if we had."

"I mean I wish the old days were still here."

Alea, who had watched the fitting on of the armour with eyes wide open with astonishment, went up to Ned and patted him on his iron shoulder.

"Good-bye—brave boy!" she said.

Chippy Chunks, having cast a final eye over his work, exhibiting his satisfaction on his beaming face, hurried the ladies out, and bade them retire to the chamber occupied by Tom and his wife at night.

"I'm head of this business," chuckled Chippy Chunks, hilariously, left alone in the courtyard, "and when them blackamoors come I must dissemble, like the chap in the play. Ha! ha! I took 'em in once as a Mardy, and now I'm on another tack. What a blessed lot of innocents they are!"

.   .   .   .

While this little drama was being enacted Si Hamick and the leper had gone their way.

The former had a shrewd idea of what would be the outcome of this new rising. Whichever way it went it would go badly for him if he were found in the castle.

He was no favourite with the Cherif, but quite the reverse, and his lot under that ruler would never be a happy one.

If victorious for a time it would not better things, for Si Hamick knew that the rising would fail eventually, as others had done before—and the policy of the French was to destroy all rebels that fell into their hands.

Si Hamick's nationality would be his condemnation, and he would be shot or hanged to a dead certainty.

Hence his desire to depart, and he was cunning enough to know that Tom Tartar would not be sorry to get rid of him.

Rejoicing in his chance of finding a place of security, and lying *perdu* until the worst was over, he hastened away.

The leper had told him that he knew of a hiding-place not far distant where they could remain for days undiscovered.

He had, indeed, been preparing for his own flight thither, and had stored away some provisions for the time of concealment.

There are many people who would not care for a leper as a companion, but one gets used to such things in the East, and Si Hamick was not fastidious.

Leading the way up a narrow path that diverged from the main one, the leper finally struck a track between two hills, which had the appearance of being little frequented.

He and Si Hamick talked in their native tongue, and we give a translation of as much of what they said as the necessities of our story require.

"It is not far," the leper said, "but as the place is accursed no man wanders thither."

"And why accursed?" asked Si Hamick.

"One day, years ago, the great prophet Shalak visited it, and lo! a lion leaped out upon him."

"And ate him, bones and all, I suppose?"

"So it is said," returned the leper, "and all men cursed the spot on which he lost his life, for he was a great prophet."

"What did he prophesy?" asked Si Hamick.

"He was coming to the people to prophesy when the lion ate him," answered the leper, simply.

Si Hamick chuckled.

There was something very humorous in the idea of a prophet being eaten up before he had time to prophesy.

"It may be," he said, "that this prophet was poor of heart, and failed to show a courageous front to the beast."

"Ah! I know not," replied the leper. "The lion ate him. That is the commencement and the end of the story."

A few moments later he pointed out a small opening in the rocks some distance ahead.

"It is there," he said, "we hide."

As they drew near Si Hamick saw it was a cave, which could be easily discovered by anyone seeking him.

But he had no fears on that score.

It was away from the line of march, and he could hide there in the full sense of security.

The leper bounded forward and reached the cave first. He was stooping down to enter when a low growl came from its depths—an ominous, well-known sound—that caused him to turn and flee for his life.

A moment after a huge lion bounded out and pursued him. The leper darted past Si Hamick, who stood still, gaping with terror, until he felt himself knocked down by one of the huge paws of the beast.

He fell upon his side, but rolled over on his face.

There he lay shivering for a moment, and then the king of the desert put its two paws upon him and, raising its head, gave vent to a terrific roar.

"The lion spared not the prophet," moaned Si Hamick, "and it will devour me. Oh! fool, to flee from a lesser evil to the jaws of certain death!"

As he gave vent to his anguish in these words darkness came over his eyes and he fainted away.

THE TWO TARTARS:

Or, Tom and Ned among the Moors.

CHIPPY CHUNKS WAS IN AN AGONY OF TERROR AND REMORSE THROUGH THE ACCIDENTAL FIRING OF THE RIFLE.

No. 30.

Price One Penny

CHAPTER XL.

THE SUMMONS—A VAIN SEARCH—THE SUSPICIOUS CHIEF—DISCOVERY.

HE voice of the Cherif crieth for the young lions. Let them come forth!"

A majestic-looking man, with a drawn sword in his hand, blazoned forth this summons in the castle. There was no response. With slow, imposing strides he entered the courtyard, and was about to repeat the cry when he saw Chippy Chunks lying at full length upon his face, with his arms and legs spread-eagled on the ground. It is the attitude Eastern men take up when awe stricken or overcome with despair. The chief gazed at him earnestly, and then, with slow steps, approached him.

"Servant of the white prophets," he said, "where are your masters?"

Chippy Chunks moaned and rolled over, exhibiting a face in which a pair of eyes were showing a lot of the whites.

"Speak—where are they?"

Chippy got up slowly, and tossed his arms up, to signify that Tom and Ned had vanished somewhere beyond the castle walls.

A puzzled look came over the face of the chief.

He was a stranger to Chippy, but he spoke the English tongue. His summons was uttered in the language that we are told is, by and bye, to be universal.

"Gone?" he said, interrogatively.

"You are too late," replied Chippy; "they went away with the others—those who were sent by the Sheriff."

"I am his messenger," returned the chief; "there has been no others."

"You are mistaken," said Chippy, firmly; "my masters were called to the Sheriff an hour ago."

The chief's face wore a puzzled look.

"It cannot be," he replied; "the entrance has been guarded."

"Search the place," said Chippy Chunks—"there's only me and the ladies left."

"It is a lie!" thundered the chief, furiously; "it cannot be."

Chippy simply bowed and spread out his hands, after the manner of men in the East who wish to keep cool when their veracity is impugned.

"You seem to know all about it," he said. "Find 'em."

The chief took a pistol from his sash and fired it into the air. In a little while twenty swarthy men had gathered round him.

He uttered a few words in Arabic, and immediately they scattered about the castle.

The chief remained near Chippy Chunks, who took up one of the Cherif's cigars, and having lighted it he began to smoke placidly.

"You will understand," Chippy said, "that you are not to harm the ladies."

"The women are naught to us," was the abrupt reply.

The chief evidently suspected something, and while his men scoured the castle he kept a close eye on Chippy Chunks, who, conscious of the necessity for a cool demeanour, smoked with the affected ease of a Bond-street dandy, drawing slow whiffs and sending a fine column of smoke into the air.

To vary the monotony of the proceeding he presently sent the smoke through his nose, while the chief looked on with a feeling akin to astonishment.

One by one the men came back with their reports. No sign of the missing ones had been found.

Two places only remained to be searched. One was the chamber occupied by Lottie and Alea, into which the men dare not intrude—the other was the armoury.

With a gloomy face the chief looked at Chippy, who remained passive.

"It may be that the women conceal them," he said.

"Come with me," replied Chippy; "I'll soon show you different."

Cocking his cigar so that the burning tip was almost level with his eyes, Chippy put on a swagger and led the way to the chamber where the women were anxiously awaiting the result of the search they knew was going on.

Hearing Chippy's voice they came out, and the chief bowed low before them.

"He wants to see if you have hidden the gentlemen,' said Chippy.

Lottie, who knew that a high bearing had its weight with such men as the one before her, haughtily swept her hand round, as an invitation for him to enter.

He bowed again apologetically, but he did not shirk his duty.

The search was soon over, and he came out with a disturbed look upon his brow

"They are not here,' he said, "and I have but one place more to search. If that fails me, I must go to my chief and tell him our prophets have been stolen from us, and the cause is lost."

"I wouldn't give 'em up all at once," said Chippy Chunks, hopefully. "Perhaps they are not far away."

Disdaining to give an answer to him the chief sauntered back slowly, deeply thinking It seemed as if he knew he was being humbugged, but could not get hold of the faintest notion of how it was done.

Slowly—slowly, with Chippy in his wake, he left the room. Lottie would have followed, too, but the old man gently waved her back

All was not yet over, and it might be that serious work would be necessary. If it should be so women would be better away.

On reaching the armoury Chippy saw to his dismay that the men who had searched the castle were swarming within it. But they were doing little more than walk up and down.

On seeing their chief they drew towards the door and went slowly out—their manner conveying the impression that nothing was to be found there.

Chippy did not dare to look directly towards Tom and Ned, but in a sidelong way he had a glance at them. They were standing side by side—erect and still.

"It must be mighty trying," thought Chippy Chunks. "I hope he won't be long here—"

The chief walked up to the further end of the

armoury, then turned slowly back, and retraced his steps until he came opposite to where Tom and Ned were standing.

His eagle glance was fixed upon the closed vizors, and the light of a discovery leaped into his eyes.

Raising his head, he gave out his summons again, in a voice as ear-piercing as the blast of a trumpet.

"The voice of the Cherif crieth for the young lions. Let them come forth."

Chippy saw that the hiding-places of Tom and Ned were discovered, and, weak with new-born terror, he bowed himself low, shivering as one with the ague.

CHAPTER XLI.

THE CHIEF DISABLED—ANOTHER MAN IN ARMOUR— THE BOOM OF THE GUNS.

HATEVER may have been the emotions of Tom and Ned as they heard the trumpet-like cry of the Arab chief, they were certainly not affected by it.

Neither stirred hand nor foot.

Chippy Chunks lost his head for a moment, and sought his favourite weapon, with the idea of doing a mortal injury to the man who had penetrated the secret of their hiding-places.

But he was deterred by the thought that, if all the other men were armed, no good would come of assailing the leader.

Seizing him by the arm, he went upon another tack.

"Chief," he said, "why do you cry out? Where are the—the—gentlemen you want?"

"Have I eyes?" was the answer. "Cannot I see? Have I ears? Did I not hear the breathing of the chief of the prophets?"

"You must be mistaken," said Chippy, holding tightly to him; "it can only be their ghosts. They're gone—taken away."

The chief wrenched himself free, and, raising his clenched hand, cried aloud—

"They are here, and if your people are deaf, and do not listen to my voice, I must go to my people and say 'Come, see the young lions hiding.' It shall be so. If they will not go forth to battle they must be taken there. Away, dog of a servant of the prophets."

"Here! who are you calling a dog?" said Chippy, with his blood rising. "I'll precious soon let you know that I am as good a man as you are— Oh! you will, will you?"

The chief was striding towards the doorway, which he had just reached, when Chippy Chunks overtook him.

And only just in time.

The chief put his hands to his mouth, and was about to send forth a cry that would have brought a score of armed men to his aid, when Chippy, both alarmed and exasperated, brought out his pet weapon and struck him down.

So swiftly was it done, and so quietly did the chief subside, that a sentry standing a few yards away neither saw the blow nor heard him fall.

Chippy cast a quick glance about him.

Nobody else was near. Only Tom had seen the deed by which he had silenced a man who would have been very troublesome.

A moment only was wasted, and then Chippy laid hold of the senseless chief by the heels and dragged him back into the armoury.

It was a "big job" as he called it, but he did it. The perspiration started upon his forehead and ran down his face in little streams.

"It's tough work, gentlemen," he said. "What shall I do with him?"

"Is he dead?" asked Tom, his voice sounding hollow behind his closed vizor.

"No, sir—only in a state of comictose, as the doctors say," replied Chippy Chunks; "but he'll soon be coming round."

"Gag and bind him," suggested Ned.

Chippy Chunks went to work, and he soon had the chief secured. Hands and feet were tied together, and a good gag thrust into his mouth. The next thing was what to do with him.

"If any of his people come in they will be sure to see him," thought Chippy.

Then a place of disposal flashed upon him.

"I have it!" he almost yelled.

Again he moved the prostrate form, dragging it near to one of the suits of armour, which he went to work upon, taking it to pieces.

This, with all his late experience, was soon done. The next thing was to get the armour upon the fallen man, and Chippy, with fevered haste, took the task in hand.

Piece by piece he fitted the armour upon the chief's inanimate form, riveting, screwing, buckling, until it was done.

Lastly he rolled the figure into the corner, where it had the appearance of having been cast down by accident.

These proceedings were watched by Tom and Ned through the bars of their visors with the keen interest one would attach to any movement on which a life or lives depended.

Completed at last, they complimented Chippy Chunks upon his work.

"Don't talk, gentlemen," he said, wiping his heated forehead, "it isn't all over. I've the rest to tackle, and I'd better do it outside."

Away he went, and first of all addressed the sentry near the armoury.

"Why do you stop here?" he said. "Your chief is gone and the young prophets too. Both took away by evil spirits."

The sentry stared at him in dumb surprise. He could not understand him.

But he soon comprehended the signals made by Chippy that the other men were wanted there, and putting his hand to his mouth he uttered a peculiar cry, which rang through the castle like the wild scream of a jackal.

It brought the men who were searching the place swiftly to the spot, and Chippy Chunks, with the most imposing bearing he could get up for the occasion, was waiting to receive them.

"Halt!—front!" he cried; "stand in a row, or anyhow, if you don't know what a row means— now then, all who understand me step forward."

The group of men, a little more than a dozen in number, had two in their body who understood what Chippy was saying.

They stood out, and by a motion of their heads implied they were waiting to be addressed.

"You want the prophets," said Chippy, "don't you?"

They bowed.

"Well, they're gone," replied Chippy. "I told your chief so, and he disbelieved me, but now he's gone, too."

"Will my lord say where?" asked one of the men.

Chippy waved his hand aloft, to indicate that all had flown away.

"Swept up—carried away," he said; "but you will find 'em all right with the Sheriff. If you don't believe me search the place."

"My lord," was the answer, "we have searched it through and through."

"Everywhere?"

"Everywhere, my lord?"

"Before going," cried Chippy, raising his voice, "it was foretold by the young proppits—I mean pro-hepts, dash it!—that all who lingered here would be blowed to pieces. Now, do as you like—go, or stay—but, whatever happens, don't blame me."

One of the men turned and rapidly translated what he had heard. A general shrinking back was observable.

The peculiarity of Chippy's vernacular did not lessen the fear his threats of being shattered to pieces inspired.

"Have we not searched, and they are not here?" said the interpreter; "and our chief—is he not gone? Why, then, should we linger?"

As he spoke the booming of a big gun was heard among the mountains.

Ere its echoes ceased another and another was heard. The battle had begun.

And these men knew the purport of those sounds.

The Cherif Bouzian, while marshalling his forces to attack the French on the plain, had been assailed by the advancing foe.

They had either been led treacherously into his vicinity or by some means discovered it.

Then came the rattle of small arms and the yells of men engaged in desperate conflict.

These were sounds they could not resist. The boom of the guns was as a voice calling them to battle, and with fierce shouts, brandishing their swords, they broke away and vanished from the courtyard.

"Done 'em!" cried Chippy Chunks, exultingly. "Done 'em, by Jingo!"

Half-wild with excitement, he dashed back into the armoury, and told Tom and Ned they were free to emerge from the burden of armour they bore.

"You needn't hide any longer, gentlemen," he said, "for there's a big fight going on outside. I don't wish the Sheriff no harm, but I hope he and his party are gone from here for good."

As soon as Tom and Ned were let loose they both expressed their delight at the ability displayed by Chippy Chunks, which he put aside with a laugh.

"It must be a poor fool who couldn't get over these derluded creatures."

"By George!" exclaimed Ned, "a little more of it and I must have been stifled."

The echo of the booming of the guns could now be still more distinctly heard—a terrific fight seemed to be going on.

As the two hurried out of the armoury the hapless chief encased in armour made a movement to attract their attention.

"All right," said Chippy; "you will be let out by and bye, when your friends come home."

Then Tom went off to seek his wife, while Ned and Chippy ran up to the top of what they now called the Tower of Observation.

CHAPTER XLII.

THE BATTLE—FLIGHT FROM THE CASTLE—CHIPPY CHUNKS TO THE FRONT ONCE MORE.

FROM the summit of it they had a view of an impressive, awe inspiring scene.

The trysting-place of Cherif Bouzian's men had been a comparatively open space in the hills, and they were gathering there when the French force suddenly burst upon them.

The hapless Arabs were caught like a number of rats in a huge cage, but, though they were suffering terribly from the concentrated fire of the disciplined troops, they fought desperately and bravely.

To add to their discomfiture the Frenchmen had succeeded in getting some good-sized field-guns into a position on the hills, from whence they could fire upon the seething mass of swarthy men.

The whole thing was a horrible slaughter.

No quarter appeared to be given or asked.

"I can't look upon this scene, Chippy," said Ned—"it is too awful. These wild, fanatical people are being *murdered*."

"And, after all, it's their own country, aint it, sir?" said Chippy.

"It is," said Ned. "Come down. Yet stay a moment—one more look, Chippy. I think we shall be able to get out of here. Do you see?—the Moors are being driven back and the French are following up. If the road by which we came is clear— Chippy, come on—there is a chance of escape."

Down ran Ned, with Chippy Chunks after him, as fast as his aged legs would permit.

They passed the armoury, just peeping in to see the chief who had been so unceremoniously treated by Chippy still lying bound and helpless upon the floor.

On they went, through the castle, to the rooms they had lately occupied. Tom, Lottie, and Alea were just coming out to meet them.

"Tom," said Ned, "I think we may get out of here. There's a big fight going on outside, and they are retreating towards the castle. If we try the west we might find a clear bit of country. Anything is better than staying here."

"You are right, Ned," replied Tom; "but there is a long way to go, and we have no food or means of travelling."

"We have risked everything before and must do so again," urged Ned. "The Cherif is licked—beaten into a cocked hat, poor fellow—and if an excited lot of French soldiers find their way in here what do you think would happen?"

"Lottie, dear," said Tom, "what do you say?"

"Let us go," she answered, firmly; "anything is better than lingering here."

They left as they were, with nothing but their arms, which consisted of the revolvers purchased by Tom and Ned.

The door leading to the cavern was unfastened, and, opening it, Tom led the way, descending the flight of steps with caution, lest some foe should be hanging about below.

But all was clear.

There was no living thing in the cavern nor in the first part of the ravine beyond, but they could hear the sounds of the battle that was raging still.

Bearing westward from the scene of conflict they hurried on, over broken ground that sorely tried the feet of the women.

Tom took Lottie's arm and helped her along. Ned could do no less with Alea, and Chippy, hobbling, brought up the rear.

They passed the turning which Si Hamick had taken with the leper, keeping straight on until they came to smooth ground, and then by a comparatively broad way to an open plateau that commanded a view of the sandy plain beyond.

In the distance they could see a number of tents, which might be a camp of the Arabs or the French. The distance was too great to tell which.

Between the fugitives and the tents there was nothing but the barren sand.

Ned called Tom's attention to two or three curious-looking structures away to the left. They had the appearance of being native houses, such as were to be seen on the outskirts of Algeria—habitations of the former people.

"We might find friends there," he said.

"At least we shall obtain water," replied Tom.

He shrewdly guessed that these houses were built near a well, and some dervish, who levied "backsheesh" upon all who came, might possibly reside there.

He saw no occasion to be afraid of one man, or two or three for the matter of that, and he elected to go thither.

There was about two miles of sandy ground to cover, and Lottie was already giving out. Alea also looked as if she had had enough of travelling.

But urged by the cheery voices of their companions they started again, and with the endurance women often show under the most trying circumstances, they uttered no sound of complaint.

Behind them the firing could still be heard, but it was getting fainter and fainter.

The Arabs were evidently retreating and the French were in full pursuit.

Dreadful work was going on among the hills, and Tom's heart ached for the Cherif, who had certainly shown himself to be a gallant, chivalrous gentleman.

At length the two miles of ground were covered, and drawing nigh to the houses they saw they were three in number—poor little dwellings, with a sort of stable attached to one of them, a few posts, and a roof to keep off the rays of the sun.

There were no signs of any inhabitants until they had reached the well, which was a hole dug deep in the sand down to the rocky bed.

It was fenced round with stone-work on three sides, and the other open, with a rough flight of steps down to the water.

At the bottom, filling a pitcher, was a man, whose scanty attire and general wild appearance proclaimed him to be a religious dervish.

Hearing the sound of their footsteps as they drew near and peered down at him, he looked up, but exhibited no signs of alarm or surprise.

Having filled the pitcher he came slowly up, and, bowing low, offered it to Lottie to drink.

She had need of it, and gratefully accepted the offer. Her thanks in English were unheeded. He did not understand the tongue.

As the pitcher passed round Tom tried him in French, but all the response was a bow and a deprecatory motion of the hands, which plainly said "I do not understand."

Having all drank, he emptied the pitcher, after having carefully washed the brim, and then went down to refill it.

This time he drank himself.

It was not, to our way of thinking, exactly polite to show that he had a strong objection to drink after his guests, but the ways of his caste were familiar to our friends, and it did not trouble them.

Reascending the steps, the dervish, by signs, asked them if they desired to eat, and, receiving a sign in the affirmative, he went into one of the low houses near and brought out a piece of matting.

On this he placed a coarse kind of bread and some dried fruit, signifying by a bow that it was all he had.

Little as it was it was very welcome, and they all partook of it heartily.

When they had finished, the dervish brought out another piece of matting, on which he spread his own food, and in silence and alone he ate his evening meal.

For evening now was coming on—the sun in an hour would be gone—but still from the mountains there came at intervals the booming of guns.

The fight was reduced to a series of conflicts with broken-up parties, but it was not yet over.

"I wonder," said Tom, "if we could be allowed to sleep here?"

Whether he was understood by his action or tone, or his desire was anticipated, is uncertain, but his wish was gratified by the dervish rising and leading the way to one of the other houses.

The door was open, and after glancing curiously at Tom and the ladies he signalled for him to go in.

Lottie followed, and a moment afterwards Tom's voice was heard—

"You had better all come in. We must not be separated."

So they went, and found a cool room, lighted by one small window in addition to the doorway. There was nothing but mats to lie on and coarse pillows for the head, but they were sufficient in that warm climate.

In the darkest corner Tom placed the two women, and with his male companions lay down near the door.

The dervish did not enter. Having seen them within the house he went back to his own abode.

"I don't know who our friend is," said Ned, "but I should say he is a thorough good fellow."

"Some repentant sinner doing penance for a crime, perhaps," replied Tom; "but whoever he is we are tolerably safe. If a scouting-party of the

French come upon us they will surely believe our story."

"I hope so," returned Ned.

"There is one I should very much like to see," said Tom, thoughtfully, "but I fear there is very little hope of coming across him again."

"Very little," said Ned.

They were thinking of Lieutenant Carmean.

Not much chance, indeed, was there of setting eyes upon their gallant young friend again.

But one never can tell, and it is unwise to give up all hope whilst any doubt of the fate of a person remains.

A few whispered words were exchanged among the party, and then, as the sun went down, they fell asleep.

CHAPTER XLIII.

THE CRY OF DISTRESS—A WOUNDED HERO'S LAST MOMENTS—THE DARKEST PERIL OF ALL.

OM TARTAR was the absolute nearest of the three to the door.

As the elder of the brothers and the leader of the party he felt it his duty to be there—to be the first one to discover and bear the brunt of any peril that might arise.

He fell asleep quickly, and went right away into the land of dreams, wandering among a jumble of events, some of which he had been mixed up with, and others of the wild, impossible nature, such as comes to us when in sleep.

After awhile he found himself in the thick of a battle, and was amazed to find that the rattle of arms was no more than would be made by three or four men walking to and fro.

The great majority of the warriors were fighting in a soundless way, which so completely astonished him that he awoke.

Outside there was a sound of armed men marching slowly, but they were as yet some distance off.

Rising, he stepped to the doorway and peered out, but as there was simply the light of the stars he could only see a shadow of mixed men approaching.

They were coming on slowly, as if by stealth or bearing some heavy burden. After a close inspection of the advancing mass he came to the conclusion that it was the latter.

Who were they?

What were they bringing to the desert home of the dervish?

The others were all sleeping quietly and soundly, and he hesitated to awake them until he knew there was danger in the coming of these men.

Slowly they came nearer, and Tom was soon able to distinguish a faint moan from their midst, the nature of their burden being thus revealed.

A wounded man was being brought thither.

Nearer and nearer the party came, until Tom could make out they were Arabs, and this threw light upon their stealthy movements.

Some chief had been brought from the lost battle-field to the haunt of the dervish, either to give him water or to obtain for him the last religious consolation of the sick.

The dervish had heard them advancing, and came out of his house with a quiet step that was ghost-like.

He showed no signs of excitement until the party had drawn near him and he could see the wounded man.

Then a great cry burst from his lips—a cry that awoke the night stillness of the desert and floated far away, dying down to nothing in the distance.

One word only escaped his lips—

"Bouzian!"

And Tom knew that it was the Cherif who had been brought thither.

How gladly would he have gone to his assistance, but he dared not. He could not tell how the Cherif might view his non-appearance on the battle-field.

Perhaps he had placed the weight of the disaster upon the shoulders of the "young prophets" who had failed to appear.

His high-bred, sensitive nature would inevitably be touched by the apparent cruel desertion by those whom he fanatically loved and trusted.

But what could Tom or Ned do?

By what right could they lift a hand against the French? To espouse the cause of the Moors was to meet with a violent death, for assuredly, if not killed upon the battle-field, they would have been taken prisoners, and short their shrift and sure the deadly shot would be.

The dervish brought out some matting, and they laid the dying Cherif—for it was, indeed, the gallant Bouzian—upon it. With water from the well they offered him drink, with which he just moistened his parched lips, and then he spoke in French to his followers thus :—

"All is lost. The young prophets have gone astray and left us to the wild beasts of the desert. On their heads may the wrath of Allah fall! May they wander in the desert and find death, and may the lions eat their flesh!

"All is lost," he said again, after a pause. "My people are dead or scattered, and in the halls of my mountain home the foe drink, and scream, and laugh. It is fate. I do not complain. Allah judge the young prophets. If they wantonly failed me let the curse of a broken people rest upon them. If they could not aid me peace and rest be theirs."

Once more he lapsed into silence, and the heaving of his body, as he breathed heavily, showed that the end was near.

Waking up from a temporary lethargy, he made an effort to rise, and one of his followers placed a hand under his head.

"Forget me," he said; "let not the sword be sheathed until the prophets are found. Then let them be examined and judged. If they sold my people to the enemy, then thou knowest what to do with them; but if—"

He stopped short, and made another effort to rise higher, but it was his last.

There was a sharp catching in his throat, and, his head falling back upon the supporting arm of his follower, the end of a noble life had come.

They laid him down, while the dozen or so of men who had brought him thither uttered a simultaneous wail, and drawing their swords mingled them together aloft in the starlight.

In short, but impressive chorus they spoke a

dozen words or so in Arabic, and then resheathed their weapons.

"A vow of vengeance," thought Tom, drawing a deep breath.

He trembled for a moment, thinking of Lottie and Ned, and then was calm again.

That their presence was not suspected was clear, for no movement was made towards them—the question was how long would they remain undiscovered.

The dervish had been kneeling by Bouzian, and when the last spark of life had died away in that gallant body he arose and went into his room.

From there presently came sounds of tearful wailing and a beating of hands upon the walls—the Eastern lamentations for the dead.

Meanwhile the Arabs had gone away, but not far. A hundred yards distant they dug a hole in the sand with their swords, drawing the gritty particles aside with their hands, until they had a grave deep enough for him to lie in.

Then they came back, and raising him in their arms bore him to his resting-place.

In a few minutes the last offices for the dead were finished, and the men came back sadly to the well.

The lamentations of the dervish had ceased, and he came out to them again.

A few words were exchanged, and then he put himself at the head of the party and led them towards the hut in which the fugitives were.

"It's all over!" hissed Tom, between his clenched teeth.

He stooped down and touched Ned lightly on the shoulder.

The boy instantly awoke.

"Ned," whispered Tom, "we are discovered. Enemies approach. Get your weapons ready, and let every shot tell."

CHAPTER XLIV.

THE WHITE DERVISH OF THE WELL—A STRANGE STORY.

A HASTY man would have fired at the approaching Arabs, with the result that the whole of the party sleeping within the house would have been sacrificed.

But Tom was prudent, and never did anything rash. Ned invariably followed his brother's lead, and so it transpired that no mischief was done.

The dervish was not bringing the Cherif's followers to attack Tom. He was simply ushering them to the third house, where they could lie down to rest.

As the men filed past Tom saw the mistake he had made, and congratulated himself upon the caution he had shown.

The men all went by without suspicion of his presence, and in a few minutes were housed and the door shut upon them.

Then the strangest thing of all that had occurred that night took place.

Instead of going straight back to his own abode the dervish came up to the door of the house occupied by Tom, and in clear English accents said—

"I desire to speak with you. Come forth!"

Wondering, Tom and Ned obeyed, and the dervish, with a sweeping motion of his hand, indicated his desire that they should accompany him to his abode.

This request, added to his speaking English, was, of course, a complete surprise. In silence Tom and Ned obeyed.

Nothing could be more simple than the inside of the home of the dervish.

It was a small, square room, with a feebly-flickering lamp hanging from the ceiling. On the floor were spread several mats, and that was all.

There was an inner room, probably his store-house, but that strangers never entered.

"Be seated," the dervish said.

They sat down, and he also took a seat on a mat facing them. After a pause of nearly a minute he spoke again—

"You wonder to hear me speak your tongue," he said, "but that will be dispelled when I tell you that I am of your nation, although it is but a name to me ; in fact I have never seen it, to remember it, although I know I was born there.

"My story is a short one," he resumed, after a moment's rest, "and my enemies are yours, so you may know the motive I have in assisting you as I intend to do. From what I learnt from my father I know I am a native of England, having been born on the borders of Wales. My mother was a Welsh woman.

"Shortly after I came into this world my father had occasion to go to Egypt. He was a mining engineer, and obtained an appointment from the Khedive to carry out some works at Cairo. Unfortunately the captain of the vessel got aground on this coast. A party of Moors fell upon the passengers and crew, slaughtered several, and carried the rest into captivity. My mother was among the slain, and she died by my father's hand. It was by her earnest entreaty that he saved her from the Moors.

"My father and I," added the dervish, "were carried away as slaves. He spent the rest of his days in a captivity so horrible that I never think of it without my blood boiling in anger. Enough! he died. I lived to grow up a slave."

The dervish paused, with bowed head, indicative of the emotion that troubled him. Tom and Ned kept silent.

Appropriate words which they had in their hearts failed to reach their lips, so unbounded was the interest and astonishment the narrative created.

"My father taught me his tongue," pursued the dervish, "and when alone we spoke no other. His captivity was a hopeless one, and mine was the same. It is so now, although I have played cunningly with them. When quite a boy I began to talk of visions and things I saw until I obtained credit for possessing occult gifts. In short, I practised upon their credulity until I became what I am. In appearance I was a Moor, for I was naturally dark, and the sun burned my skin to the native hue. Strange natives always took me to be one of their people, and only a few—a very few—remember now that the Dervish of the Well has alien blood in his veins.

"I chose this place, and I have given up my life to helping those who fall into the hands of the Moors. I cannot do much, but now and then I help a victim to regain his freedom. Judge of my joy when I saw you approaching last evening. It was as if a full harvest had come to the husbandman."

"You have fairly overwhelmed me with your story," said Tom; "forgive me if I cannot frame the words of gratitude I fain would speak. We are thankful."

"I am a dervish in habit, but not in heart," continued the strange man. "Through all I have kept the faith my father taught me, but I have to be wary in what I do—not that there was need to palm any subterfuge upon you. All that I intended to do was to make the moment of your escape a complete surprise. Your joy would have been ample payment for me."

"We are refugees," said Ned, "but you have yet to learn our story."

"I know it," replied the dervish; "it has been brought to me piecemeal by the mountain men. You may grieve for Bouzian, for he had a noble heart. While he lived your lives would have been safe, but not after. You cannot trust the people. And now," he added, rising, "steps must be taken for your escape. An hour's journey from here I can procure camels to bear you back to Algiers. As soon as possible get away from there, and if you are wise you will never set foot in this land again."

"Will you not go with us?" asked Tom. "It would be something to have so true a friend to take back with us."

"No," was the somewhat sad reply; "my place is here. What could I do in England? I know it not, except by name, as I told you. Its people are strange to me. The habits of the country, the climate—everything would clash with my early training."

"For all that I would you went with me," urged Tom. "You would soon become used to us."

"No," firmly replied the dervish; "my place is here—my work is here. What am I fit for, and what could I do so well as what I have now my heart set upon? I remain here, and, believe me, I shall live and die content."

"But suppose the Moors should discover the work you do?"

"They would slay me. But what of that? It would be an honourable death."

"At least tell me your name," pleaded Tom, "that we may reverence it."

"Again I must say no," was the quiet reply. "As the White Dervish of the Well let me live and die in your memories. And now you must hasten. Those dogs are soundly sleeping, and we must get away. Go, rouse your friends at once, and let us begone, for I must be back by dawn."

CHAPTER XLV.

THE CAMEL-OWNER—STORY OF A VISION—A START FOR FREEDOM.

UT a small Moorish village, it was yet a sort of posting-station for those who travelled on camels or horseback to the hills, and the name of the keeper of the camels was one Horab Effendi.

He was sleeping the sleep of a just man, dreaming of houris and all the joys of paradise, when a hand was laid upon his shoulder, and, starting up, he saw a figure by his side.

It was the practice of Horab Effendi to sleep with a light in his room, and by its aid he saw a figure that was familiar to him—the White Dervish of the Well.

"Ah! son of the Prophet," he cried, "what brings you here?"

"I have had a vision," replied the dervish, "and in it I was commanded to hire three camels of thee."

"Whither to go, and for whom?" demanded Horab Effendi.

"It is not for me to say," replied the dervish, "but so it must be; and lo! in the vision it was recorded that in four days the camels should be returned to thee, with shekels of silver and gold to their full worth."

"Say, oh! son of the Prophet, was it a clear vision?" asked Horab Effendi, doubtfully; "one that will not deceive."

"Question not the voice of the Prophet," returned the dervish, sternly, "for it was shown in the vision that if thou saidst nay thy camels should die, and leprosy fall upon thy flesh. What sayest thou?"

"The camels shall be thine," sighed Horab, "and I will pray that the shekels shall not be all a dream."

"Go—caparison the beasts," said the dervish. "Tether them together, and I will lead them forth."

As Horab slept in his everyday attire, which consisted of a simple linen robe, turban, and sandals, he wasted no time in making his toilet.

"It is good to work for the son of the Prophet," he said, with a sly glance at the dervish, "for, verily, great gifts come of it."

"Hasten with the camels," was all the response he received.

Horab Effendi kept his camels at the back of the house in a large enclosure, part of which was under shelter.

The greater portion of it, however, was open to the air.

About a dozen camels were lying about in attitudes of contented ease, and Horab proceeded to rouse two or three of the nearest by kicking them in the ribs.

"See that the best are chosen," said the dervish.

"In the name of the Prophet—yes," replied the camel-owner.

In a few minutes he had three ready side by side,

tethered together by the head. The dervish took charge of them.

"Rest content," he said to Horab Effendi—"they will return."

"May I not see those who are blessed by riding them?" asked Horab.

"It was not so pointed out in the vision," calmly answered the dervish.

As he moved away Horab Effendi gazed after him with a most malevolent expression of face.

"May the tortures of the lost seize upon all vision-makers!" he growled. "I would I knew if thou hast lied or not. But the vision of the White Dervish of the Well must be obeyed, lest ill befall me. Yet have I done some good unto myself, for of the camels two are lazy, as if hamstrung, and the third is a rogue. They have need of the spirit of the Prophet to make their beasts worthy of hire."

The dervish, in utter ignorance of the class of camel which had been palmed off upon him, led the animals away to a spot a short distance from the village, where Tom Tartar and his party were eagerly awaiting his return.

Alea was speedily mounted upon one camel—the smaller of the three—and Tom and Lottie upon another.

These two beasts were tethered together. Ned and Chippy Chunks took possession of the third, the last-named modestly choosing a rear seat.

Tom and the dervish shook hands.

"Farewell, friend," said Tom. "If not in name you will in person live in our memory."

"May you safely reach home," responded the desert recluse, "and, once there, look around you and thank Heaven you are a native of the freest and greatest land the world has ever seen."

"Once more—will you not come with us?"

"No—my duty lies here. In any other place on earth I should be a poor, useless creature. Farewell."

A kind word to each of the others and the adieus were over.

He turned, and, as it seemed to Tom, wrenched himself from them and melted away into the gloom.

He had already given Tom instructions how to guide the camels by the stars. When morning came they would possibly be out of danger.

Alea's camel was a poor, dejected little beast, but Tom's was inclined to go. As the pair were tethered together, where the second went the first had to follow.

Taken altogether, they got along very well for a time, until the camel bearing Ned and Chippy Chunks showed a strong inclination to lie down.

Ned was furnished with a stick, and he used it with no sparing hand, but he could not keep up with Tom.

Seeing this, Tom called back to him—

"Hurry up, old fellow; we must keep together!"

"Go ahead!" cried Ned; "we may be behind for a bit, but we shall get there all the same. Don't forget who is with you."

Tom knew it would be wrong for him to linger, but for Ned's sake he would have gladly done so for awhile. As things were he could not help himself in the matter. His camel had made up its mind to go, and it went—just *went*.

The long-legged beast proceeded at a great pace, dragging its smaller companion after it.

The jolting motion effectually stopped all con-

versation, but the riders bore it bravely. They were on the way to safety.

CHAPTER XLVI.

PURSUED BY ARABS — A CAMEL CRAWLER — THE VOLLEY.

HIPPY, can you see them?" asked Ned, It was early morning, the sun on the point of rising, and a grey light in the sky.

Ned and Chippy, on their camel, were crawling along, the brute oblivious of all adjurations, blows, or digging of heels.

"No—they are gone clear out of sight, sir," said Chippy, "and I hope as they're all right. But when we are going to get to Algiers on a creature like this *I* don't know."

"No more do I," growled Ned. "Come up, you leather-hided brute. A policeman going his round could give you six hundred yards in a mile and beat you by half the distance."

"Master Ned," said Chippy, looking back, "there's some parties on foot coming along after us."

Ned scanned the plain and saw quite a crowd of natives bearing down in their direction; but as yet they were only little specks, being at least a mile-and-a-half away.

Still, it was an ugly fact. They were being pursued, and the camel could only crawl.

"Chippy," said Ned, with a groan, "give the beast a touch just on the top of his tail with the hammer. Use the small end."

"I'm holding on with both hands, Mister Ned," replied Chippy, "and if I let go I'm bound to fall off."

"Then don't let go," said Ned.

They both shouted at the brute they were riding, but with 'no more effect than would have been apparent had they been on a rocking-horse.

With slow, regular movement it put out one leg after the other, just crawling along.

Ned plied his stick until it was broken into three pieces about the length of a rolling-pin, but there was no addition to the speed exhibited.

It was like travelling over a bog with leaden feet.

On came the Arabs, gaining some ground, but not so quickly as Ned expected, for after all the camel took long strides and got over a fair amount of space, only his action seemed to make the movement a dismal crawl.

"Chippy," said Ned, "this is worse than a sudden rush upon us."

"It is, sir—like dying by inches. What will you do when they come up?"

"I never make plans now, Chippy; they always get upset. Anyway, we'll have a bit of a fight for it ere we die. I'm glad Tom and the women have got away."

"You ought to have ridden with the lady," suggested Chippy.

"Well," replied Ned, with a short cough, "I thought not. It was hardly proper in the dark; but if I had done so it wouldn't have helped you."

"I don't know about that, sir," said Chippy. "Maybe this 'ere lopping creature was only made for one rider. Come up, you catamunk, you wall-eyed, boxing-glove-footed beast."

The camel uttered the peculiar cry its species give out when it begins to feel distressed.

It so startled Chippy Chunks that he nearly fell off behind.

"Hold on!" cried Ned, cheerily.

"I don't think I can for long, sir. I'm a-going to drop off."

"It won't do, Chippy. You are going to sacrifice yourself so that I may get away; but I won't have it. Both or neither of us must be saved."

This was exactly what had just entered Chippy's mind, and he was sorely discomfited by Ned having discovered his intention.

"But if I can't hold on, Master Ned?" he asked.

"You've got to hold on," said Ned, "or I shall fall off with you."

"Very well, sir," returned Chippy, "I'm a limpet. But they're a-coming up, sir. I fancied I heerd 'em holler."

Ned looked back, and saw that half the original distance between them was gone.

The Arabs, with the steady, swinging trot of the sons of the desert, were slowly but surely overhauling them.

It was a bad look-out behind and no better ahead.

Away on the horizon, many miles off, he could see a haze, such as might be hanging over a great city at early morning, but he could not make sure that it was enveloping Algiers.

And, even if it were, he could not expect, without considerably accelerating the pace of the camel, to escape from his pursuers.

He was well aware that the Arab could keep on at his swinging trot for many hours. Speaking humanly, he never tires.

There are men who, with a few dates and a piece of bread in their sashes to eat at intervals, can keep on from sunrise to sunset. They have been known to run without sensibly flagging through a day and night.

A more hopeless position it was hardly possible to be in.

He had his revolver with six shots, which might or might not mean six lives, but that would not avail him.

The Arab does not fear death, because he believes it to be the beginning of a better existence. Apart from that he is naturally brave, and in addition he is remorseless to a foe.

Ned had no hope of mercy or consideration from them. As for Chippy, his French uniform would certainly seal his fate.

The camel flagged instead of increasing its pace, and the snorts of distress became more and more frequent.

"They're putting on a spurt, sir," said Chippy. "They see we can't go."

"What arms have they?" asked Ned.

"Every man seems to have a gun," replied Chippy.

"Then all I hope is they will use them," said Ned, gloomily, "and put us out of our misery. How do you feel, Chippy?"

"Quite perky, sir. I ain't afeard of 'em. I don't believe they can shoot straight."

Once more Ned looked back. The Arabs were gaining on them fast. In a little while—a quarter of an hour at the outside—they would be upon them.

Fifteen minutes is not a long time in which to recall one's life, but Ned made the most of it, and he managed to pass a lot of events in review before him.

Like an honest, sensible fellow, he was not satisfied with what he recalled.

His life had not been perfect.

He had been rather troublesome at home, and occasionally a little wrong outside.

There were many things he would like to take back—much he would like to undo—but it was now too late.

"They're close upon us," groaned Chippy, "and are going to fire."

"Very well," was all Ned said. "Good-bye, Chippy."

"Good-bye, sir!"

Then a volley rang out, and the bullets went screaming by.

Ned and Chippy were untouched, but the camel snorted viciously, and, staggering forward, fell upon its knees.

CHAPTER XLVII.

THE STIMULATED CAMEL—A HAPPY REUNION—ALGIERS.

NED thought it was all over with them, and he was about to jump off the camel and defend his life to the last when it rose again from its knees and set off at a tremendous pace.

It was all the work of a moment, and ere another volley could be fired two or three hundred yards were placed between the camel and the Arabs.

Ned was too much surprised at first to do more than hold on, and called out to Chippy to know if he were still there.

"A-a—all ri-i-i-ght, si-ir," was the reply.

"Stick to him," said Ned; "we may get away yet."

The Arabs must have had nothing better than muzzle-loaders in their possession, for two or three minutes elapsed ere they began to fire again in an irregular fashion.

The sound of the rifles had a galvanising effect upon the camel, for the hitherto stubborn, lazy brute put forth all its energy, and exhibited a lumbering trotting power that was not to be despised.

Ned's spirits rose again.

It was like receiving a new lease of life, and after a while he looked round to see how Chippy Chunks was getting on.

He was clinging like a leech to the camel—toe-and-nail fashion—and as his eyes met Ned's a broad smile spread over his face.

"I ca-a-an ho-old on-n-n, sir," he said.

The Arabs were already far behind, and there was an appearance of the pursuit being given up.

Some of them were tailing off, and the others were not by any means keeping up the original pace.

"Saved," thought Ned, "if the brute will only keep up for half an hour—that is, if we are going the right way."

The bare possibility of being taken further into the desert was enough to turn him cold, and he cast an anxious glance around the horizon, seeking some signs of the mountains. To his joy he could now make them out, far away behind him, and a glance ahead showed him faint outlines of the highest buildings of Algiers.

He was almost certain he could recognise the form of the grim Cabash.

It was a long time ere the camel gave any signs of flagging, and when it did so the Arabs had given up the chase and been lost in the distance.

When the eccentric animal fell into a walk Ned was able to converse with more freedom with Chippy Chunks.

"I suppose the brute is not used to fire," he said.

"Bless you, sir, it wasn't that alone," replied Chippy; "one of the bullets grazed him in the flank, and just cut through the skin. You can't see the wound—it's too far behind—but that is what stimerlated him."

"I had almost given myself up for lost," said Ned.

"It looked as if we had to draw our back day, sir," replied Chippy, "but after this I'll never give in until I'm dead and buried."

Ned laughed merrily.

He was naturally light-hearted under the circumstances, and when the camel showed a disposition, an hour later, to lie down and rest awhile, he did not object.

They had a little food with them, which Ned brought out and shared with Chippy Chunks.

The camel had to rely upon the natural storehouse within himself.

A rest of half an hour did them all good, and at the end of that time Ned had no difficulty in inducing the beast of burden to resume its journey.

Furthermore, it seemed to scent a haven of rest ahead, and, putting its best leg forward, got over the ground at a great rate.

It was terrible work riding in such heat, but the knowledge that they were going back to freedom inspired both riders, and they kept their seats bravely, enduring their agony in silence.

Later in the afternoon they were within easy hail of Algiers, and might expect to reach it before or shortly after dusk.

Ned was speculating on the time it would probably take the camel to complete the journey when it suddenly gave a joyous snort and redoubled its exertions.

"What on earth is the matter now?" thought Ned.

The mystery of its accelerated movements was soon revealed. About a mile ahead were the other two camels with their riders—safe, but anxious about Ned and Chippy Chunks.

Ned's camel had sighted its companions ere its riders had done so, and sped forward to join them.

It was a happy reunion all round, and when the general greetings were over the whole party started once more for Algiers.

About half an hour after dark they were outside one of the gates of the city awaiting permission to enter.

It was necessary at that time for the French garrison to exercise some discretion in the matter, but Tom Tartar, having expressed a desire to be taken to General Boureau, the governor, the party was allowed to pass in.

One of the soldiers of the guard attended upon them, to act as guide to the general's residence.

From this man Tom learnt the joyous fact that his yacht, the White Wing, was still lying at anchor near at hand.

Captain Starfish had been on shore daily to inquire after his lost employer, but no tidings of the fate of the missing ones had ever reached the city.

And there was yet another good piece of news given him.

Lieutenant Carmean and some of his garrison had escaped from the little fort upon the mountains, having found a way down the cliff to a ledge of rock, that finally led them to a place where they hid awhile.

The lieutenant had joined the fighting party which had met and defeated Bouzian and his followers.

The residence of the French governor was in the heart of the city.

He was at dinner when Tom's party arrived, but he came out at once to see them and to give a hearty welcome to all.

"You must be my guests to-night," he said.

"In this garb?" asked Tom, exhibiting his well-worn attire.

"Why not?" he said. "I have some guests to whom your story will be interesting, especially if it is told in costume. Even our friend here," indicating Chippy Chunks, "must not think of casting off the uniform to which he is a credit."

Notwithstanding the fatigue of the day and night's ride, all were so elated with their escape that they had no sense of being tired.

A bath and a brush-up sufficed to put them in order ere they saw the governor's guests.

But first they had a quiet dinner to themselves, and when refreshed thereby they were ushered into the drawing-room.

About a score of guests, mostly people of rank, were there assembled, and great was the interest shown in those who had practically "returned from the tomb," as one of them put it.

Tom was the narrator, and he told the story of their adventures briefly but clearly.

"Something must be done to put a stop to the selling of white people into slavery," said the governor. "Abdul-ab-Bourad shall be summoned before me to-morrow. I shall ask those who have suffered at his hands to attend as witnesses, and you," to his friends, "to be silent in this matter until I have him in my power. If he gets wind of what is in store for him he may fly from the city. There are a thousand places in the country where such a scoundrel can hide, and I want badly to put him in a place of security."

CHAPTER XLVIII.

THE EMIR TROUBLED—HE FINDS THE CLOUDS OF ADVERSITY GATHERING AROUND HIM.

ALONE, seated on his favourite pile of cushions, reclined Abdul-ab-Bourad, Emir and governor of the Cabash, smoking a hookah and meditating.

The meditations of this important functionary were not at all agreeable, for of late matters generally had gone wrong with him. Long before this he expected Si Hamick would have been back, with the price of the white slaves he had been commissioned to sell in his pocket, but now that one of the frequent hillside wars had broken out there was little chance of his getting a shekel.

This was a bad look-out with his coffers as empty as the sarcophagus of King Cheops.

Abdul-ab-Bourad also missed Alea, his wife.

It is true that she had laughed at, derided, and scornfully treated him, but, although that was very mortifying, the fact remained that she was very pretty, and he had not been able to find one to compare with her.

Nay, he had not been able to obtain one in her place at all, for among the Moors a penniless man has to whistle for a spouse. They do not believe in love in a cottage in that sunny clime.

Last of all, he had reason to know that he was out of favour with the French governor, General Boureau.

Some time had elapsed since that important functionary had consented to see him. Thrice had he called and been told that his excellency was "engaged," which really meant, "My good man, you are not wanted here."

Therefore was the Emir gloomy.

He sat for awhile puffing at his pipe and reflecting on the advisability of calling again upon the general, but the possible outcome of it did not offer him an inducement to do so.

"A blight lay on all the infidel dogs!" he muttered.

The curtains at the door of the room quivered for a moment and then were parted. A slave stood at the entrance.

"Ah! dog," said the Emir, "what brings you here?"

"Oh! my lord, a messenger from the Frank," replied the slave.

"Admit him."

The slave retired, and presently the rattling of a sabre was heard.

Enter a French officer in all the glory of full uniform.

A careless salute was given the Emir, and then came the message—

"The governor desires to see you, Emir."

"I am at my lord's pleasure," replied Abdul-ab-Bourad. "At what hour?"

"Now."

"Is it to be an official visit or only that of a friend?"

"Official, I believe," replied the officer, with a dry smile.

Abdul-ab-Bourad was pleased to hear it. He liked official visits. They impressed the people in the streets, and led them to note what an important man he was.

Rising, he clapped his hands, and when the slave reappeared—which he did with magical rapidity—he bade him order his conveyance of office, a sort of palanquin borne on the shoulders of slaves, to be got ready without delay.

In addition he commanded all his available men to turn out as an escort, remarking to the officer that "all things were to be done in honour of the mighty general."

"For myself," he said, "I care not for display."

"It is well," replied the officer, with another smile. "One can never tell when it is to be dispensed with."

They left the apartment a few minutes later and walked down to the courtyard of the Cabash.

There the officer's horse was awaiting him, with the palanquin for the Emir.

About thirty men, in a variety of Moorish costumes, mostly bordering on a state of decay, were waiting to act as guard.

Their arms were the curved sword of the Moors and old-fashioned firelocks.

As the party emerged from the gate he saw a further escort of mounted French soldiers awaiting him.

This was an honour he did not expect, and he professed himself to be more than delighted.

Indeed, he entirely recovered his spirits, and for a time was quite gay.

Down the sloping, winding road the party travelled, with little or no talk to liven the way.

The French soldiers closed round the palanquin, the officer rode in front, and the straggling men of the Emir brought up the rear.

Down to the city and through the narrow streets they went, with many a curious eye cast at the Emir and his escort.

A few saluted, but the majority simply stared, and a few laughed. The spirits of the Emir began to fall.

"This is no visit of pleasure," he muttered. "Can it be that I am in disgrace?"

On arrival at the Embassy he was bidden to descend. Instead of being led into the state apartments he was escorted down a long passage to a chamber used as an office.

The general was seated at a library table, engaged in writing. By his side stood an armed sentry.

Instead of saluting the Emir as a great potentate he took no notice of him beyond pointing to a place where he was to STAND.

The heart of Abdul-ab-Bourad was now rapidly getting into the region of his slippers.

Besides the young officer two of the men remained as an extra guard, but they all stood some distance away, so that the Emir was alone.

He tried to look haughty and proud, but the attempt was rather a failure. He was completely cowed by the unexpected position he found himself in.

General Boureau calmly finished the document he was engaged upon, blotting and folding it, and finally placing it in an envelope ready for post.

Then he at last addressed the prisoner.

"Emir," he said, sharply.

"My lord," was the faint reply.

"Some time ago two Englishmen were here in Algiers. They came hither in a yacht, and mysteriously disappeared. Know you aught of them?"

"May the dust of the desert eat into my bones if I have set these eyes of mine upon them!" fervently answered the Emir.

"A lady—wife of one of the Englishmen—is also missing," pursued the general. "When did you see her last?"

"By the beard of the Prophet I have not seen her at all."

"A servant of theirs is not to be found. What has become of him?"

Abdul-ab-Bourad, with upturned eyes and outstretched hands, vowed by all that was dear to him and to the world that he had not so much as heard of the man.

"You swear it?"

"By the beard of the Prophet."

"Let the accusers of this liar enter," said the general, curtly.

The officer opened the door and let in Tom and Ned, who walked boldly across the room and sat down.

An expression of utter amazement sprang into the face of the Emir. His eyes had perfect white rings round them, so wide open were they, and the words he would have uttered stopped short on his quivering lips.

"You know these gentlemen?" said the general.

The open eyes opened still wider, but beyond this there was no reply.

"Tell your story," said the general.

Then up rose Tom and denounced the scoundrel who had brought so much misery upon them.

Every word of his story told, and as he went on, putting the net of evidence around the Emir, that old scoundrel gradually sank upon the floor in a posture of abject humiliation, and pleaded in broken tones for mercy.

But Tom did not intend to be merciful to him.

He had learnt the nature of men of his class, and knew that it would be useless to extend the hand of forgiveness to him.

It would simply be giving him a new lease of villainy.

It was not so much his own wrongs as those of Lottie that Tom remembered.

True it was that she could now be considered safe from further harm, but the possibility of what might have happened was in Tom's mind, and right heartily did he denounce the Emir.

"Our lives would have been forfeited," he said, by way of conclusion, "but for his cupidity, and in dooming us to a fate worse than death he had no thought of mercy. Revenge and avarice were the mainsprings of his motives."

When he had finished and resumed his seat Ned arose, and simply said—

"I support and endorse every word my brother has said. He has not deviated one hair's breadth from the truth, and I echo his demand for justice."

CHAPTER XLIX.

THE GOVERNOR'S DOOM—CHIPPY GOES ON BOARD THE WHITE WING—A MATRIMONIAL AGENCY.

"RISE, Abdul-ab-Bourad," said the general, "and let us hear what you have to say in your defence."

Slowly the Emir got upon his feet, and with bowed head stood before the man who was to judge him.

"It may be," he said, "that I have done these things, but I do not remember them."

"How so?" asked the general, with a frown.

"I have been bewitched with the evil eye," replied Abdul-ab-Bourad, "and know not what I do, save at intervals."

"Ah! then, for the sake of others," returned the general, severely, "you are well out of the world. Emir, we have tolerated you too long."

"Oh! my lord."

"Much too long. It is such men as you who breed revolutions and encourage assassination. It is time that a lesson should be taught you."

He signalled to the officer, who was standing some distance away from the prisoner, and in a twinkling the Emir was secured by the arms.

He made no resistance, but when he was pinioned staggered back a pace or two and fell into the arms of the soldiery behind him.

"What an abject cur!" muttered Tom, scornfully regarding him.

"If I might speak to my lord," said Abdul-ab-Bourad, "he of the dimpled face and tender heart, on whom my Alea cast an eye of favour—"

"You would waste your time," interposed Ned. "Personally, I think hanging too good for you."

"Ah! then I spit upon—despise you!" hissed the Emir, with sudden ferocity.

He would have suited the action to the word but for the look on Ned's face as he sprang to his feet.

"Take him away," said the general.

"Have mercy—mercy!" gasped the Emir, once more losing heart.

He would have thrown himself down again, but the soldiers seized him, and he was dragged away crying for mercy.

Even after he was out of the room and the door closed his appeals to be set free could be heard, but ere long they died away.

"You may consider him disposed of," said the general, rising; "and now we will return to the ladies."

"What shall I tell them?" asked Tom.

"That the Emir has been dismissed from his post."

"Dismissed?"

"Aye, sir," said the general, coolly, "dismissed, for he will return to it no more. Dismissed, and—ruined. But who will care? Of what value is human life to these people?"

"Will he have no further trial?" asked Tom.

"None," was the reply.

"But who will say that he is guilty? Who will be judge and jury?" asked Tom.

"I am the judge and jury too," replied the general. "You are shocked."

"I do not quite like it," returned Tom.

"Such a way of dealing with a man like him is necessary; but," said the general, "he deserves his fate, and if he simply disappears nothing more will be heard about it. A further trial would lead to complication."

"You will hang him, then, in secret?"

"I beg of you not to inquire too closely into his fate," was the polite reply.

While this scene was being enacted, Chippy Chunks, still wearing his uniform, had taken a boat, and desired the man to row him to the White Wing, which lay about half a mile from the shore.

Chippy was commissioned to fetch Captain Starfish ashore.

Now, it so happened that the worthy captain, in his many anxious visits of inquiry to the city, had made himself a bit obnoxious to the Frenchmen, and something approaching a rupture had arisen between them.

It was therefore with no very pleasurable feelings that the captain of the White Wing saw one whom he took to be a French soldier approaching.

"I'll be hanged," he said, "if I don't think they've sent him to arrest me! He don't come aboard here. Hi! one of you men fix the fire-hose and get the pump ready for action."

It was done before the boat was within hail, and Chippy, thinking the movements on deck were those of curiosity, arranged a surprise for the captain.

Lowering his head, so as to hide his features, he told the man to pull with all his might and bring his boat under the stern of the yacht.

"Hi! you. Stand off there, Froggy, or I'll play the hose on you."

"What?" cried Chippy, in a feigned voice.

"Keep off here!" said the captain, leaning over the side. "We don't want any of your breed here. Why, as I live, it's Chippy! Hooroar!"

You might have heard him bellow as he gave vent to his delight.

Over the side went the rope-ladder, and up came Chippy, to be embraced as fervently as if he had been a prodigal son just returned to the parental nest.

Chippy scrambled on deck in a somewhat breathless condition. Excitement and the enervating tendency of his recent adventures had made him weak.

They were all glad to see him, but the seamen kept at a distance while their captain was busy shaking hands with him.

"So you've 'listed, have you?" said Captain Starfish. "A bit old in the tooth for that fun; but, of course, any Englishman is good enough for the French army."

"I haven't 'listed," said Chippy. "What I've gone through has brought me down to these clothes. Oh! it's a rare story. But never mind me now. The governor—"

"Do you mean to say he's alive?" gasped Captain Starfish.

"I do," replied Chippy.

"But Mister Ned—he's gone, aint he?"

"No—he's all right. And Missus—"

"What, all of 'em right?" said Captain Starfish. "Oh! this is a bit TOO much. Come downstairs and have a drink; I must have one before I can listen to any more. All alive and hearty, I hope?"

"Yes, and coming aboard this afternoon," returned Chippy.

Captain Starfish turned to the men to tell them the story, but he saw by their faces that they had heard all.

"You may cheer, my lads—once," he said, "but save most of your breath for when they come aboard by and bye."

The men gave a cheer, as permitted, and afterwards threw one in on their own account without being called to task for it.

Chippy and the captain went below.

"Starfish," said Chippy, as the captain put a bottle and some glasses on the table, "you are a single man, aint you?"

"Widderer," replied the captain.

"Same thing, but more lonely like," continued Chippy. "Would you like to marry again?"

"I've thought of it," replied the captain, musing. "It's nice when you go ashore to have your Polly to meet you—but there's a lot of chance in it. You mayn't get a good one."

"I can put you up to a wife," said Chippy, "a bloomer, beautiful as a butterfly—a widower, or as good as one."

"Friend of yours?" said the captain.

"Yes."

"French, perhaps?"

"No—a native, eyes like sloes, handsome as paint, gentle as a dove. I aint a marrying man myself, but I'd like to see her settled. She aint a bad sort in the main. Will you come ashore and see her?"

"I will," said the captain.

"Then just let me get at another suit of clothes," said Chippy. "I've left my Sunday best in my box, and I'm tired of being a sham soldier. As soon as I'm dressed we'll be off."

Chippy went away to dress, and when he reappeared in a Sunday suit of pepper-and-salt, in which he looked something like his old self, but not quite, the captain was ready.

"I suppose, Chippy," he said, "there's no gammon in this business?"

"Not a bit of it," replied Chippy.

"No wice in the widder?"

"Not an ounce."

"And really beautiful?"

"She could sit for the picture of an angel," replied Chippy; "leastways, I've seen some who couldn't hold a candle to her."

"All being according to catalogue," said the captain, resolutely, "I'm on the job. I'll make her Mrs. Starfish."

CHAPTER L.

HOME AGAIN.

HERE is no doubt that Chippy Chunks, when he lured Captain Starfish ashore to see Alea, meant the whole affair to be a joke.

Chippy, elated by the escape of his beloved master and mistress from the toils of the Moors, was in a jocular mood, and thought there was no harm in giving vent to a jest at the old salt's expense.

But many a joke has a serious ending, and it was destined to be so in this case.

The captain was a gallant man, and when, after an interview of a very gratifying nature with the restored adventurers, he was introduced to Alea, who was now to all intents and purposes a widow, his gallant heart was set on fire.

"She's a foreign craft," he said to Chippy, in confidence, "but as trim built as here and there one of our own make."

So he set himself the task of winning her smiles, and succeeded beyond his expectations.

During the next few days the Tartar family were the recipients of much hospitality and kindly attention from the French residents at Algiers.

At first it was their intention to get away from the place without delay, but they were induced to remain under the assurance that no repetition of the outrages they had endured could possibly take place.

"Abdul-ab-Bourad is at peace," said General Boureau, significantly, "the outbreak of the hillmen is at an end, and no one in this place dare raise a finger against you or yours."

"Of course it is my wife I am thinking of," said Tom. "But for her being a brave little woman she must have sunk under the ordeal she has been subjected to."

"She is admirable—a queen!" returned the general, enthusiastically.

Indeed, Lottie was favoured with so much attention from the French officers that a little jealousy on Tom's part would have been excusable.

But he knew his wife too well to doubt her for a moment, and she loved him too dearly to give him any cause for uneasiness.

So the time passed—a week or more—and then one morning Tom was startled by a request from Captain Starfish to be allowed to take home a wife with him.

"In Heaven's name, man!" exclaimed Tom, "whom do you think of marrying?"

"The lady who's been about so much with Mrs. Tartar," said Captain Starfish. "She's a widder, sir, although a recent one, and I don't think the man, who I've heerd has been hanged in prison, as he deserves to be, was in any way the right sort of husband for her. She isn't going to put on any weeds for him."

"Isn't it rather sudden?" asked Tom, who had lost sight of Alea for a week, as she was not a sharer in the hospitality of the French.

"Well, sir," said Captain Starfish, "I've kept on steady courting all the week, say seven hours a day, and I think that's as good as three months' occasional visiting."

Tom laughed, and said he supposed so. As far as he was concerned he had no objection to the proposed marriage, and he was sure Mrs. Tartar would be very pleased.

There was no difficulty in getting married, as there was both a Protestant and a Roman Catholic place of worship in the town.

So Captain Starfish was united that very afternoon to Alea, whose ambition to marry an Englishman was at last gratified.

We may here say that she made him a very good wife, and on their return to England fell into our ways with great adaptability.

They never had any children, but they made a very happy pair, as Chippy Chunks, who is a frequent visitor to their little home at Battersea, can testify.

To return for a moment to Algiers.

At last the day came when the Tartars were to leave, and they were making a round of calls, by way of adieu, when, passing through the great thoroughfare, Bab-el-onad, they came upon a car drawn by a man, in which another one was lying—a cripple.

Changed and shrunken as the latter was, they all recognised him instantly. It was Si Hamick.

Deeply as he had injured them, they could not gloat upon him lying there, and Tom, with a motion of his hand, stopped the car.

"Oh! my lord, strike me not," murmured Si Hamick.

"I should be sorry to do so," replied Tom. "How came you in th[illegible]te?"

"I was ren[illegible]n pieces by a lion, generous master," rep[illegible]mick, "but it was scared from me by the [illegible]ng of cannon. He who is my friend," looking at the man holding the shafts of the cart, whom Tom saw with a shudder was a leper, "brought me away."

"And why do you come here?" asked Tom.

"We must beg—and shall we do so in the desert?" asked Si Hamick. "But if my lord betray me I shall hang, even as I am."

He looked piteously at Tom, who took out some coins from his pocket and dropped them into the car beside him, saying—

"You have sinned, but have been terribly punished. If I were ten times more revengeful than I am I would not wish you a more awful fate."

"My lord," said Si Hamick, with tears in his eyes, "was ever noble and great. If I had not been a fool, but served him faithfully, I should now be walking proudly in the sunlight, and not lying here."

Tom turned away with a look of compassion in his face, and so they parted, never to meet again.

The next day the White Wing spread her sails and put out to sea. A little powder was used by the courteous Boureau as a parting salute, and the tricolour was run up at the fort.

At last a salute was exchanged by the dipping of the Union Jack on board the yacht, and then the word was given.

"England, as fast as the wind will take us, Captain Starfish!" said Tom.

And with very favourable weather on the whole

they returned to the old country, without a halt, save at Gibraltar for a few necessaries.

With unmeasured delight they put foot on shore and sped away home, where a reception that was all they could desire was awaiting them.

Having had enough of adventure—for some time, at least—Tom resolved to settle down and enjoy the sweets of domestic life.

Ned was also of opinion that he could make himself content wit' more comfortable surroundings than he had recently experienced, and so we leave them.

We have only to add that Chippy Chunks has a moderate pension which suffices for all his wants.

You can guess where it comes from.

But, of course, Chippy is not idle. It is not in his nature to be. With a hammer and a tack or two, or maybe a nail, he is always at the beck and call of his f   who may have some little repairs needed in their nomes.

It   Chippy to carry them out and save the expense, so both parties are gratified.

In short all our friends who have figured in this story are satisfied with their present lot, and who, being a friend of theirs, could wish them more?

THE END.